PRAISE FOR CAR

The Perfect Dress

"Fans of Brown will swoon for this sweet contemporary, which skillfully pairs a shy small-town bridal shop owner and a softhearted car dealership owner . . . The expected but welcomed happily ever after for all involved will make readers of all ages sigh with satisfaction."

—*Publishers Weekly*

"Carolyn Brown writes the best comfort-for-the-soul, heartwarming stories and she never disappoints . . . You won't go wrong with *The Perfect Dress!*"

—*Harlequin Junkie*

The Magnolia Inn

"The author does a first-rate job of depicting the devastating stages of grief, provides a simple but appealing plot with a sympathetic hero and heroine and a cast of lovable supporting characters, and wraps it all up with a happily ever after to cheer for."

—*Publishers Weekly*

"*The Magnolia Inn* by Carolyn Brown is a feel-good story about friendship, fighting your demons, and finding love, and maybe, just a little bit of magic."

—*Harlequin Junkie*

"Chock-full of Carolyn Brown's signature country charm, *The Magnolia Inn* is a sweet and heartwarming story of two people trying to make the most of their lives, even when they have no idea what exactly is at stake."

—*Fresh Fiction*

Small Town Rumors

"Carolyn Brown is a master at writing warm, complex characters who find their way into your heart."

—*Harlequin Junkie*

"Carolyn Brown's *Small Town Rumors* takes that hotbed and with it spins a delightful tale of starting over, coming into your own, and living your life, out loud and unafraid."

—*Words We Love By*

"*Small Town Rumors* by Carolyn Brown is a contemporary romance perfect for a summer read in the shade of a big old tree with a glass of lemonade or sweet tea. It is a sweet romance with wonderful characters and a small-town setting."

—*Avonna Loves Genres*

The Sometimes Sisters

"Carolyn Brown continues her streak of winning, heartfelt novels with *The Sometimes Sisters*, a story of estranged sisters and frustrated romance."

—*All About Romance*

"This is an amazing feel-good story that will make you wish you were a part of this amazing family."

—*Harlequin Junkie* (top pick)

"*The Sometimes Sisters* is [a] delightful and touching story that explores the bonds of family. I loved the characters, the story lines, and the focus on the importance of familial bonds, whether they be blood relations or those you choose with your heart."

—*Rainy Day Ramblings*

The Strawberry Hearts Diner

"[A] sweet and satisfying romance from the queen of Texas romance."
—*Fresh Fiction*

"A heartwarming cast of characters brings laughter and tears to the mix, and readers will find themselves rooting for more than one romance on the menu. From the first page to the last, Brown perfectly captures the mood as well as the atmosphere and creates a charming story that appeals to a wide range of readers."

—*RT Book Reviews*

"A sweet romance surrounded by wonderful, caring characters."
—*TBQ's Book Palace*

"[A] deeply satisfying contemporary small-town western story . . ."
—*Delighted Reader*

The Barefoot Summer

"Prolific romance author Brown shows she can also write women's fiction in this charming story, which uses humor and vivid characters to show the value of building an unconventional chosen family."

—*Publishers Weekly*

"This story takes you and carries you along for a wonderful ride full of laughter, tears, and three amazing HEAs. I feel like these characters are not just people in a book, but they are truly family and I feel so invested in their journey. Another amazing HIT for Carolyn Brown."

—*Harlequin Junkie* (top pick)

The Lullaby Sky

"I really loved and enjoyed this story. Definitely a good comfort read, when you're in a reading funk or just don't know what to read. The secondary characters bring much love and laughter into this book—your cheeks will definitely hurt from smiling so hard while reading. Carolyn is one of my most favorite authors. I know that without a doubt that no matter what book of hers I read, I can just get lost in it and know it will be a good story. Better than the last. Can't wait to read more from her."

—*The Bookworm's Obsession*

The Lilac Bouquet

"Brown pulls readers along for an enjoyable ride. It's impossible not to be touched by Brown's protagonists, particularly Seth, and a cast of strong supporting characters underpins the charming tale."

—*Publishers Weekly*

"If a reader is looking for a book more geared toward family and long-held secrets, this would be a good fit."

—*RT Book Reviews*

"Carolyn Brown absolutely blew me away with this epically beautiful story. I cried, I giggled, I sobbed, and I guffawed; this book had it all. I've come to expect great things from this author, and she more than lived up to anything I could have hoped for. Emmy Jo Massey and her great-granny Tandy are absolute masterpieces not because they are perfect but because they are perfectly painted. They are so alive, so full of flaws and spunk and determination. I cannot recommend this book highly enough."

—*Night Owl Reviews* (5 stars and top pick)

The Wedding Pearls

"*The Wedding Pearls* by Carolyn Brown is an amazing story about family, life, love, and finding out who you are and where you came from. This book is a lot like the *Golden Girls* meet *Thelma and Louise*."

—*Harlequin Junkie*

"*The Wedding Pearls* is an absolute must-read. I cannot recommend this one enough. Grab a copy for yourself and one for a best friend or even your mother or both. This is a book that you need to read. It will make you laugh and cry. It is so sweet and wonderful and packed full of humor. I hope that when I grow up, I can be just like Ivy and Frankie."

—*Rainy Day Ramblings*

The Yellow Rose Beauty Shop

"*The Yellow Rose Beauty Shop* was hilarious and so much fun to read. But sweet romances, strong female friendships, and family bonds make this more than just a humorous read."

—*The Readers Den*

"If you like books about small towns and how the people's lives intertwine, you will love this book. I think it's probably my favorite book this year. The relationships of the three main characters, girls who have grown up together, will make you feel like you just pulled up a chair in their beauty shop with a bunch of old friends. As you meet the other people in the town, you'll wish you could move there. There are some genuine laugh-out-loud moments and then more that will just make you smile. These are real people, not the oh-so-thin-and-so-very-rich that are often the main characters in novels. This book will warm your heart and you'll remember it after you finish the last page. That's the highest praise I can give a book."

—Reader quote for *The Yellow Rose Beauty Shop*

Long, Hot Texas Summer

"This is one of those lighthearted, feel-good, make-me-happy kind of stories. But, at the same time, the essence of this story is family and love with a big ole dose of laughter and country living thrown in the mix. This is the first installment in what promises to be another fascinating series from Brown. Find a comfortable chair, sit back and relax because once you start reading *Long, Hot Texas Summer*, you won't be able to put it down. This is a super fun and sassy romance."

—*Thoughts in Progress*

Daisies in the Canyon

"I just loved the symbolism in *Daisies in the Canyon*. As I mentioned before, Carolyn Brown has a way with character development, with few, if any, contemporaries. I am sure there are more stories to tell in this series. Brown just touched the surface first with *Long, Hot Texas Summer* and now continuing on with *Daisies in the Canyon*."

—*Fresh Fiction*

the Banty House

ALSO BY CAROLYN BROWN

CONTEMPORARY ROMANCES

The Family Journal
The Empty Nesters
The Perfect Dress
The Magnolia Inn
Small Town Rumors
The Sometimes Sisters
The Strawberry Hearts Diner
The Lilac Bouquet
The Barefoot Summer
The Lullaby Sky
The Wedding Pearls
The Yellow Rose Beauty Shop
The Ladies' Room
Hidden Secrets
Long, Hot Texas Summer
Daisies in the Canyon
Trouble in Paradise

CONTEMPORARY SERIES

THE BROKEN ROAD SERIES

To Trust
To Commit
To Believe
To Dream
To Hope

THREE MAGIC WORDS TRILOGY

A Forever Thing
In Shining Whatever
Life After Wife

HISTORICAL ROMANCE

THE BLACK SWAN TRILOGY

Pushin' Up Daisies
From Thin Air
Come High Water

THE DRIFTERS & DREAMERS TRILOGY

Morning Glory
Sweet Tilly
Evening Star

THE LOVE'S VALLEY SERIES

Choices
Absolution
Chances
Redemption
Promises

the Banty House

CAROLYN BROWN

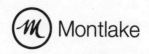 Montlake

Published by Montlake, Seattle

www.apub.com

Amazon, the Amazon logo, and Montlake are trademarks of Amazon.com, Inc., or its affiliates.

ISBN-13: 9781542018814
ISBN-10: 1542018811

Cover design by Laura Klynstra

Printed in the United States of America

In memory of my grandmother
Edna Rhoades Gray
March 5, 1910–September 25, 1974

Chapter One

*C*hange is a good thing.

Kate Carson wished she had the person who had first said that by the throat. She'd choke them until their face turned blue and then slap them for being that color. She didn't like change. First her little town had lost its post office, and then the saloon was blown away by a tornado and the cotton mill went out of business. All that had happened in the past fifty years, and just two weeks ago, her hairdresser had up and dropped graveyard-dead.

They hadn't had a bit of forewarning, and now the Carson sisters had to drive almost three miles to the Hondo Cut and Curl just to get their hair fixed on Thursday mornings. Used to be they only had to walk one block down Main Street, turn left, and their beauty shop was right there in the garage beside the second house on the right. They'd figured Estelle, their old hairdresser, would outlive them all, being as how she was only sixty-five and the youngest of the Carson sisters was more than a decade older than that.

Next thing would be that God Himself wasn't interested in sticking around Rooster, Texas, either, and He'd send a tornado to wipe out the only church left in town. Kate muttered about that idea as she put on her best sweater that cool April morning and crossed the dogtrot from the house to the garage to get the car backed out so they could go drive to Hondo. Lord only knew that she couldn't let Betsy or Connie drive their mama's car. Connie would get to daydreaming and drive them through a barbwire fence. Betsy drove like a bat set loose from the bowels of hell. She wouldn't only drive them through the fence; she'd kill a cow or two in the process.

Kate remembered the first time she had gotten behind the wheel of the turquoise 1958 Lincoln. Her mama had brought it home from the dealership down in Hondo, and she'd let each of the girls have a turn at driving it around the block. She told them that she had picked out that color because it reminded her of Easter, which was the very next Sunday.

"And here we are sixty-two years later," Kate said as she started the engine. "Easter is this coming Sunday, and this old girl"—she patted the steering wheel—"still runs like a jewel." She looked up toward the pale-blue sky with no clouds in sight. "You done good, Mama, when you bought this car."

Betsy came out of the big two-story house first and crawled into the back seat. "I hate seat belts, and I still say that having the damn things installed has ruined the value of Mama's car."

"We didn't have much choice after the third time the cops pulled you over for speeding and we had no seat belts so he doubled the fine," Betsy replied.

Connie opened the passenger door and slid into the wide bench seat next to Kate. "Cops are everywhere these days. Don't know why they can't stay on the highways where they belong, and leave the farm roads alone. Next thing you know they'll be camping out at the edge of Rooster."

"I doubt that." Kate put the car in gear and made a right-hand turn onto Main Street. "We're pretty much all that's left of Rooster, and they know we've got seat belts now. Besides, no one needs to be scared, because you don't drive anymore, Connie."

"I would if you hadn't let my license expire," Connie fumed.

"Don't fuss at me. You can always get it back if you take the test," Kate reminded her for the hundredth time.

"If this damn seat belt wasn't holdin' me down, I'd reach over this seat and slap you silly," Connie told her.

Kate turned on the radio and found the classic country music station they all liked. Every time Connie said something else, she jacked up the volume a little more. Pretty soon they were all wiggling their shoulders to Johnny Cash's deep voice singing "Folsom Prison Blues."

By the time Patsy Cline had finished "Walkin' After Midnight," Kate had parked the car in front of the new hairdresser they'd chosen. Of course, it had taken two hours of discussion before they'd decided to give her a try. Connie had had to get out her gemstones and toss them around on the table, and Betsy had had to call the woman and talk to her for thirty minutes. It was a wonder that Lucy hadn't hung up the phone when Betsy asked her age, weight, and marital status.

Her younger sisters wasted no time getting out of the car, across the gravel parking lot, and into the beauty shop. Everything had always been a contest for the two of them, except in what each of them called their area of expertise. Betsy made the best jellies and jams in Medina County, and Connie never met a speck of dust she couldn't conquer, so she took care of the house. Betsy hated to clean, and Connie, bless her heart, couldn't boil water without setting off one of those newfangled smoke alarms. Kate made sure that she had locked the car and then followed her sisters into the beauty shop.

"There you are." Lucy, a short, round woman with a lot of salt in her dark-brown hair, smiled when Kate came into the shop. "Since Connie got here first, I'll get her shampooed and under the dryer."

Connie stuck her tongue out at Betsy and sat down in the chair. "You're gettin' slow."

"I let you win so you wouldn't pout like a baby," Betsy shot back at her.

Lucy wrapped a plastic cape around Connie's neck and asked, "Are y'all ready for Easter?"

"We've got our new dresses and white gloves all ready, and we'll get our ham when we do our shopping after we get our hair done. I wouldn't be caught dead in the grocery store lookin' like I do now." Connie leaned her head back. "Betsy might need her roots touched up. I can see a gray peeking out."

Lucy glanced over at the middle sister. "I'll check her out."

"Well, go ahead and do what needs doin' anyway. I don't want them showin' for our Easter picture," Connie said.

"Y'all take an Easter picture, do you?" Lucy wet Connie's hair and then worked shampoo into it.

"Have every year for our whole lives," Kate answered. "Mama started it the Easter after I was born. She made me a little pink dress and a cute bonnet. I was only three weeks old that year. The next year, Betsy was a few weeks old and she wore that same dress and bonnet, and when I was two, Connie wore it. Mama had all of us a year apart. She said it was like raisin' triplets, so once a year, she dressed us like that."

"Until I was a teenager, I lived in their outgrown clothes," Connie sighed. "Except for Easter, and then we all got new dresses."

"And they were exactly the same," Betsy said. "Mama thought it was cute to dress us alike, but we did get different hats."

"So every year"—Kate sat down and picked up a magazine—"we buy identical dresses and hats of our choice, and we have our picture made for the Easter photo album."

"That's adorable," Lucy said. "I wish I had a sister or two and we had a tradition like that."

Kate had two sisters that she'd gladly give Lucy if she'd just take them off her hands.

❖   ❖   ❖

Ginger Andrews picked up the small suitcase containing all her belongings and stepped off the bus in Hondo, Texas. Other nineteen-year-old girls might be scared out of their wits to be in a strange town without a single penny to their name, but this wasn't Ginger's first rodeo. Different town and different street, but living on the streets was all the same. She'd survived for the past year, and she'd live through this experience, too. She sat down on a bench and put a hand on her very pregnant stomach. She just hoped that she at least found a shelter before the baby came.

She caught a whiff of hair spray and permanent solution and turned to see that she was sitting in front of a beauty shop. Her reflection in the window showed her stringy blonde hair and gaunt cheeks, which left no doubt that she was a homeless kid. What little pride and dignity she'd had a couple of weeks ago was gone in her time on the road, and the only thing she had left was the baby. She'd vowed from the day the pregnancy test had come up positive that she'd be a good mother and that her child would never go into the system.

"Well, hello there." An older gray-haired woman sat down beside her and lit up a cigarette. "They won't let me smoke in the beauty shop, so I have to come out here for my nicotine fix. You waitin' on a bus?"

"No, ma'am." Ginger pulled her frayed denim jacket tight around her protruding belly.

"Someone goin' to pick you up, then?" The woman took a long drag on her cigarette, and turned her head to blow the smoke away from Ginger. "I'm Connie Carson. What's your name?"

"No one is pickin' me up, and my name is Ginger Andrews, ma'am." Most folks wouldn't even sit down beside someone who might be homeless.

"Then what are you doin' sittin' on a bench here in Hondo?" Connie asked.

"Just restin' up a minute before I get out on the highway to try to hitch a ride." Ginger told the truth. "I've run out of money."

"Good God!" Connie gasped. "Don't you have relatives?"

5

"No, I just don't." Ginger shrugged. "Been in foster care my whole life up until a year ago. The gover'ment don't pay for kids past eighteen, so I been on my own since then."

"Where's your husband, child?" Connie looked over at Ginger's big belly.

Ginger put her hand on her bulging stomach. "His name was Lucas and he got killed seven months ago, before he ever even knew that I was pregnant." It felt good to talk to someone, even if the woman reminded her of Marie, the mama from that television show about everyone loving Raymond. Connie even wore bright-red lipstick and had her hair all frizzy like Marie did in the show.

"Where are you from?" Connie asked.

"Kentucky, I guess. That's where I was born, according to my birth certificate. My mama was in prison at the time, so I went into the system," she replied with another shrug. "Guess I'd best get on my way now. Nice talkin' to you."

"Whoa!" Connie almost dropped her cigarette. "You can't be hitch-hikin'," she gasped. "Don't you watch them crime shows on the television? Someone could kidnap you so they could steal that baby when it's born, and you'd never see it or daylight again. Why did you leave Kentucky?"

"Nothing for me there but bad memories."

"How far you plannin' on goin' to get away from them ugly memories?" Connie asked.

The woman was sure nosy, but then, she was old. Most of the elderly folks who were regulars at the café where Ginger had worked until they'd closed the doors asked lots of questions, too.

"Until I run out of land," she answered as she stood up. "You have a nice day, now, ma'am."

Connie shook her head and set her mouth in a firm line. "I just can't bear to think of you out there travelin' in your condition. You're comin' home with us."

"Us?" Ginger asked.

"Me and my two sisters, Betsy and Kate. They'll be out of the beauty shop in a few minutes. I'm calling a rule number one," Connie said.

"You think you should ask them about that first? And what's a rule number one?" The woman was crazy for sure. No one took in a complete stranger. Ginger thought of herself as a good person, but for all Connie knew, she could be a serial killer—or for that matter, Connie might be one.

"Come on with me." Connie put what was left of her cigarette in a bucket beside the bench. Then she got Ginger by the hand and tugged. "We'll go ask them together, but I'm tellin' you right now, they'll say yes. They have to, because of Mama's rules."

"Which are?" Ginger stood up, wondering if Mama was the cult leader. Connie seemed to be a little crazy, so maybe it was hereditary.

"The Banty House has rules," Connie said. "You'll have to abide by them. Anyone who walks through the doors has to, but don't worry—they ain't hard to uphold. I been doin' it for my whole life, and I'm still alive and kickin'. Rule number one is the one about takin' in strangers."

Ginger's first instinct was to grab her ratty suitcase and run, but then she thought about her situation. Surely one night with three old women wouldn't hurt anything. She'd probably get to sleep in a real bed and have a real meal. Then tomorrow she'd sneak out and hitch a ride on out West—Texas was a good distance from Kentucky, but it was not far enough. She hadn't forgotten anything yet.

One of her foster mothers had had a standing appointment on Mondays at a local salon, but Ginger couldn't remember which town she'd lived in during that short period of time. She'd never been inside a beauty shop in her entire life. She drew her brows down and tried to get a picture of the woman—somehow it seemed very important that she remember. She had spent a birthday—her fourteenth birthday—in that house and was the oldest of the five children in the home. She was pretty much the in-house babysitter for the four smaller kids. The foster mother had been a tall brunette who'd smoked a pack a day. She had been one of the indifferent ones. She wasn't interested in the kids, but she didn't fuss at Ginger or punish her for not knowing what the preacher said on Sunday morning. She followed Connie inside the shop and was amazed that it looked exactly like she'd imagined it would from the pictures in the magazines that her various foster mothers had left scattered around the house. Sometimes she had imagined herself sitting in one of the chairs like those in front of a mirror, but she had always known it was just a pipe dream.

"Look what I found sitting on the bench out front," Connie said. "Her name is Ginger Andrews, and I've invited her to come home with us since she ain't got no place to live."

Kate looked over at Betsy and raised an eyebrow. "Rule number one?"

"I guess so," Betsy said. "Well, Miz Ginger, do you have a driver's license?"

"Yes, ma'am, but it's from the state of Kentucky," she answered.

"I don't reckon that will matter for a few months. Kate"—she nodded toward the tall lady with short dark hair sprinkled with gray—"is the only one of us who's still got a license. You could earn your keep by drivin' us and helpin' me with makin' my jams and jellies."

"Hey, now," Connie protested. "I found her, so she gets to help me with the cleanin'. You know how I'm gettin' down in my back and all."

Kate giggled. "Maybe we should ask Ginger about all this before we start arguin' about who gets her first."

"Y'all are offerin' me a job?" Ginger asked. "You don't know me, and I'm pregnant and not married." Good Lord! Connie wasn't the only one in the bunch who was crazy.

"Darlin', we all make mistakes, but our mama set down the rules, and we've abided by them all these years. The rules ain't never failed us, not one time," Betsy said. "So soon as we pay our bill in here, you're welcome to come home with us and help out at the Banty House, at least for the rest of today and tomorrow. Then you can be on your way if you want to."

Ginger wasn't sure whether to agree or to run, but the baby kicked hard right then. She took that as a sign that she should go home with them. Besides, it seemed like fate that Connie had chosen the very moment Ginger had gotten off the bus to need a smoke. She started to ask what the Banty House was, but when it came right down to it, she didn't care if it was a floral shop, a restaurant, or a bakery. They had offered her a job, and even if all she got out of it was room and board, it sure beat sleeping in a park or in an abandoned house.

Chapter Two

Friday was Sloan Baker's favorite day of the whole week. That was the day he worked for the Carson sisters. Usually he was up and going, trying to keep his mind busy, but that morning, he awoke in a cold sweat from the recurring nightmare that he'd had since he was sent home from the army.

He and his teammates made up the bomb squad, and in the dream, they were going into a tent where there'd been a threat. He went in first, located the bomb, and was about to dismantle it when the timer started clicking off minutes, not seconds. He turned to tell his buddies to run, but he couldn't open his mouth. He awoke with his hands over his ears, trying to block out the sound of the explosion.

He crawled out of bed and spread the covers out until there wasn't a single wrinkle. He got dressed in faded camouflage pants, an army-green T-shirt that had seen better days, and his combat boots. The things that he'd brought home when they'd sent him back to the States a little more than two years ago were about to wear out—all but the boots. He figured he could get another five to ten years out of them.

He made a pot of coffee, poured himself a mug, and carried it out to the front-porch swing. "It was just a dream," he said out loud.

Real or nightmare—it didn't matter. His buddies had been blown up in an explosion that he could have prevented if he'd only been with them. He was glad to see the sun peeking up over the horizon, giving shape to the tombstones in the cemetery right next to his place. When daylight came, he didn't have to worry about the dreams and he could stay so busy that sometimes he even forgot about the guilt he carried with him. He got into his twenty-year-old pickup truck and ate half a dozen cookies while he listened to the radio and drove the half mile up to the Banty House.

Washing their fancy car was his first job on Fridays. Most of the time the car didn't even need to be cleaned, but Connie could find a fleck of dust hiding in a dirt pile. And she *knew* they stirred up all the dust driving into town on Thursdays for their beauty-shop appointment and their grocery shopping. After it was cleaned up, he'd check the oil and everything under the hood to be sure that nothing was needed there. Then he'd go on to mow the huge lawn and take care of Connie's flower beds. Beyond that, they always found a few odd jobs to keep him busy the rest of the day—sometimes helping Kate in the cellar or maybe doing whatever Betsy needed to make her jams or jellies, or even helping Connie on the days that she decided to move everything out of a guest bedroom to clean it.

They always paid him well for his day's work, but what he liked best was that they invited him to eat dinner with them at noon. Betsy was a fantastic cook, and her biscuits reminded him of his granny's. He parked in his usual spot in front of the house and checked the rose-bushes on his way across the yard to see if they needed any buds clipped. He whistled as he made his way up the four steps onto the porch and knocked on the doorjamb. He expected to hear someone yell for him to come on in, but that morning the door flew open and there stood the cutest and the most pregnant little blonde woman he'd seen in a while.

"I'm Sloan. I'm here to work for the Carson sisters today," he said.

This was the first time in his remembrance that they'd brought home a pregnant stray. Usually, it was older women or sometimes men who needed a place to stay for a day or two while their house was being fumigated, or maybe just before they were about to make a move from their home to a nursing facility.

"Hello, Sloan." She stuck out her hand. "Betsy told me that you would be coming this morning. I'm Ginger."

"Pleased to meet you, ma'am." He shook her hand and then dropped it.

"Come on in," Betsy called out from the kitchen. "Have you had breakfast? We've eaten, but there's plenty of leftovers."

"Yes, ma'am, I've eaten." Sloan removed his cap and wiped his feet before entering the house. He slid a sly look over toward Ginger again. Had the old ladies completely lost their minds? This was more than following the first of their deceased mother's rules—the one about not turning away strangers. What if that woman had the baby before they could get rid of her? She might weasel her way right into their hearts with a baby and then rob them blind.

Betsy poked her head around the kitchen door. "I see you've met Ginger. She's stayin' with us. Today she's helping me make elderberry jelly."

"You about to use up all that juice we put up last summer?" Sloan reached for the key to the garage.

"Not quite. I figure it'll last until harvest in late August, and then we'll be ready to start all over. Folks sure like it," Betsy said.

"You should've put in a café years ago," Sloan told her as he headed across the kitchen floor. "If people ever got a taste of your biscuits with elderberry jelly on 'em, they'd swarm the café like ants to an open sugar bowl."

"I'm too old to manage a café, and besides, I'd have to keep a schedule. With my jams and jellies, I just make them when I want to, and folks come to me to buy them. I sold the last of my wild plum the first of the week, so we may make a batch of that today, too," Betsy said.

"If you ladies need me, just holler." Sloan slipped out the door and closed it behind him. He'd have to keep a good eye on the ladies for sure, and see to it that this Ginger woman left in a day or two at the most. Poor old souls were so damn gullible that they didn't know people in the modern world could be conniving.

❖   ❖   ❖

Ginger pinched herself on the leg, and it hurt like hell, so she was definitely not dreaming. She'd had a bath in a big claw-foot tub the night before—one so deep that she could sink all the way down to her neck, leaving her pregnant belly the only thing poking up out of the water. She'd slept in a bed with sheets that smelled like flowers and laid her head on a soft feather pillow, and she'd awakened to the smell of coffee and bacon floating up the stairs to her bedroom.

The bedroom was an absolute dream, with a hand-quilted spread on the four-poster bed, a pretty crystal lamp on the bedside table, and even one of those long velvet chaise lounges against one wall. She felt like a queen when she sat on it and propped her feet up to read a book before she went to bed. To put the icing on the cake, there was a bookcase that reached from one wall to the other, and what shelves weren't filled with novels had decorative things on them. She particularly liked the figurines that looked like little children, but she was afraid to touch them.

Sloan had looked at her like he could see through her—all the way to her soul—and he didn't like what he saw. But then, if she'd been in his shoes, she might have also had second thoughts about some woman the ladies dragged into their home. She unzipped three plastic bags of elderberries and poured them into the pot that Betsy brought out from the cabinet.

"I thought Sloan would be an old gray-haired man," she said.

"Why would you think that?" Betsy barely covered the elderberries with water and started smashing them with a potato masher.

"You said that he lives alone and does odd jobs," Ginger answered. "Most guys his age have a job like in a factory or a business of some kind."

"He's a good man, that Sloan is, but . . . ," Betsy said.

Connie butted into the conversation as she headed over to the pantry and brought out a fresh can of furniture polish. "But he went into the military right out of high school, and they sent him home more than two years ago."

"What happened back then?" Kate asked as she opened the door and came up from the basement to join them.

"Sloan came home," Connie said.

"That's right." Kate nodded. "His granny said that he didn't do anything wrong, but there was some kind of trouble over there, and he's been kinda like a hermit ever since. He don't talk about the time he was in the army, but his granny said that it all happened when they sent him to Kuwait, or maybe it was Iran—one of those foreign places, anyway. We don't get much into politics here at our place."

"Why does your house have a name?" Ginger caught a whiff of alcohol and cinnamon mixed together when Kate walked past her to get a cup of coffee.

"It's like this . . ." Kate sat down at the table and blew on her coffee. "Rooster hasn't ever been very big, and it's kind of out of the way, what with it being on a dead-end road that stops at the Cottonwood Cemetery. Way back there at the end of the Civil War, just south of us was a black community named Mission Valley."

Connie poured herself a mug of coffee, added a heaping spoonful of sugar and a lot of whipping cream to it, and then sat down beside Kate. "Grandma Carson told me that it was named that because there was a Baptist church and a Methodist church, both of the missionary type, down in that area."

Ginger didn't want a history lesson. She only wanted to know how they came to name their home the Banty House. Something like the

Sisters' Mansion sounded more fitting to her than the name of a little male fighting chicken.

"So anyway, the Mission Valley community and both churches are gone now. The cemetery is still down there." Betsy set the pot of elderberries off to the side, poured herself a cup of coffee, and joined them. "And it was all grown over. Folks that come to find their relatives had to walk through weeds and cockleburs and hope there weren't no rattlesnakes hiding in all that until Sloan came home. He devotes a day a week to mowing and keeping the little graveyard looking decent."

"Our family is buried there," Kate went on. "Grandma and Mama, and there's plots for each of us."

Ginger wondered what all that had to do with the name of the house, but she'd learned through the years to be patient. The ladies seemed to be enjoying the reminiscing about the area. Maybe the cemetery itself had something to do with the name of the house.

"Anyway . . . ," Connie sighed, "back then Rooster had a bank, a post office, and a general store. Our great-grandparents, Elizabeth and Rooster Carson, were instrumental in starting the town when they put in the general store and built this house. And yes, that was his real name—it's right there on his tombstone. Rooster was his mama's maiden name, so that's where they got it, but from what we hear of his reputation, he was a short man with a real cocky attitude."

Okay, Ginger thought, *so we've narrowed down the topic from the whole area to a ghost town that only has half a dozen houses left and no businesses.*

"They only had one child, our Grandma Carson, and she inherited this place when they died during that big flu epidemic back in 1919," Betsy went on. "When Grandma Carson passed on about the time the Great Depression started in 1929, she left Mama this place. Y'all know something?" She drew her dark brows down in a frown. "We should get our house put on the historical registry. I'm going to have Sloan look into that."

Kate pointed a finger at her. "You really want them fancy bitches from one of them historical societies knowin' our business? Comin' in here and checkin' everything out to see if we've added on to the house. Goin' down into my basement?"

"I guess not." Betsy sighed.

Kate continued. "Mama and Grandma had a real nice seamstress business going here in Rooster. Folks down in Hondo didn't have much to do with Grandma since she had Mama out of wedlock, and since—"

Connie butted in. "Might as well go on and spit it out. Mama was a quarter black. Folks back then called her a quadroon, when they weren't callin' her meaner stuff. That makes us an eighth black."

"Some of my foster siblings were mixed race," Ginger said. "I never thought much about the color of a person's skin."

"A person should look at the heart first." Betsy pointed in Ginger's direction. "Why don't you get yourself a glass of milk from the refrigerator? And then sit down here with us. You don't need to be drinkin' caffeine in your condition, and milk will be good for the baby."

"Thank you." Ginger got a glass from the cabinet and filled it with milk. Then she sat down across from Connie.

"Folks today would call Mama mixed race," Kate said. "Grandma never married, but the love of her life was a man whose mama was black and his daddy was white. His name was Malachi James and he was the preacher at one of those missionary churches that used to be here. Anyway, I guess it was a good thing that old Rooster was dead and gone by the time Grandma gave birth to our mother, or he might have shot her and the preacher both. Grandma said he was a hard man who thought he was above the black folks that did business with him at the store."

"Havin' a baby out of wedlock is not a killin' offense," Ginger said.

"It *was* back in the time when Mama was born," Connie told her. "Lots has happened in this old world in the past hundred years."

"After Grandma died," Betsy said, "Mama tried to keep things afloat with her seamstress business. The hoity-toity folks in Hondo might not want to be her friend, but they sure loved her fine sewing skills. The Depression hit Texas right hard at that time, though, so no one had money for anything. Food and shelter took the place of fancy clothing to wear to church, and Mama's business was going under fast. Taxes were due on the house and things were getting bad. Prohibition was still in effect, and . . ." Betsy stopped to take a sip of her coffee.

Connie picked up the story. "And Grandma had taught Mama how to make moonshine, just like her mama had taught her and so on and so on back down the line. It wasn't legal, but word soon got out that folks could buy their liquor here, and the whole town had an interest in it being secret. The way Mama told us the story was that it didn't quite keep the bills paid, town or no, so she hired six girls and turned the house into a brothel."

Ginger almost choked on the milk.

Kate stood up, went to the sink, and rinsed her cup. "Since Rooster was the name of the town and since most men are like little banty roosters, she had that sign made that still hangs out there on the porch—the Banty House."

"And then she made the rules that still hang on the wall above the piano," Connie said.

Ginger made a mental note to reread the whole list of rules she'd seen when she crossed what the ladies called the parlor. Connie had quoted the first one to her on the way to Rooster from Hondo the day before: *Do not forget to show hospitality to strangers, for by so doing some people have shown hospitality to angels without knowing it. Heb. 13:2*

Ginger wondered why that was the first rule in a brothel.

❖　❖　❖

Sloan made sure there wasn't a fleck of dust anywhere on the car, and then he rapped on the back door and went inside. The smell of sweet elderberry jelly filled the whole place. A dozen pint jars sat on the counter. Once the people in the area knew that they were available, they'd fly out of the house pretty damn fast.

No one was in the kitchen, so he poked his head through the basement doorway and yelled, "Kate, you down here?"

"I am, but I'm on my way up, so stay up there," she yelled. "And I've got dibs on you for the whole afternoon."

"Yes, ma'am." If he'd been a drinking man, his mouth would have watered at the aroma of apples and cinnamon floating up the stairs. But Sloan would rather have an actual apple pie than a double shot of moonshine.

Thank goodness the law down in Hondo never bothered much with Rooster, and not even the most conscientious police officer would lock up an eighty-year-old woman for brewing shine for nothing but personal use.

Kate took the steps a little slower than she had when he'd first come home, but she didn't need to pull herself up by the banister by any means. "I want you to plant our cornfield today. It's two weeks since the last frost. I saved seed from last year's crop, so we're ready to go. Come harvest time, I'll be gettin' almighty low on my supply of corn for mash. Since I been makin' flavors, seems like I can hardly keep up."

He held the door for her and then closed it behind her. "You've got everything all safe, and you've double-checked your vent pipes, haven't you?"

"Every week, regular as clockwork, just like Mama taught me, but thanks for reminding me," she said. "Have you met Ginger?"

"Yes, I surely have. Will she be needin' a ride to town later this evenin'?"

Kate shook her head. "No, I don't reckon so. We're going to keep her another day or two."

"How'd you find this one?" Sloan asked.

"Connie found her sittin' on the park bench in front of the beauty shop yesterday." Kate went on to tell him the rest of what had happened.

"I've told y'all before that pickin' up strangers isn't a good thing." Sloan followed her into the kitchen.

"Now, just exactly what could one little bitty pregnant woman do to harm the three of us?" Kate protested.

"She might not be as innocent as she looks," Sloan warned her.

"Well, she's good help in the kitchen, and she says she knows her way around a mop and broom. We may keep her for a while instead of our usual just two or three days."

"Why is that rule so important anyway?" Sloan asked.

"Mama said that we wouldn't want to turn away someone that might be an angel sent from God to help us get through a difficult time," Kate answered.

"Just be careful," Sloan told her.

"Always." Kate patted him on the back. "Shhh . . ." Kate put a finger over her lips. "I hear them all talking in the dining room. Betsy will set the dinner table in there since there's five of us now. Speakin' of that, since the garden is comin' on, reckon you could give us another day a week, like maybe Saturday?"

"Yes, ma'am." He nodded. "Starting tomorrow?"

"That would be great," Kate told him.

"What would be great?" Betsy heard the last word as she came through the door separating the dining room and kitchen. She picked up a basket of biscuits. "We've got everything on the table but the sweet tea. By the time y'all get washed up, we'll be ready for grace."

Sloan took his time washing up, then fished a comb from his back pocket and ran it through his black hair. He wore it a little longer these days than he had in the service, but lots of things had changed since then.

He was the last one to the table, and they'd seated him right beside Ginger. He sat down and bowed his head. Betsy said a short grace; then they began to pass the food around the table.

"The rules say that we always bless our food," Kate said. "You figured that out last night, Ginger, but we didn't tell you that we take turns. When Mama was alive, we divided it by oldest to youngest." Kate put a fried chicken leg on her plate. "I say the breakfast prayer. Betsy does the noon one, and Connie takes care of supper."

"Fried chicken is my favorite meal." Sloan was glad they never asked him to pray. He and God hadn't had much of a relationship since he'd lost all his buddies over there in the sandbox.

"Mine, too," Ginger said. "I never learned to fry it like this, though."

"The secret is in being patient. Some things you just can't hurry along." Betsy smiled across the table at her. "The sisters and I've decided that if you're willing, maybe you'd stay through Sunday. That's Easter, you know, and we'd hate for you to be out on the road all alone on a holiday."

"Are you serious?" Ginger asked.

She seemed genuinely surprised at the invitation. Maybe she wasn't out to fleece his friends after all and was really what she claimed to be—just a woman down on her luck.

"Yes, we're very serious. Mama wouldn't want us to turn you out right here at Easter. It was her favorite holiday," Kate offered.

"You barely know me," Ginger said.

"They're pretty good at reading people." Sloan dipped deep into the mashed potatoes when they came his way. "I've seen them follow rule number one a lot of times." They'd sure looked after him plenty of times since his grandmother died.

"And the next morning, we sometimes feed our stranger and send them on their way," Betsy said as she picked up the gravy boat and handed it to Sloan. "Mama said that the rule said we could tell within twenty-four hours if we had an angel or just a passerby."

Connie shot a smile across the table toward her. "I've been wearing a lapis lazuli next to my heart since you got here. It leads to enlightenment and wisdom. In the dream, I saw us all four hunting Easter eggs together. I never go against a dream, just in case it's Mama talkin' to me in spirit form."

She'd given Sloan a small chunk of rose quartz when he first came to work for them. He was supposed to keep it with him at all times, and according to Connie, it would heal all emotional problems. He'd thrown it in the dresser drawer with his socks when he got home and had forgotten all about it until that moment.

"Are you Wiccan?" Ginger asked.

"Not really," Connie answered. "Mama taught me the healing powers of the stones. I didn't even know that it was a part of Wicca until I was grown."

"It's bad enough that everyone has thought our blood was tainted for all these years. We sure don't want them thinking that we're witches." Kate passed the green beans to Connie.

"I'll be glad when we can start gathering garden vegetables. These green beans aren't bad, Betsy, but fresh ones are so much better." Connie sighed.

"You'll have to come up here in the evenings and snap beans with us when they start coming in," Kate told Sloan.

"Be glad to," he said.

Working more than one day a week occasionally in the spring and summer wasn't anything new, but they'd never invited him to sit on the porch and snap beans or shell peas with them. Maybe Connie had consulted her stones and decided that he wasn't getting enough social life.

"Just so y'all know," Kate said, "I've already asked Sloan to start helping us on Saturdays, and he belongs to me that day. We've got to get the corn in the ground, and I'd like to enlarge our garden, especially the strawberry patch for Betsy's jams."

Betsy turned her head slowly and gave Kate the old stink eye. "And I bet you want those strawberries for your moonshine, don't you?"

"Thought I might experiment with it a little," Kate said.

Sloan chuckled. "Sounds like it might be good."

"My best seller is the apple pie, but I thought about trying some different things, like maybe wild grape and even buttered pecan if I can figure out just how to do it all," Kate said.

❖   ❖   ❖

Ginger couldn't believe that she was sitting around the table with three old ladies who looked like they'd be strict Sunday-school teachers and they were talking about moonshine. That shouldn't have been a surprise since they lived in an old brothel, but it shocked her nonetheless.

"So when's the baby due?" Sloan asked right out of the blue sky.

Ginger shrugged. "I'm not real sure."

"Didn't the doctor give you a due date?" Connie asked.

Ginger shook her head. "I haven't seen a doctor yet. I just bought one of those drugstore tests and it was positive." She hadn't given much thought to the time when the baby would be born. Up until she sat down on that bench in front of the beauty salon, she'd just been trying to get through a day at a time.

"Good Lord!" Kate gasped. "I'll call Doc Emerson and make an appointment for you."

Ginger felt the heat crawling from the back of her neck all the way to her face. She was sure if she looked in the mirror, she'd have two bright-red circles on her cheeks. "I should wait until I have enough money to pay him."

"We've been bartering with Doc since before Mama died, and she passed almost sixty years ago. He does like his shine, and he doesn't like to pay for it, so . . ." Kate shrugged.

"Thank you," Ginger said. If she was dreaming, it went far beyond anything she'd ever imagined, maybe short of winning the lottery. She reminded herself that she'd be leaving on Monday morning, so she shouldn't get too attached to these sisters.

"So, where do you come from, Ginger?" Sloan broke the moment of silence.

"All over Kentucky," she answered. "The latest place was in Lexington, but most of my life was spent in and around Harlan County."

"I knew a guy in the army who had an accent like yours." Sloan buttered another biscuit. "Man would use five hundred words when five would do the job."

"I've known folks like that." Ginger passed the platter of chicken to him.

She didn't even have to close her eyes to get a clear picture in her head of Lucas Dermott. He'd promised her the moon, the stars, and half the universe if she'd leave the shelter and live with him. He'd delivered the first two all right. She could see them through cracks in the dirty windows in the last apartment where they'd lived before he was shot and killed. At first she'd tried to keep the windows clean, but that proved to be an exhausting job. Dust and dirt from the gravel business nearby, plus all the grime that flew up to the second-story windows from the car-repair shop below them, collected on the windows on a daily basis. Using his ability to sweet-talk, Lucas would run a few scams occasionally, but that money went for what he wanted to buy. The paycheck she brought in as a waitress had paid the rent and put food on the table.

"You don't say much, do you?" Sloan nudged her shoulder with his.

"Neither do you," she shot back.

"Maybe we'll have to work on that." His shoulder touched hers again.

The sparks from his touch brought her from the past to the present in a split second. "I was just enjoyin' this fine meal and y'all's company. Last time I sat down in a dinin' room like this was in Harlan, Kentucky.

A little girl became my friend at the new school and invited me to have supper with her family. My foster mother said it would be all right."

"What happened?" Connie asked.

"That was the only time I was invited. Guess they figured out that I wasn't going to be a cheerleader." She raised a shoulder in a shrug.

"Funny how that works, isn't it?" Connie's smile didn't quite reach her eyes. "I wanted to be a cheerleader, too, but Mama's reputation and the fact that we didn't have one hundred percent white blood in our veins put a stop to that."

"The past is gone. The future is iffy. That means the present is all we've got, so we'll dwell on that," Kate said.

"You sound just like Mama," Connie told her. "And she was always right. So let's talk about the peach cobbler that Ginger helped me make for dessert. We've got fresh whipped cream for the top. If everyone is ready, I'll bring it out."

Ginger pushed back her chair. "I'll carry the dessert bowls for you."

Connie laid a hand on her shoulder when they reached the kitchen, and then she leaned over and whispered, "Sloan don't usually talk as much as he has today."

"I didn't think he said all that much," Ginger said in a soft voice, wishing she could get to know him better.

"We've gotten used to one-word answers from him and very little conversation." Connie picked up the cobbler in one hand and the bowl of chilled whipped cream in the other and headed back to the dining room.

Ginger followed her with dessert dishes and clean spoons. "How do you girls stay so slim eating like this every day?"

"Honey, we appreciate the compliment, but Kate is the only skinny one among us." Betsy giggled. "She's built like our father. Me and Connie took after Mama."

Ginger had always wondered what her biological mother and father might have looked like. Her father had been shot in what they called a domestic abuse situation. Her mother was pregnant with her when she was sent to prison for killing him. Six months after Ginger was born, her mother died. She'd never even seen a picture of either of her parents.

She helped Connie in the kitchen all afternoon, and they had supper at the dining room table again. The conversation seemed to center on growing corn for the moonshine business, and evidently they were going to sow it over a lot of ground.

"Just how big is this place?" she asked.

"The house and yard cover about two acres," Connie said.

"That's what we figure we've got fenced in anyway," Kate told her. "The house sits at the front of our hundred acres. We've got a garden and the cornfield out behind us. We gave up growin' a steer or two for beef and the hogs and chickens about five years ago. Figured that with just the three of us, we could buy or barter for our meat and eggs as cheap as we could grow it, and besides, we was gettin' too old to go out every mornin' in the winter to feed and milk the cow."

"If we'd have known Sloan was coming back home and we could've hired him to help us more than a day or two a week, we might still be doin' all that, but hindsight is the only twenty-twenty vision most of us get." Betsy sighed. "I did like having my own beef and pork in the freezer. You never know what that meat we get in the market might have been treated with."

"Probably lots of salt to make us live longer." Connie giggled so hard that she snorted.

Betsy rolled her eyes. "She always says that because Mama wasn't even sixty when she died. She always had the garden and the livestock to help feed her girls when she ran the brothel. She didn't have much bought food, so she didn't eat all the preservatives that we do these days."

"She said it gave her girls something to do in the daylight hours." Kate's tone sounded like she was telling Ginger that the price of corn was going up that year. "Now it gives us something to do other than just sitting down and waiting to die."

"Don't talk like that," Betsy scolded. "We've all three got lots of good years left on this old earth. I'm planning on living to be a hundred, myself."

"Me and God got us an agreement. Long as I keep that commandment about cleanliness bein' up there next to godliness, I get to keep dustin' and cleanin' this house and workin' in the flower beds," Connie said.

Sloan chuckled. "Did you get that agreement in writing, Miz Connie?"

"Nope. I figured God's word was good enough," she shot right back at him.

Ginger was glad that she'd just swallowed a big sip of sweet tea, or she would have spit it all the way across the table.

Chapter Three

*G*inger could feel the expectancy in the house when she awoke on Saturday morning. There wasn't anything particular that she could put her finger on, but the feeling surrounded her. The only way she could describe it was by comparing it to that year that she'd stayed with a foster family by the name of Williams. The Christmas tree had been set up in the corner of the living room and each of the three kids in the house had two presents under it. She felt the same anticipation that morning as she dusted all the furniture and knickknacks in the living room.

"We'll just do this room today," Connie told her, "because right after we finish eating at noon, we get to dye our eggs. Betsy boils a dozen for each of us, and then we get to decorate them."

"What do you do with them?" Ginger asked.

"Why, honey"—Connie stopped cleaning the window ledges—"we pay Sloan to work for us after church tomorrow. He gets a good Sunday dinner that way, and then his job is to hide our eggs so we can hunt them. Rules say that they have to be inside the yard fence. We're too old to be traipsing out to the barn to find an egg in an old chicken roostin' nest."

"I've never hunted Easter eggs," Ginger admitted. "I hid them once for the younger kids, but the foster homes I lived in didn't do anything special at Easter, or Passover for that matter."

"Well, you're in for a treat. Whoever finds the most eggs gets a hundred dollars as the big prize." Connie went back to cleaning an already spotless window.

"If you get the prize money, what do you do with it?" Ginger asked.

"I tuck it away and give it to the church missionary fund the next Sunday," Connie whispered.

"Did your mama give you that much money when you were a little girl?" Ginger couldn't imagine having money that wasn't needed for bills and food—dollars that she could spend on whatever she wanted.

"No. Mama gave us five dollars, and we had to give at least one of those to the church the next Sunday. In those days you could buy something nice with four dollars, but now you can't buy a bag of sugar for that. So we upped the prize a few years ago. What are you going to do with the money if you find the most eggs?" Connie sat down in an old wooden rocking chair and set it in motion.

"I dreamed I would hunt eggs with y'all, and now it's coming true." The thought of even the possibility of having that much money in her hands was mind-boggling.

"Honey, we all hunt eggs on Easter." Connie frowned. "Well, maybe not all of us. Sloan says that it wouldn't be fair since he's the one who hides them, and that we're payin' him to do that."

"Well, then I expect if I wind up with that money, I'll use it to buy a bus ticket to take me the rest of the way to California." Ginger finished the last of the dusting. "What do we do now?"

"It's half an hour until we eat dinner, so I expect we'd better go set the table for Betsy. Poor old Sloan has been out there plowing and planting corn all morning. He's going to be hungry." Connie eased up out of the rocking chair. "Kate's too damn old to be raisin' her own corn for the shine. She needs something to keep her busy, so I don't fault her for makin' the stuff in the basement," Connie said. "I don't even mind that she grinds it herself and makes her own mash, but she could buy the corn in the husk. The planting and harvesting is getting to be too much for her."

Ginger didn't know anything about making moonshine, so she kept her mouth shut, but she couldn't help but think about that prize money. Would it get her all the way to California?

"Why did you decide to go west rather than east?" Connie asked as she made her way to the kitchen. "The silverware is in the drawer of that buffet over there."

"I want to see the ocean, and I want my baby to know that there's a world outside of Kentucky." Ginger opened a buffet drawer and brought out the silverware.

"I used to feel like that when I was your age." She took the dishes from the china cabinet. "I wanted to see if there was a world outside of Rooster, Texas, but after Mama took us to Medina Lake for a campout one weekend, I decided that Hondo was as far as I wanted to get from my home."

"What happened at the lake?" Ginger asked.

"Nothing catastrophic." Connie set out the gravy boat and four serving dishes. "I just hated being out there in the wilds. I didn't like sleeping in a tent, and I hated the mosquitoes. I just wanted to be in my own bed, in my own clean room, and eating food that Betsy and Mama made in the kitchen rather than what they tried to make on an open fire."

"But you made a memory, right?" Ginger wanted her baby to have good memories, and most of all grow up knowing that it would never spend time in the system.

"Oh, yeah." Connie laughed out loud. "I had mosquito bites that took a week to heal, but Mama read to me every night and put her special salve on them to keep the itch at a minimum."

Betsy came from the kitchen with a big bowl of salad in her hands. "Is she tellin' you tales about the time Mama took us camping? That was so much fun. I learned about cooking over an open fire. Me and Mama burned the chicken, but the inside wasn't too bad. If the end of times renders us without electricity or runnin' water, at least we know how to fend for ourselves."

"You sound just like Mama did," Connie told her.

"I'll take that as a compliment. I hear Kate and Sloan comin' in the back door. Y'all come on in here and help me get the meal on the table," Betsy said.

"We're starvin'," Kate said as she came into the house. "I forget from one year to the next how much work is involved in the corn plantin' business."

"Well, I keep tellin' you to buy the corn," Connie argued.

"I might buy it another year just to shut you up about it," Kate fussed.

"She gets like this when she's tired," Betsy whispered. "Lord only knows that she's downright sassy when it comes to her moonshine. We never did know our father real good. Connie was just a baby when he died, but Mama had a picture of him up in her bedroom, and Kate's like him. Tall and thin and stubborn as a cross-eyed Missouri mule."

"I'm standin' right here." Kate glared at her.

"And I can see you plain and clear," Connie said. "Go wash your hands."

"Don't boss me," Kate threw over her shoulder.

Ginger had seen children act like that, but never adults. It was almost funny, but she was careful not to laugh. She picked up the serving bowls and hurried into the kitchen to help Betsy bring the food to the table.

After grace, Kate began to pass food around the table. First the platter of pot roast and then a bowl full of potatoes and carrots. Ginger wondered if fried chicken was always served on Friday and pot roast on

Saturday. Betsy had told her already that she was planning to make the traditional Easter ham on Sunday.

You wanted memories, the little voice in the back of her head said loud and clear. *No ocean or anything you could look at could provide memories like this. Fate led you to this place. Enjoy it while you can.*

She caught Sloan staring at her just as she nodded in agreement with the pesky voice. She flashed a smile his way, and his head bobbed once, as if he had read her thoughts and knew exactly what she'd been thinking. She was more than a little intimidated by him. The way he looked at her made her feel like he could read her mind.

"I've got a question," Ginger said. "So, was there a school here in Rooster at one time?"

"Oh, yes, honey," Connie answered. "It wasn't ever very big, and when we were in high school, there were only maybe thirty or forty white children that went to it, but we had our school."

"When they finally shut it down about forty years ago, there were only six seniors. The next year, the Hondo school system ran buses out here to get the kids." Kate sighed. "That was a sad fall for all of us. We lost the post office a few years later. Once those two things are gone from a community, it's all but a ghost town."

"If the majority of the kids were black, then why did you have trouble being a cheerleader?" Ginger placed her hand on her stomach. Lucas had come from Cajun folks down in Louisiana. He'd told her that his nanny when he was in preschool had been French. She should have realized then that he'd grown up in a different social world than she did.

"Honey"—Connie patted her on the arm—"if we'd been black we might have stood a better chance. Neither race, black nor white, really wanted us."

"We're sure glad that times have changed," Betsy said.

An awkward silence followed her statement. Ginger thought about Lucas. If it hadn't been that she was carrying his baby, things could have gone different for her. She might have found another waitress job when the café she'd been working at closed down, but no one wanted to hire a woman who was visibly pregnant.

Lucas had said that he loved her when he talked her into moving out of the shelter and into the ratty apartment with him, but his actions often hadn't matched his words. He'd lose his temper if her tips were a few dollars less than they'd been the day before, and twice he'd slapped her. She couldn't even find tears to cry when the police came to tell her that he was dead, because down deep, she'd been relieved that she was out of the relationship. She had never known that any of his relatives were alive, but his parents had claimed the body and taken it home with them for burial.

"So did y'all get the corn planted?" Connie changed the subject.

"About half of it. We'll take care of the rest of it Monday afternoon. We've got other things to do when we're finished eating," Kate answered.

"I'm thinkin' that Ginger can wear my dress from last year," Connie said.

Kate cocked her head to one side and eyed Ginger. "It just might fit her at that. I'm glad this is my year to choose the Easter dress, so we don't have to wear those flowing things you always choose."

"Hey, just because you're skinny and nothing binds up your waist don't mean me and Betsy want to have to wear a girdle and a waist-length bra to look good for the picture," Connie fussed.

"She's right," Betsy agreed. "Last year's dress was so comfortable that I felt like I was wearing a nightgown."

Ginger took a deep breath and let it out slowly. She didn't want to offend them, but Lord have mercy—she sure didn't want to wear one of their dresses if it looked like a nightgown, either. "I have something I can wear, but thank you for the offer."

"If you change your mind, it's a cute little pink linen with butter-fly sleeves," Connie said. "I'll show it to you after we eat and you can decide."

"That would be great." Ginger managed a smile and decided that if the dress came close to fitting her, she'd wear it. So what if it made her look like Dumbo's baby sister? Church services would only be for one hour, and if it made Connie happy, then it would be worth it.

❖   ❖   ❖

A vision of the dresses from last year flashed through Sloan's mind. He didn't know a blessed thing about fashion, but in his mind those dresses sure didn't look like something Ginger would wear. Both days that he'd been around her she'd worn tight-fitting britches and a faded knit top that hung almost to her knees.

Kate interrupted his thoughts when she passed the platter of biscuits to him. "Are you going to church with us tomorrow?" she asked.

"Now, Miz Kate, who'd hide the eggs if I went to church?" he asked.

"You could do that job while I get dinner on the table," Betsy told him.

"Then you'd all be peeking out the windows trying to see where I put them." He chuckled. "I know you, Miz Betsy, and how much that hundred-dollar prize means to you."

"Busted!" Betsy giggled. "But you are welcome to go with us anytime that you want. Your granny wouldn't be happy that you don't attend."

"I know that, and I hate to disappoint her, but," Sloan said in a slow drawl, "God and I have got some things to straighten out before I don't feel like a hypocrite sittin' in His house."

Kate reached over and patted him on the shoulder. "When you get it right with Him, you're welcome to sit with us on our pew."

"Thank you." Sloan didn't expect that he'd be attending church anytime soon, but it was nice of Kate to offer her support. Before he enlisted, he'd gone every single Sunday morning and sometimes on Wednesday nights with his granny. He'd gone to chapel a few times, but only in basic training. After that, it was hit and miss, depending on whether he was in the field or not and whether he was hungover on Sunday morning. When his buddies were all killed in one fell swoop, he blamed himself—and then he questioned God. If the Almighty Maker was all that great, how could He let a bomb take out Sloan's entire team?

"Where did you go to church, Ginger?" Connie asked.

"Depended on what foster family I was with," she answered. "I seldom stayed more than a year with any one of them, sometimes even less. I remember one that was pretty religious, and we went every Sunday morning. On the way home, the lady would ask us questions about the sermon. If we couldn't answer them, we were punished."

Sloan's hands knotted into fists under the table. No child should suffer because of something like that. It would make them hate God even worse than he did.

"I didn't think foster parents were allowed to whip kids." Connie's chin quivered.

"There's lots more ways to punish a child than to use a belt or a paddle," Ginger told her. "The punishment if we couldn't answer the questions was that we had to go to the bedroom, get down on our knees, and pray the whole time the rest of the family was eating dinner. Now"—Ginger's smile didn't reach her pretty eyes—"tell me how we go about decorating the eggs this afternoon. How do y'all color them?"

"We've got all kinds of things, from glue and glitter to dye kits and pretty little decals." Betsy stopped what she was doing and gave Ginger a quick hug. "Decorating the eggs has always been such a big afternoon for us. We don't get in a rush, and we bring out all our artistic abilities, and, honey, you'll never miss a meal here at the Banty House."

Sloan glanced over at Ginger. "I have trouble hiding the eggs because they sparkle in the sunlight as it is. It takes me the whole hour and a half that they're gone to get the job done."

He liked that he'd made her smile and her brown eyes had taken on a sparkle. He couldn't imagine how hard her life must have been, or how he would have survived without his grandmother's support after his mother and dad were both killed.

❖   ❖   ❖

When the dishes were all done and put away, Kate gave Sloan orders for what she wanted done in the rest of the corn patch, and then she hurried downstairs to check on the mash she had setting up. Betsy started two pans of eggs to boiling, and Connie took Ginger upstairs to try on the pink dress.

Ginger would rather have stayed in the kitchen with Betsy or even gone to the moonshine room with Kate. Truth was she'd take going to the cornfield with Sloan over all that. Sloan had a mysterious air about him that made her want to get to know him better. His eyes said he'd known pain and his smile was guarded, but she loved it when he slid one eyelid shut in a wink. She felt as if they were sharing a secret that no one else had any idea about.

As she climbed the stairs behind Connie, she compared Sloan and Lucas. Both were good-looking guys. Lucas had black, curly hair that he wore a little too long and brown eyes that were constantly darting around. Now that he was gone, she could see that he was always looking for an easy way to make a dollar—legal or not, it didn't seem to matter. He'd sweet-talked her into moving out of the shelter where they'd both been living and into an apartment with him about a year ago. He'd told her that in a few months he'd have enough money to buy them a house.

"This is my room." Connie threw open a door. "Come right on in and we'll see what the dress looks like on you."

Ginger followed her inside, trying not to stare, but it was impossible. Wallpaper with trailing pink roses surrounded her. The full-size canopy bed had a pink-and-white checkered ruffle around the top and a matching bedspread. The stool in front of the vanity was covered with pink velvet, and pillows of every shade of pink were scattered on the bed.

"I like pink," Connie said. "I've had that bed since I was a little girl. I only wish that I could talk Kate and Betsy into digging a hole big enough in the Cottonwood Cemetery to bury me in it."

Ginger shivered at the idea of Connie dying, but when it happened, she'd probably never even know. Her time at the Banty House would be over on Monday morning.

Connie went to her closet and found the dress, pulled the plastic bag up over the hanger, and laid it on the bed. "Are you too modest to try it on in front of me?" she asked. "I can step out into the hallway if you are."

Ginger bit her tongue to keep from giggling. Connie couldn't know that she'd slept in shelters that had as many as sixteen women in one room. "I'm fine with you being in the room." She jerked her shirt up over her head and kicked off her shoes. Then she stripped out of her jeans, removed the dress from the hanger, and slipped it over her head.

Connie took one look at her, fell back on the bed, and laughed so hard that she got the hiccups. When she could finally talk, she said, "Darlin', you look like a bump in a tent."

"I can wear what I have." Ginger couldn't see a long mirror anywhere, so she had no idea just how she looked. However, she felt exactly like what Connie had said. She started to take off the dress, but Connie slid off the bed and took her by the hand.

"Honey, it can be fixed. We'll just go on over to the sewing room. I already have ideas about it." Connie led her to the last room on the left and opened the door. "Mama insisted that we all learn to sew. I'm not as good as she was, but in thirty minutes I can easily turn that dress into something that will look good on you."

"How?" Ginger asked.

Connie took her by the shoulders and turned her around to face a floor-length mirror. The corners of her mouth turned up slightly, and then she giggled. She truly did look like a bump in a tent. There was no way that Connie could ever make this dress usable—especially in thirty minutes.

"First, we'll take the sleeves out. I only picked out this dress because all three of us have old-women arms. I call them bat wings because they flap in the air when we raise them. We needed something with sleeves," Connie said. "And then we're going to remove the collar. You've still got a nice firm neck, so you don't need a stand-up collar. When I get those jobs done, I'll put a little bit of elastic under your boobs. That way it will fit right above your tummy." She talked as she helped Ginger remove the dress. "I've got a belt with pretty diamonds—well, not the real things, but sparkling stones—that will finish it off."

Ginger couldn't see that any of those things would help. "But, Miz Connie, it will ruin your dress."

"Honey, my closet is so crammed that I'll never miss one dress," she said as she got out a tiny pair of scissors and went to work. "I'm thinking that we need to cut two inches off the bottom, too. I can do that after we dye eggs. You've got good legs. Enjoy them, girl. They'll turn cheesy when you get old. I'll have it all done by bedtime and you can try it on again. What size shoes do you wear?"

"Seven," Ginger answered.

Connie cocked her head to one side. "I think you probably wear about the same size shoes as Mama did. She's got a lovely pair of white satin flats that will work. Don't worry, darlin'. She never wore them. I wouldn't want to wear a dead woman's shoes, either, not even Mama's, but she bought them to wear the last Easter she was with us, and then she passed before the holiday." She rattled on as the sewing machine buzzed.

"You're really good at sewing," Ginger said.

"Mama insisted that we be self-sufficient as much as possible." Connie glanced down at Ginger's hands. "You must have white gloves, but don't worry, I've got a drawer full. I've got a pair of pretty lace ones that will go perfect with this dress." Connie laughed. "I feel like I'm dressing Cinderella."

"A very pregnant Cinderella." Ginger went to the window and looked out over the field where Sloan was riding on a small tractor. He sure wasn't Prince Charming on a big white horse, but then, it had been years since Ginger believed in fairy tales.

Chapter Four

*G*inger had thought that dyeing eggs was going to be a two-hour job, but she was dead wrong. The dining room tablecloth had been removed and replaced with newspaper. Four place settings had been arranged with paintbrushes, glitter, glue, all kinds of cute little stencils, and everything that could be imagined to decorate the eggs.

"All this just to put the eggs in the grass and then eat them tomorrow?" Ginger asked.

"Honey, the real prize isn't the end; it's the journey itself," Kate told her. "This is one of our traditions, and we love this part of it as much as hunting the eggs."

"And after they're decorated, we put them in the refrigerator," Betsy told her. "That way, it's safe to use them tomorrow. We always, always have egg salad sandwiches for supper on Easter night."

Ginger made a mental note right then to have lots and lots of traditions for her baby, and one of them would be decorating Easter eggs. She pulled out a chair and sat down. "What do I do first?"

"You are the artist," Betsy answered. "If you want the background to be a color, then you start dipping like this." She picked up a boiled egg, settled it into a wire loop, and slowly submerged it in a bowl of blue dye. "The longer you leave it in there, the darker the color that you'll get."

Kate giggled under her breath.

"What's so funny?" Connie asked.

"I was just wonderin' if I'd be totally white if I soaked myself in buttermilk for a whole day," Kate replied. "Maybe then I'd look like Edith Wilson, and I could have gotten a husband like Max."

"Honey, you never would have had a chance with someone like Max Wilson. No way would a budding preacher man want a woman who came from the Banty House." Connie laughed out loud.

"Or who had black blood in her veins, but I do remember the buttermilk days." Betsy laughed with her sister.

"What's so funny?" Ginger asked.

"I read about women soaking their hands and using buttermilk compresses on their faces in an old magazine I found in the attic back when we were little girls." Connie dried her eyes on a paper towel.

"And she took a whole gallon of buttermilk up to the bathroom and Mama caught her smearing it on her arms and neck and face." Kate drew a design on an egg and started painting a lovely picture of a little duck swimming in water.

"Did it work?" Ginger asked.

Connie shook her head. "Nope. I'm still not one thing or another."

"I'll tell the rest of the story," Kate said. "We had one of our sister meetings in my bedroom, and we figured the lady in the article got it all wrong. It had to work from the inside, so we all three asked for buttermilk every night with our supper. I gagged with every swallow and still hate the taste today."

"How long did you do that?" Ginger asked.

"About a week, and then one night at supper, Mama told us that it didn't matter what we were on the outside," Kate said. "What mattered was what we were on the inside—in our hearts and how we treated other people. I was so glad that she said that, and I've never put buttermilk in my mouth again."

"Your mama was a smart lady." Ginger put an egg in a little wire holder and dipped it in red dye just long enough to turn it pale pink. Maybe if she made sure all her eggs were shades of pink and decorated to please a little girl, her wish for a daughter would be granted.

"Yes, she was." Connie picked up the silver glitter.

"It was after the buttermilk week that I asked her who our father was," Kate said.

"You didn't know?" Ginger asked.

"Not until many years after that. She just told us that he was a good man who'd died a hero, and that satisfied us until we were teenagers," Betsy answered.

"But on her deathbed, she said she'd only ever loved one man, and that was the sheriff of Medina County. That includes Hondo and Rooster and a few more little towns around us, and he was the father to all us girls." Connie sighed. "He died a few months after I was born."

"I'm sorry," Ginger said.

"He wanted to marry Mama, but she'd have none of it. She said being married to the madam of the Banty House would ruin his career. So they had about five years of love before he got killed during a bank robbery, and she never forgot him," Kate said. "Too bad none of us ever found that kind of love."

"Thank God we didn't." Connie rolled her eyes toward the ceiling. "We've done very well taking care of the Banty House without a man telling us what to do."

"You've got Sloan," Ginger reminded them.

"Oh, honey, he's like our shared son. That's different from a husband who'd always be meddling in our affairs." Connie made squiggle designs on her egg with glue and rolled it in glitter.

"More like our grandson," Kate told her. "If he was a son, we'd have to keep him in the house. But a grandchild is different. We can spoil him and send him home. Shhh . . ." She held a finger to her lips. "The tractor has stopped, so he'll be coming in for a break."

Ginger drew a princess crown on her pale-pink egg with glue and then shook gold glitter on it. "I so hope this baby is a girl."

"Got a name picked out?" Kate asked.

Ginger shook her head. "I wouldn't know what kind of name to give him or her. What if I picked out Grace and that didn't fit her at all? Or maybe Ross if it's a boy and he looked more like a Declan? I'll just wait until I'm holding the baby in my arms and then make the decision."

Sloan came into the house through the kitchen door. His dark hair was stuck to his forehead and was flattened at the place where his hat had been. "I'm going to help myself to a glass of lemonade. Any of y'all want one?"

"Pour up four and bring them in here," Connie said. "Want to take a break and decorate eggs with us?"

"No, ma'am," he called out.

"We always ask him, but I reckon he'd soon as be out there sweatin' on that tractor as gettin' his hands all messed up with glitter and paint," Kate whispered softly across the table toward Ginger.

Ice crackled in the glasses filled with homemade lemonade as he carried them to the table and set one at each place. Ginger's breath caught in her chest when he pulled out a chair at the end of the table and sat down. His biceps strained the sleeves of his chambray shirt, and sweat had mussed up his hair. The temperature in the house seemed to rise by at least ten degrees, and Ginger's hands shook when she dipped another egg, this time in green dye.

Dammit! She thought. *I'm pregnant and ugly as a mud fence right now, and I vowed I'd take care of my own self and this baby first. I don't need a man in my life—not after Lucas.*

"The rest of the field is plowed, and corn is in the ground." Sloan took a long drink. "Anything else y'all want me to do this afternoon?"

"Nothing I can think of," Kate said.

"Then I'll be goin' on home. Tinker will be missin' me," he said.

"That's his dog," Betsy explained to Ginger. "It's an ugly little mutt that his grandma adopted when it showed up on her porch one day several years ago."

"The eggs will be in the refrigerator tomorrow when you get here, and you might turn off the oven so the ham doesn't get too done," Betsy reminded him.

Connie looked up and said, "Don't forget your phone. Past two years have been the best pictures we've had to go in our album, and you got them with your fancy-shmancy cell phone."

"Got to have it so I can listen to music. I'll see y'all tomorrow a little after noon," he said as he stood up and started for the door.

"You could come on back up here for supper after a while," Betsy said. "We're havin' waffles and chicken, and I know how you like that."

"Thanks, but no thanks. Me and Tinker need to get some things done around the house, but I sure appreciate the offer." He pulled a camouflage cap from his hip pocket and put it on as he left by the kitchen door.

❖ ❖ ❖

Tinker came from around the house, tail wagging and head down, wanting to be petted when Sloan got out of his truck. The dog looked like maybe one of his parents had been a Chihuahua and the other a small poodle. The hair on his sides was smooth, but what was on his back was kinky curly, and he had a tuft on his head. He probably didn't weigh more than seven or eight pounds, but he had a big bark, especially when someone was coming around the house. Sloan stooped down and scratched Tinker's ears. "Did you hold the place down for me today, old boy?"

Tinker yipped and led the way up onto the porch and then rushed inside when Sloan opened the door. He went right to the sofa and jumped up on his favorite spot. Sloan hung his cap on the rack inside the door and sat down on a ladder-back chair to take off his combat boots.

"The sisters have taken in a new stray. She'll be gone Monday. I guess since they don't go to town except on Thursday, they'll ask me to take her to the bus stop. 'Course, they've started talkin' about getting a new cat, so it could be that they'll make an exception and go twice in one week."

Tinker's tail thumped on the worn sofa.

"I agree with you. It is what it is, whether I take Ginger to the bus stop or they do. She'll be gone. I kind of feel sorry for her. There she is pregnant and no family. At least when I hit rock bottom, I had Granny to come home to . . . and you." Sloan laid his phone on the coffee table, picked up Tinker and gave him a kiss on the head. Then he set him back down on the sofa. "What'll it be tonight? You want some classic country or new modern country?"

Tinker looked up at him with big round brown eyes.

"All right, classic country it is." Sloan touched the screen and Waylon Jennings began singing. He pulled his shirt up over his body and carried it with him to the bathroom, where he put it in the hamper and adjusted the water in the shower. A visual of the rush to the showers after he and his team had been out on a long mission flashed through his mind. A cold shower and a bottle of bootleg whiskey sent from home in a mouthwash bottle were the two most important things in those days. He finished getting cleaned up and went to the kitchen to open a can of dog food for Tinker. Then he poured himself a glass of sweet tea and carried it to the living room. Surfing through the few channels on the television, he finally settled on reruns of *NCIS*.

Somewhere in the middle of the last half of the episode, he turned off the television. "I'm restless tonight, Tinker. Let's go for a walk. I need to clear my head of all these thoughts rumbling around up here. It's a jumble of things that happened over there in the sandbox and what's going on at the Banty House with that new girl." He touched his forehead with his forefinger.

The dog hopped off the sofa and headed toward the door. He waited patiently until Sloan got his boots on and tied and slipped on a hooded jacket, but when the door opened, he bounded outside and ran toward the end of the short lane.

County Road 4404 was a little less than half a mile long and ended at Cottonwood Cemetery. The tiny community of Rooster was set just off County Road 442, and that was where he and Tinker usually went if they felt like an evening walk. The dog was getting up in years, so Sloan always gave him a rest at the halfway mark, where an old scrub oak had fallen over beside the road.

Sloan kept an eye on the dog when he chased a rabbit into a mesquite thicket, but he didn't seem to be panting too hard when he came back to the edge of the road. He was sure enough ready to flop down and catch his breath when they reached the log, though, and Sloan sat down. They weren't there but a few seconds, when Tinker's head popped up and he growled down deep in his throat.

"What is it?" Sloan glanced over his shoulder, expecting to see a squirrel or maybe even a slow-moving possum. A movement to his left startled him, and he whipped around to see Ginger not ten feet from him.

"Well, hello." She sat down on the log about two feet away. "Is that Tinker? He's kind of cute."

"Beauty must be in the eye of the beholder," Sloan replied. "But to answer your question, yes, this is Tinker. He's gettin' up in years, so when we take a walk from our place to Rooster, we take a little rest right here."

Ginger nodded but didn't say anything more for several seconds. Other than the sisters at the Banty House and their occasional guest, Sloan hadn't socialized since he'd come home to Texas. Sitting there with Ginger so close should have been awkward, but it wasn't, and that surprised him.

"You just out for an evening walk?" he finally asked.

The setting sun put sparkling highlights in her blonde hair when she nodded. "The way the ladies are feeding me, I figured I'd better get out and get some exercise, or I'll be rolling by the time this baby is born."

The night air was so still that Sloan could hear a dove cooing in the distance and a coyote howling somewhere beyond the cemetery. Then the thump of an oil well as it started pumping overshadowed every other sound.

"What's that noise?" Ginger asked.

"Oil wells. If you listen, you can hear several different ones starting to work. There's one on my property and two at the very back of the land that the Carson sisters own, way back behind the Banty House," he answered.

"So that's where they get their money," she mused.

"Some of it," he replied.

"I wondered how they could live on what they made from moonshine and jelly," she said.

"Connie sells her jelly and jams, all right, but they use the moonshine to barter with. That's what upset them so much when their hairdresser died. They'd been paying her with shine. Kate says it's against the law to sell homemade brew, but she can't find a single place that says she can't barter with it." He chuckled. "I'm not sure that the law is really written that way, but I'm not about to argue with Kate."

"You are a smart man, Sloan. I wouldn't disagree with Kate, either. If she wants to make moonshine and use it for haircuts and shampoos, I ain't sayin' a word." Her brown eyes twinkled with humor.

"So where are you going next?" he asked.

"As far as wherever my paycheck takes me. I don't expect much, and I sure won't never find anyone who'll treat me like I've been taken care of since I got here, but I've got some good memories," she answered. "Do you ever get the urge to go somewhere else?"

"Been there, done that, got a pair of well-worn combat boots to prove it." He held up a foot. "So, no, ma'am. I'm content to be a hermit right now."

"If I was goin' to settle in one spot, I wouldn't mind this being the one," she said.

"But? I hear a *but* in your voice," Sloan said.

"But until now I ain't never been outside of Kentucky, and I want my baby to have more than I did," she told him. "I got to see Tennessee, Arkansas, and a little of Oklahoma before I got to here, though, so that's something."

"How did you wind up in Hondo?" he asked.

"I ran out of money in Oklahoma City, so I hitched a ride with a trucker and wound up in Dallas. He gave me some money when he let me off, and I asked the ticket person how far I could get with that amount. She said I could make it to Hondo, which was west of San Antonio, so I paid the price and had enough left to buy a sandwich and a carton of milk for my lunch," Ginger explained.

"That's sure traveling by faith," Sloan said.

"Faith has nothing to do with it. *Determination* to get as far away from Kentucky as I can is the right word," she told him.

"I had that feeling when I went into the military right out of high school. I couldn't wait to get away from Texas," he admitted.

"And now you don't want to go anywhere? What happened?" she asked.

"Life happened." He wasn't ready to go into detail about what had happened in Kuwait. Part of it was classified, anyway, and like his granny said so many times, "Let sleeping dogs lie."

"Amen to that," Ginger agreed, standing. "I'd better get on back to the house."

"Tinker and I are going that way. Mind if we walk with you?" Sloan asked.

"Not a bit, but I have to warn you, I don't go too fast these days," she answered.

"Tinker doesn't either," Sloan replied.

Tinker took his cue from Sloan when he stood to his feet and started back to the house. Sloan whistled, and the dog whipped around and plodded along between him and Ginger.

He tried to think of something to start a conversation, but nothing came to mind. When the Banty House was in sight, she finally said, "I can't imagine a white community and a black one living this close together and still being segregated."

"It was the times," Sloan said. "Mission Valley was all black. Rooster was less than a mile up the road and was all white. The residents met at the grocery store in Rooster. Each little town had their own churches and schools since those weren't integrated back then, and other than buying groceries, each side pretty much kept to itself."

"I read about such things in history classes in school, but I can't wrap my mind around that kind of prejudice," Ginger said. "I'm glad that I live in today's world instead of that one."

"Me too," Sloan agreed. He'd seen prejudice when he was in Kuwait for those two tours, both inside the military and out, so he knew it was still in the world, but if Ginger wanted to believe it was all gone, he sure wasn't going to burst her bubble.

They reached the sidewalk leading up to the house, and she turned around to face him. The sun was nothing more than a sliver of orange on the horizon, but the shadows and light blended together to form a halo right above her head.

"If Tinker needs to rest again, you could sit on the porch swing with me for a little while. I suppose it would even be all right if I offered you a glass of sweet tea or lemonade," she said.

He heard a familiar sound, and his pulse kicked into high gear. He glanced down just as Ginger took another step and her foot landed right behind a six-foot rattlesnake's head.

"Don't move," he said. "Don't take another step, or even breathe."

"What?" She looked up at him with questions written all over her face.

"You are standing on a snake. If you can, put more pressure on your foot, but don't pick it up for any reason," he whispered as he pulled his pocketknife out and flipped the longest blade open.

"What are you going to do?" She gasped when she looked to the side.

"I'm going to cut its head off, but you have to be still and put pressure on the body to hold it still, or else it could bite one of us," Sloan told her.

The snake's body and tail twitched and jerked as it tried to free itself from her weight. When it wrapped its tail around her ankle, all the color left her face.

Sloan dropped to his knees and laid the blade of the knife in the narrow space between the head and Ginger's foot. Tinker must've realized what was happening because he began to growl and bite the snake. The creature writhed even more, as the dog tried to kill it by chewing on its middle while Sloan worked on holding it down right behind the head and slicing away with his knife. One slip of the knife and he'd cut the edge of Ginger's foot. If that happened, she would no doubt jump and the rattler would turn and sink its fangs into Sloan's hand.

"I've got a leg cramp," Ginger said.

"Just another second or two." To say that Sloan was sweating bullets was an understatement. He hadn't been so tense since he'd come home to Texas in a numb state, devoid of any kind of emotion.

"Please hurry," she said.

He could hear the sob in her voice just as he got through the last of the skin and used his knife to flip the critter's head out to the side of the road, so Tinker wouldn't mess with it. "It's all right to take a step forward," he said as he wiped the blade of his knife on the grass beside the road and straightened up.

Ginger blinked a couple of times, then let out a whoosh of air and started to fall forward. He tossed the knife on the ground and caught her. If she hadn't been pregnant, he might have thrown her over his shoulder like a bag of feed, but he scooped her up like a bride and carried her up the sidewalk to the porch. He managed to ring the doorbell, and time stood still. Ginger was still breathing, but fainting like that couldn't be good for the baby. In reality, Kate opened the door within a minute, but it seemed like hours to Sloan.

"What happened?" She motioned him inside.

"She fainted." Sloan's voice sounded to him like it was coming from a tunnel as he crossed the foyer and headed toward the living room.

"Put her on the sofa in the parlor." Kate barked orders to the others. "Connie, get a cold rag. Betsy, bring the smelling salts."

By the time he'd crossed the room and gently laid her down, Connie was hurrying back across the floor. Betsy came from a different room carrying a small bottle in her hand. Both of them rattled off questions so fast that it made his head swim.

Connie sat on the edge of the coffee table and began to wash Ginger's face. Her eyelids fluttered yet didn't open wide, but when Betsy waved the contents of the bottle under her nose, she sat straight up and started coughing.

"Good girl!" Betsy quickly capped the smelling salts and set them on the mantel above the fireplace. "Now, tell us what happened."

"Do we need to call the doctor or take you to the emergency room?" Betsy asked.

"She stepped on a snake." Sloan hovered close by the end of the sofa.

"Sweet Jesus!" Kate groaned. "I'll get the snakebite kit."

Sloan shook his head. "No need for that."

"How did I get in here?" Ginger finally asked.

"Sloan carried you." Kate picked up the receiver of the old rotary phone from the end table. She tapped her foot as she waited for someone to answer and then said, "Hello, Dr. Emerson," and then she went on to explain what had happened.

"I'm fine," Ginger said over Kate's conversation. "I'm terrified of snakes, and that thing wrapped its body around my leg, and . . ." She shuddered as the sentence trailed off.

Kate laid the receiver back on the base. "Okay, then. Dr. Emerson is out of town. Thank goodness he gave me his cell phone number for emergencies. He will see you on Thursday when he gets back, but for now you are to make sure the baby is moving at least every hour and drink lots of fluids and be careful where you walk."

"I'll take the first watch," Connie said.

"What?" Ginger frowned.

"We have to be sure the baby is moving, so I'll take the first watch through the night," she explained.

"You ladies need to be fresh for Easter tomorrow. I'll sit with her all night. I did lots of all-night guard duty in the service," Sloan said.

❖   ❖   ❖

Ginger slung her legs off the sofa and shook her head. "No one is sitting up with me. The baby is kicking right now, so it's all right. I was scared out of my mind, and my leg began to cramp, and I thought Sloan would never cut through that ugly thing's head, but it's over now."

Lord, have mercy! She had never had to hold her foot on a snake or fainted before, but she'd lived through equally harrowing situations. "I'm going to the kitchen to get a glass of sweet tea. Can I pour one for anyone else?" She stood up, and the room swayed a little before she got her footing.

"I'll get the tea," Connie said.

"You sit down and tell us all the details," Kate demanded.

"Why don't I tell y'all and we can give Ginger a break? I was hopin' she couldn't see anything from right above the snake." Sloan stood in the middle of the living room, back straight and shoulders squared off like he was about to talk to his commander.

Connie headed to the kitchen with Betsy right behind her.

"Don't you say a word before we get back," Connie demanded. "Do you hear that?"

"Sounds like someone out on the porch," Ginger said, hearing a scuffling sound.

Kate cocked her head to one side, then got up and went to the front door. She eased it open and said, "Tinker, you can come inside, but you leave that thing on the porch."

As if he understood her, he raced into the house, went straight to the sofa, and jumped up onto Sloan's lap. Ginger sat down on the other end of the sofa, and the dog moved over between them.

"He thinks he killed that snake, doesn't he?" Ginger smiled.

Sloan scratched his ears. "He probably does, and we'll let him think he's a ferocious dog."

Connie returned carrying a tray with five glasses of tea on it. "Y'all didn't start without us, did you?"

Betsy came in behind her with a full pitcher. "I was afraid Connie would stumble and fall with a heavy tray. She's not too steady on her feet."

"Speak for yourself, Elizabeth Carson." Connie shot a dirty look toward her sister.

"Elizabeth?" Ginger asked.

"Betsy is Elizabeth," Kate said. "The name on my birth certificate is Katherine, and Connie's is Constance. Mama thought we needed a dignified name in case we ever wanted to become doctors or lawyers, but she liked shortened names for what she called everyday livin'. Now that we're all here, tell us this snake story."

Just hearing the word made Ginger remember how that creature felt wrapped around her bare leg. With a shudder, she nodded toward Sloan. "You tell them. You were the hero."

Sloan's face went blank for a split second. Ginger had learned at a young age to read people's expressions, and it had benefited her very well in her formative years. She'd learned to tell if a new foster mother or father was angry and how to sidestep the issue in whatever way she could. Sloan was remembering something bad, and it took him a minute to shake it off.

"Well." He rubbed his chin and went on to tell the story, ending with, "I was just glad that Ginger stepped on it where she did and not halfway down the body, where it could have flipped over and bitten her."

"Me too." Ginger picked up a glass of tea and sipped it, then laid her free hand on her stomach. "The baby just kicked very hard. Matter of fact, I can tell that it was a knee or an elbow just by the way it feels. So he or she is fine, too."

"She's probably tellin' you that she wants to meet all of us before you take her away to some other place," Connie said.

Ginger moved her hand to the other side. "And there's another one. I do believe that she likes sweet tea."

"A true Southern lady." Kate smiled.

"Now that I see you're all right, I should be going." Sloan picked up the last glass of tea and downed it with one long drink. "Thanks for the tea, and I'm right sorry about that scare."

"Don't be," Ginger told him. "Like I said before, you're the hero. You saved my life and my baby's life and even kept me from falling. Thank you from the bottom of my heart. But one more thing—will you please throw what's left of that snake across the road as you leave?" She stared at him and wondered if there was a Superman cape and outfit under his camouflage.

"Yes, ma'am." He gave her a slight nod as he stood up and headed to the door with Tinker right beside him.

"Well, now." Connie sighed. "That's a lot of excitement for old ladies."

Kate's index finger shot up in a blur. "Who are you callin' old? None of us have earned that title, and for your information, baby sister, I don't ever want it. I'm going to be young until the day I die."

Ginger chuckled. "On that note, I'm going to go upstairs and take a long, soaking bath before I go to bed."

"You be careful gettin' in and out of that tub, young lady." Connie shook a finger at her. "You could slip, and Dr. Emerson won't be back until Thursday."

"And I'm leavin' on Monday, remember?" Ginger said.

"Oh, no!" Kate shook her head. "We can't let you do that. Rule number two."

Ginger drew her brows down and tried to remember the second rule on the list in the living room. "What's that one?"

"Help people in distress," Connie sing-songed.

"But I'm not in distress," Ginger argued.

"You were when you fainted, and now we're going to take care of you like Mama would if she was still here. You're in no shape to be travelin' on a bus." Connie shivered. "Or hitchhiking. You never know about truckers. I watch them cop shows on the television. I'm going out on the porch for a cigarette. Lord only knows I need one to calm my nerves when I think about how near you came to bein' snakebit."

Ginger didn't really want to leave, and it *would* be nice to have a doctor verify her due date and tell her what she was having . . . "Thank you, all, for letting me stay on a while longer. I appreciate it more than you realize."

"You are very welcome." Kate picked up the tray and headed for the kitchen. "I swear, Connie, Doc has told you at least a thousand times you need to stop that nasty habit."

"And he's told you"—Connie did a head wiggle that any dramatic teenage girl would envy—"that if you didn't stop samplin' your moonshine, you were going to get a bad liver."

Ginger glanced over at Betsy.

The middle sister shrugged. "I don't smoke cigarettes or drink. I will admit to havin' a little joint before I go to bed at night, but I don't buy it. I just grow a little in the backyard flower bed for personal use."

"Hells bells!" Connie turned around and frowned. "She crossbreeds the stuff and has the best shit in the county, and, honey," Connie whispered as if she were letting Ginger in on a big secret, "we ain't had to pay money for groceries since the year after she went to Woodstock."

Ginger wasn't sure how she was supposed to respond to that, so she just smiled. "Sounds like you've got the bartering system down pretty good."

"Yep, we do," Betsy said as she went upstairs. "And on that note, I'm going to my room. I'll see all y'all tomorrow morning."

"If Mama had been alive when Woodstock happened, she wouldn't have let Betsy go." Kate came back into the room. "But she'd passed years before that, and Betsy was determined to fly to New York and listen to the music. She came back telling us about smokin' pot and how it made her feel. Six months later, she was growin' it in the backyard. What could I say? I was making moonshine, and Connie had been smokin' cigarettes for years and years."

"I was just glad she didn't come home pregnant," Connie said. "Oh!" She clamped a hand over her mouth. "I didn't mean to . . ." She trailed off.

Ginger stood to her feet. "No offense taken, but why would you think she'd come home pregnant?"

"Honey, have you ever read about Woodstock? All kinds of things went on there," Kate said. "For the most part Betsy couldn't even remember what she'd done or who she'd done it with. It wouldn't have been like she'd fallen in love with a man and had a baby with him."

Ginger patted Kate on the shoulder as she passed by. "I'm not sure I was ever in love with Lucas, but he was a means to have a place outside of the shelter. Life is what it is. I can't say I haven't drank a little or that I haven't smoked a joint. Lucas did both of those things on a daily basis, but then he died and I could barely eke out a living. I wouldn't have the right to judge anyone. I was kind of glad that I hadn't been using any of that kind of shit, though, when I found out I was pregnant."

"Thank you," Kate said. "You go on up for a long bath. Breakfast will be half an hour early tomorrow, since we'll need a little extra time to get ready."

"See you bright and early, then," Ginger said as she made her way upstairs. She went to her room first to get her nightshirt and found the pink dress on her bed. With no sleeves or collar, and shortened, it was truly beautiful. A lovely pair of white flats was sitting right beside it with a note. *I found these in Mama's closet. They've never been worn, and I liked them better with the dress than I did the ballet slippers.*

"Bless your heart, Miz Connie." Ginger picked up the dress and held it against her body. She'd never had anything quite so elegant, and she wondered what Sloan would think of her all dressed up for Easter.

Who am I kiddin'? She looked at her very pregnant body in the mirror. *I'll look like a big pink elephant. No one, especially not a good-lookin' guy like Sloan, is going to think I'm pretty.*

Chapter Five

K ate was sitting on the bed, carefully pulling her pantyhose up to her knees, when her two sisters poked their heads into the room. She motioned them inside with a wrist movement and then kept working her stockings up a little at a time.

"Remember when we had to wear those uncomfortable garter belts?" She thought back on those days—the days that she was secretly seeing Max Wilson. He'd thought the garter belts and nylons were sexy.

"Yep." Betsy sat down on the edge of the bed beside her. "And then pantyhose came into vogue and I loved them. But when I gained these few pounds, I was glad to discover thigh highs. The pantyhose crotch always bagged down halfway to my knees. I just can't find a size that seems to work for my body."

"They wouldn't have if you'd bought queen size like I told you," Connie smarted off. "But oh, no, you think you're still as skinny as you were at twenty-eight when you traipsed off to Woodstock."

"Are you never going to let me live that down?" Betsy asked. "It was my one and only adventure, and I had a good time."

"You don't remember *what* you had, other than you learned that you love pot." Kate finally got her hose to her thighs and stood to work them on up her legs, only to push a hole in one leg with her thumbnail.

"Dammit to hell and back on a rusty poker!" she said as she peeled them off and threw them in the corner. "Good thing I bought an extra pair."

Connie held out her hand. "Give them to me."

Kate gave them over. "I should've brought the first pair to you."

"I've got magic hands." Connie giggled as she stretched the pantyhose until they were as tall as Kate. "Now try them."

"Why aren't you two getting dressed?" Kate pulled the hose on without a problem this time.

"Because I'm callin' a meeting." Betsy sat down on the end of the bed. "Ginger has agreed to stay until Thursday, but we've got to make her stay forever."

"I can't bear the thought of a young woman out there with no family. And I like having her around. We were fallin' into a rut around here. She spices things up, and"—Connie sucked in a long breath before she went on—"I believe that Sloan might open up to someone near his age."

"She don't judge us for our little habits," Betsy offered, "and I never told y'all, because I was afraid you'd judge me, but I'd slept around the days I was there, and I wanted a baby so bad that I didn't care who the father was. We'd grown up without a daddy. So . . ." She shrugged. "Anyway, I missed two periods and went to Doc Emerson."

"How'd you do that without us knowin'?" Connie asked.

"I told you that I was deliverin' jams to old Miz Grandy. She was a shut-in, remember, and I used to deliver to her sometimes. I really did take jam to her that day, and on the way to the doctor, I . . ." Betsy put her head in her hands and sobbed. "I lost the baby. I wasn't far enough along to even know what it was, but I just knew in my heart it was a girl. Doc Emerson did what he had to in his office, and I told y'all I had the flu so I could lay around and rest a few days. I was depressed for weeks, and saying it out loud . . ." She stopped and wiped her eyes.

"I understand." Kate felt like she'd failed in her job as the oldest sister. Her mama had told her from the time she was a little girl that she had a responsibility as the firstborn to look after her two siblings. Then she remembered that she'd kept a secret from her sisters—not as big as a baby, but still a secret.

"I figured God took my daughter from me because I'd been wild and smokin' pot when I got pregnant with her. I wasn't goin' to be a fit mama, so I didn't get a baby like Grandma and Mama did even though they wasn't married." She straightened up and wiped her eyes on the end of her nightgown. "I always imagined my baby would have had brown eyes. What chance did she ever have of having anything else with our bloodlines? But I wanted her to have long blonde hair. I didn't even care if it was stringy, or if she was fat or skinny. Then last Thursday, it was like an omen when Connie brought Ginger into the beauty shop."

"Well, I found her," Connie said. "I was the one on the park bench."

"Sister, you can't force her to stay at the Banty House," Kate said.

"But we could make it so nice here that she wouldn't want to leave, and then it would be her decision to stay. We've talked her into a few more days," Connie said. "Maybe we could get her to stay until the baby comes, and by then she'll have put down some roots."

"It's worth a try." Kate's heart went out to Betsy for keeping that secret locked up inside her all these years. "I just wish you hadn't gone through all that alone, Betsy." Her poor sister had wanted a baby so badly that she'd gone to extremes to get one, and when it still hadn't worked out, she had figured it was a sign that she shouldn't have children and she never tried again.

"I just figured that I didn't deserve any support. If I'd stayed home where I belonged"—her chin quivered—"then I mighta gotten pregnant by some guy around these parts and gotten to keep my baby. But oh, no, I had to go off and be wild, so I had to pay for it on my own. I didn't deserve to have my sisters help me get through the loss of my daughter. But I've got another chance at havin' one now, so y'all can help me with that. I'll even share my granddaughter with y'all if you will."

Connie moved over to sit beside Betsy and wrap her arms around her. "My poor sister."

Betsy sniffled and then broke down crying. "After more than fifty years, I still see a little blonde-haired girl in the store or at church and I think about my daughter."

Connie hugged her tighter, and Kate joined them for a three-way hug. "Honey, she'd be a full-grown woman, possibly with a daughter Ginger's age by now." Kate tried to think back to that time in their lives when Betsy had flown to New York and then traveled to the Woodstock site. She shook her head when she remembered the turmoil in her own life during that time. She'd been so involved with her own emotional roller coaster that it wasn't any wonder she'd never even realized that her sister was having a problem.

"I know that, but in my mind, she was always a child until I found Ginger, and now she's a grown woman when I dream about her," Betsy said.

Connie patted Betsy's arm. "You need to keep an amethyst and a rose quartz close to your body. One heals body, mind, and spirit, and the other restores harmony after emotional wounds. I'll put a couple in one of my small pouches. You tuck them inside your bra."

"I don't need stones," Betsy said.

"You've got to get over this, Sister," Connie said. "It'll break your heart when she leaves if you don't. I've kept an amethyst in my pocket since we brought her home. I handle the stone and then touch her bare skin every chance I get, so that she might find healing for all the crap she's been through," Connie said. "I've got to admit, having her with me in the kitchen is like having a breath of fresh air in the house. So, what do you say, Kate?"

"You'll get no argument out of me," Kate said. "I like having her in the house, and just thinking about a baby here with us . . ." Her eyes filled with tears. "Words can't even describe how much fun we'd all have."

Betsy pulled a tissue from a box on the nightstand beside Kate's sturdy four-poster bed and handed it to her. "Be careful or you'll ruin your makeup and have to do it all over. Now that we're in agreement, I'm going to make our traditional Easter breakfast. I'll see y'all at the table in thirty minutes."

❖ ❖ ❖

Ginger had been dreaming about the first day she met Lucas at the shelter. He'd winked at her from across the room, and she'd smiled at him. A week later they were sneaking out after lights were out almost every night to go to the park a few blocks down the street to have sex. After two months had gone by, he'd landed a job that paid enough so that he could rent the tiny apartment above an old drugstore that had been turned into a café.

When she first opened her eyes, she was surprised to see bright sunlight flowing into the room through spotless windows. For a split second, she wondered if Lucas had cleaned up the place. Then she remembered where she was and that Lucas was dead. The Banty House was the best place she'd ever lived, so she couldn't be sad about that. Guilt filled her at the realization that she didn't have some kind of emotion concerning Lucas. He was, after all, her baby's father.

She shook off the dark feeling and went downstairs to help Betsy with breakfast. She'd washed and rolled her hair on little pink sponge rollers the night before. Her last foster mother had let her take them when she was tossed out of the system like a piece of stale bread. Eighteen was the magic number, or else when she finished high school. She'd never realized true loneliness until she'd checked into the first shelter.

"Good mornin'." Betsy grinned. "Don't you look cute in those hair rollers. I remember back when Mama put my hair up in pin curls for special times."

"They're the only thing that will keep the curls in for more than ten minutes." Ginger tied an apron around the top of her belly. "I didn't know if I should get dressed before breakfast. I decided against it because I didn't want to get anything on the pretty new dress that Connie fixed for me."

"That's why we all come to the breakfast table in our robes. We've got our undergarments on and are ready to just slip into our dresses and put our hats on." She stopped turning strips of bacon and gasped. "I forgot your hat! You simply must have one, and it can't cover up your beautiful curls. I've got the cutest little fascinator hat with a lovely white silk rose on it that will go very well with your new dress."

Ginger had already learned not to argue with the sisters. She actually enjoyed having them dress her up like a Barbie doll. "Thank you for everything," she said. "I know I keep saying that, but it's all I've got."

"You are so welcome." Betsy went back to flipping bacon from one side to the other. "You've brought us a lot of joy."

"Don't all your guests do that?" Ginger asked.

"No, honey, they don't. Most of the time, they are happy to have a good hot supper and a bed for the night, but they're eager to get on the road the next morning," Betsy informed her.

"I'm glad for all the sweet memories I get to make here until next week." Ginger got out the plates and set the small kitchen table for four. "And I'm grateful that y'all have asked me to stay on until after I see the doctor on Thursday. It'll sure be good to know my exact due date and maybe find out if I'm gettin' a boy or a girl."

"You mentioned wanting a girl," Betsy said. "Will you be terribly disappointed if it's a boy?"

"No, ma'am, long as it's healthy and don't act like Lucas," Ginger replied. "I thought Lucas was like me, an orphan, until after we moved in together. I should've known that he wasn't because he had a fancy cell phone that he never got a bill for, and he dressed better than the rest of us in the shelter." Her thoughts went back to how excited she had been when she had first gotten a cell phone. It sure wasn't a fancy one, and she had to keep buying minutes for it or it didn't work.

"Was he difficult to live with?" Betsy asked.

"Not at first." Ginger finished setting the table and poured orange juice in cute little glasses for all four of them. "He was funny, always upbeat, probably because he was always high, right up until we moved in together. I think he just wanted a woman around to hold down a steady job and cook and clean for him. It wasn't until after we were living together that I found out he was as useless as"—she blushed—"as tits on a boar hog, as one of my foster fathers used to say."

Betsy chuckled. "I hadn't heard that in years, but I've sure known a lot of people just like that in my lifetime."

"Who's like tits on a boar hog?" Kate entered the room. This morning she wore a red gingham-checked robe that barely reached her knees and left three inches of slip showing at the hem.

"Lucas, my baby's father," Ginger answered. "I was saying that if it's a boy, then I hope it's not like him. I hope my son is willing to work for a living and won't always be looking for a way to make quick and easy money."

Kate pulled out a chair and sat down. "There's folks like that for sure. Is Lucas's family going to make a fuss to see the baby and have grandparents' rights?"

Ginger shook her head. "I didn't know I was pregnant when he died, but even if they did know"—one shoulder raised in a shrug—"they'd think I was just after their money, and they'd insist on a DNA test and all that. It's best that I do this on my own." The words sounded all right in her head, but the truth was that Ginger was scared his family might take her baby from her.

"They have money?" Kate asked.

"He told me that they did." Ginger shrugged again. "But that was after we'd moved in together, and I never really knew if he was telling the truth about anything. According to his story, they cut him off when he wouldn't listen to them, and he ran away from home when he was seventeen, but looking back that was a lie, because he had that fancy cell phone and he always seemed to have a few dollars to buy what he wanted. When he was killed, they came and got his body and took it back home for burial." Ginger helped Betsy bring the food to the table and then sat down in her usual spot. "I tried to talk to them, but they told me to get lost and that they were glad we hadn't gotten married."

"I guess they would be," Kate said. "If he'd married you, then you and his child would be entitled to his share of the inheritance. Your child still would be, you know, if you wanted to get a lawyer and ask for it."

Ginger shook her head slowly from one side to the other. "I don't want anything from them."

"I'm here." Connie breezed into the kitchen and took her place. "Say grace, Kate, before the cinnamon rolls get cold."

Kate bowed her head and said a simple thanks for the importance of the day and for the food. "Now let's see if Betsy has lost her touch when it comes to making our traditional Easter-morning cinnamon rolls. Have you been going to church recently, Ginger?"

"I don't reckon that I've lost my touch with cinnamon rolls any more than you've lost your touch making apple-pie moonshine," Betsy shot across the table at her sister.

Kate cut a section off the end of the steaming-hot rolls, put it on her plate, and took a bite. "They're good enough to make you slap your granny."

Ginger giggled as she held out her plate toward Kate. "What does that mean, anyway? And to answer your question, when I had to work, I'd go sit on the back pew in one of the churches on my way home. I'd just sit there on the back pew and look at the songbook." She had loved the feeling of peace when she attended church.

"Well, at least you went," Connie said.

"And 'slap your granny' means that something is so good that you'd slap your granny for a piece of it even though you knew you'd get your fanny whipped with a switch for being disrespectful to your grandmother," Kate explained. "Betsy always makes the best hot rolls and cinnamon rolls in Medina County, but she did extra good today."

"Thank you." Betsy smiled. "I put a little extra love in them since Ginger is with us."

"Then I vote we hog-tie Ginger and keep her forever," Connie teased.

Ginger took her first bite. "You really should've put in a café or maybe a pastry shop. These are better than any I've ever eaten before. We should save one for Sloan to eat before he hides the eggs."

Betsy beamed, and Ginger caught her sliding a sly wink over to Kate. They must have had some inside joke going, because she couldn't figure out why her comment would put such a glow on Betsy's face.

❖ ❖ ❖

If there hadn't been a steeple on the top and stained-glass windows flanking the double doors in the front, the little white church set back off the road would have looked like a plain clapboard house.

Ginger felt a little overdressed as she entered the sanctuary with the Carson sisters, but the feeling soon went away when she looked around at the small congregation. The ladies all wore hats and gloves. Most of the men wore creased jeans and nice shirts. Some had on sports jackets, but not many. Evidently Easter was the biggest holiday in Texas.

She felt all eyes on her as she followed Kate down the center aisle and took her seat on the second pew with them. No one else joined them on the long, polished oak bench, but then there seemed to be plenty of room for maybe another fifty people. The place wasn't nearly as crowded as the last little church she'd attended on Mother's Day before she was kicked out of the system.

She picked a hymnal from the pew in front of her and thumbed through it. From what she could remember, it was about the same as the one she'd sung from a year ago, but this cover was burgundy instead of forest green. The music director took his place behind the podium. They sang a congregational song before the church secretary reported on what the Sunday-school offering and attendance had been that morning. Then the lady compared it to the previous week and made a few comments about how good it was to see the attendance up by 50 percent that day.

Ginger glanced over her shoulder and figured that meant last week there were only about half as many folks in the building, but then Rooster wasn't a very big place, so maybe that was a good number. The sign on the edge of the city limits said it had a population of ninety-five. She'd thought it had to be a mistake until she saw just how few houses there were in the town.

The preacher took his place behind the podium, looked out over the crowd, and adjusted his reading glasses to the right place on his nose. With a deep voice, he told them that he'd be speaking about the Resurrection that morning.

Surprise! Surprise! Ginger thought, but then she began to compare where she'd been a week ago to the place she was that morning. She wasn't Jesus—not by any means. But she'd been in a very dark place for three days, just like he'd been in the tomb. She'd lost her job, was down to her last bowl of cereal, and had walked the streets looking for work. Everyone had taken one look at her rounded belly and shaken their heads. Now she'd been brought out of the dark into the light. Jesus got to ascend into heaven at the end of his days. She wondered if her final destination would feel like heaven to her.

Betsy startled her when she leaned over and whispered, "I wonder if Sloan has the eggs all hidden. Last year it took us a whole hour to find the last one."

The preacher cleared his throat, and Betsy straightened up. Ginger noticed that she'd crossed her fingers like a little girl who was either telling a lie or hoping for something.

"Eli Thomas, will you please deliver the benediction for us this morning?" the preacher asked.

An old guy on the pew behind them stood to his feet and prayed, and prayed, and then prayed some more. Ginger was sure she'd either fall asleep listening to his monotone or get a crick in her neck from trying to look over her shoulder at him before he finally ran out of air and said, "Amen." The first thing she noticed when she opened her eyes and was able to focus again was that Betsy's fingers weren't crossed anymore and that everyone was getting to their feet.

"I didn't get my wish this morning," Betsy whispered.

"What did you wish for?" Ginger asked.

"Same thing we all did," Kate answered.

Connie scanned the area around them and then said in a low voice, "We all hoped that the preacher would ask Everett Dickson to pray. He keeps things short and sweet."

Ginger bit her lip to keep from laughing out loud. "Y'all are so funny."

Before any one of them could answer, a lady touched Betsy on the shoulder. "I thought I might drop by tomorrow and pick up a few jars of jelly. Have you got strawberry and grape made up?"

"I sure do." Betsy nodded.

Several other women had approached Betsy by the time they were outside and asked if they could come by the next day to pick up jams or jellies. She graciously told them that it would be fine and then broke into laughter when she got into the car.

"I swear to God, and I do not mean that blasphemously right here on Easter morning"—Betsy took a lace-edged hankie from her pink handbag and wiped her eyes with it—"that I've never had this much business on a Sunday morning in my life. Ginger, you are my good-luck charm."

"How's that?" Ginger asked.

"They want to find out about you, so we're going to play this close to our vests. Tomorrow I want you to help Connie and stay out of sight." Betsy rubbed her white-gloved hands in glee.

"You're evil," Connie laughed, "and I love it. I bet you sell every jar of jams and jellies that you have made by next Sunday."

"I'm plannin' on it," Betsy said sweetly.

Ginger thought the whole thing was a hoot. Folks in Rooster must love gossip and drama as much as the people in the shelter had. She'd always avoided that kind of thing, but today it was more than a little humorous.

Kate parked the car in the garage, and they all went inside through the kitchen. Sloan was leaning against the doorjamb leading from the kitchen to the dining room. He was dressed in his usual camouflage pants, and his dark hair had recently been combed back. His biceps stretched the knit of his army-green shirt, and a smile barely tickled the corners of his mouth.

"Well, don't you ladies all look just like a picture out of one of those fancy magazines," he drawled.

"Thank you," the Carson sisters said in unison.

Ginger nodded, afraid that her voice would be all high and squeaky. Just looking at him had jacked up her pulse. She should feel guilty for feeling that way—after all, she was carrying another man's baby.

"Are you ready for the annual picture-taking event?" His eyes locked with hers.

"Just make me look pretty in the pictures," she whispered.

"That won't be a problem." He grinned.

"Yep," Betsy said. "We want some with us sisters, and then we want some with Ginger in the photograph with us."

"Are you sure you want me in the pictures?" Ginger asked.

"Of course," Connie said. "You're with us this Easter, so you should be in the book. Mama would like that."

The ladies posed on the porch exactly like they had in the pictures Ginger had seen in the album. They lined up from oldest to youngest, put their arms around each other's shoulders, and smiled at the camera. Their big hats would have been the rage at the Kentucky Derby, what with the huge bows and floral arrangements. Her fascinator had looked pretentious to her that morning when she'd settled it on her head, but now the poor little thing made her appear underdressed.

For the first several pictures, she stood beside Sloan as he snapped away with his phone. Every time the wind shifted, she caught a whiff of his shaving lotion—something woodsy with a hint of a fiery, spicy aroma that sent her senses reeling.

Dammit! Pregnant women don't feel this kind of thing.

Chapter Six

Easter dinner was the traditional ham, sweet potato casserole, baked beans, hot rolls, and a lovely green salad. At least that's what Betsy said it was. Ginger couldn't have proven it by her past. The only real celebration dinner she might have known had been when she was with the religious couple. That year, she couldn't answer the questions about the Resurrection, so she didn't get to eat, but one of the other children slipped her a ham sandwich after dinner was over.

The ladies removed their gloves, but they wore their new dresses and hats to the table that afternoon. Sometime during the meal, Ginger laid her hand on her stomach and silently told the baby that this was like eating with the Queen of England. The best china had been brought out of the cabinet, and the sterling silver had been polished. Ginger fingered the lace cloth that covered the table and felt the heat rising from candles. Before he died, Lucas had gotten high and told her a little about his family and how much he hated what people expected of folks who had money. She'd thought he had been affected by the pot and the liquor, but when she met his mother, it all became pretty real.

If he was so against having money, then why did he try to scam so many people? she wondered, putting another bite of ham into her mouth. She was jerked out of the past and into the present when Sloan accidentally brushed her shoulder as he reached for the bread basket to passed it down to Kate.

"What do you think, Ginger? Want to put your bet on the table?" Kate asked.

"I'm so sorry," Ginger apologized. "I was thinkin' about how beautiful the table is today and got caught up in woolgathering. What were y'all talkin' about?"

"Gladys Jones is coming by tomorrow to buy strawberry jam," Betsy explained. "She arrives about this same time every year and buys a couple of jars, but what she's really interested in is gossip. Edith will arrive next and will be the one to try to talk me into hiring a few girls to dress up in what she calls hooker clothes and sit on the front porch during the Rooster Romp. Poor old darlin' thinks no one in town knows that she got pregnant before she married."

"Not that we care," Connie said, "but the way she puts our mother down for not having a husband grates on my nerves."

Kate nodded and said, "Her son is the preacher at our church. We're bettin' on how long she'll be here before she brings up the idea of us being the daughters of a woman of the night. Edith is one of those things that you have to take with a grain of salt and laugh about, or else you might want to kill it. You want in on the money?" Kate's thought drifted over for just a moment to Max, Edith's deceased husband. She'd really bet dollars to doughnuts that she'd cried more at his death than Edith had.

"Say no," Sloan whispered.

"You hush!" Connie pointed her fork at Sloan.

"What's the Rooster Romp?" Ginger asked.

"It's our annual festival. Anyone who ever lived here or in Mission Valley, or who has kinfolk here, comes back for the Romp. We have a carnival for the kids, all kinds of vendors up and down the street from the church to the cemetery. The street is closed off to traffic, but there's golf carts to take folks down to visit the graves if they want to go. People come from all over the county," Connie explained.

"And why would Miss What's-her-name want y'all to put hookers on the front porch?" Ginger asked.

"She's watched too much television and thinks that Mama had her girls dressed in red satin and black garters. The Banty House wasn't that kind of place. Men didn't just come and go all through the night," Kate answered.

"I'll show you tomorrow what we'll be wearing," Connie said. "Since you've got to stay out of sight so that Betsy can draw out all this drama a little longer, you can help me let out one of the dresses that we wear on the day of the Romp."

"Sweet Jesus!" Betsy rolled her eyes. "I thought you'd already let that dress out as far as it would go last year."

"I'm planning to put a gusset in it," Connie told her. "Just think how round I'd be if I didn't smoke. I hear you gain about forty pounds when you give up cigarettes."

"Those things are going to give you lung cancer," Kate said.

"I'll eat what I want, smoke as many cigarettes as I want, and die when I'm supposed to, so stop bitchin' at me and pass the sweet potatoes this way," Connie said.

"Changing the subject back to the bet . . ." Ginger tried to smooth things over. "Explain it to me again."

"Edith won't be able to keep her mouth shut about how we dress, and she's coming tomorrow. So we're betting on how long it'll take her to get around to it when she gets here." Betsy smiled.

❖   ❖   ❖

Sloan could agree with Connie's statement about not knowing what the future held when it came to eating or smoking. One day he was going out into the heat and sand to defuse bombs. The next week he was being sent to doctors and psychiatrists for severe depression and PTSD. Then he'd been told to pack his stuff, and he had been put on a plane and sent home to Texas with an honorable discharge and full disability from the United States Army. He didn't want either. His dream had always been to go into the army after high school and make a career out of it. The future damn sure hadn't brought what he'd wanted.

When the meal was over and they had finished the cleanup, the ladies all hurried off upstairs. They returned hatless and barefoot and carrying the same Easter baskets that Sloan figured they'd carried from their young days. Ginger was still wearing shoes when she came down the stairs, but not for long. When she noticed that the sisters were barefoot, she kicked hers off at the foot of the steps.

"Hunting in our bare feet is a tradition." Betsy picked up a basket from the credenza, handed it to her, and said, "This was Mama's basket. You can use it today."

"Oh, I couldn't," Ginger protested. "What if I ruin it? I can just use a grocery bag."

"Nonsense," Kate said. "Mama would be glad for you to use it, and besides, we always take a picture at the end of the hunt to go in the album. It just wouldn't be right for you to be holding a plastic sack in the picture."

"Where's your basket?" Ginger locked eyes with Sloan.

"Remember—I take the pictures and hide the eggs. I don't hunt them," he answered. "But I did like the excitement back when I was a little boy. One time, I even found the prize egg at the church hunt and got a bicycle. I put a million miles on that thing riding up to the Rooster store for snow cones in the summertime."

"Okay, now you've got me wanting a snow cone," Betsy said. "Maybe after supper, we'll all take a walk to town and get us one. I like cherry. What's your favorite, Ginger?"

Kate led the way to the porch. "My favorite snow cone is blue coconut. We don't have a starting pistol, but after Sloan takes a picture of us all waiting with our baskets, we take off."

"Cherry," Ginger said as she followed behind them.

"Rainbow." Connie took her place in the lineup.

Sloan walked out past them and into the yard, where he held up his phone and took several photos, including a couple of Ginger by herself. Those he quickly shuffled into a personal folder, where he kept pictures of his grandmother and his old team members.

Maybe you shouldn't put her in that file, the voice in his head said. *Seems like folks you put there don't live much longer.*

Or just maybe, she'll be the one that breaks the pattern, he argued.

When the ladies looked at the pictures later and decided which ones they wanted, he'd send an order into a place in Hondo, and they could pick them up on Thursday when they went into town.

"All right. I believe we've gotten several good shots for y'all to pick from." He raised his voice. "On your mark."

Kate bent forward like someone who was fixing to run in a quarter-mile sprint.

"Get set," he yelled.

Betsy put one foot out and tucked her elbows to her sides.

"Go!"

Connie threw both arms out to slow her sisters down and got ahead of them by ten feet. All dignity was thrown to the wind as they began to search for hidden eggs.

"I saw that one first," Connie squealed when Kate picked one up right at her feet.

"Too bad. If you didn't smoke, you wouldn't be out of breath and you could get around faster," Kate threw over her shoulder.

"Did you sample your shine while you were takin' off your panty-hose?" Betsy asked. "That's why your face is flushed and you're so hyper, ain't it?"

"I did not," Kate protested. "My eyesight is better than y'all's, that's all."

"Bullshit!" Betsy disagreed. "You have to have reading glasses just like Connie. I'm the one with good vision."

Sloan fell in beside Ginger. "You just point at whatever you find and I'll pick it up for you."

"Thank you." She smiled at him. "That bending over business is gettin' to be a real problem."

"Kind of like trying to get past a basketball under your dress?" he asked.

"More like a great big old watermelon." Her smile widened.

"You sure you got just one baby in there?" Sloan asked.

"Nope. Could be a whole litter for all I know." She stuck her toe on a bright-purple egg with lots of glitter on it.

He put it in her basket. "What would you do if it was twins or maybe even triplets? Would that change your plans?"

"I don't know that I have anything to change *to*," she answered.

"You could stay here in Rooster," he suggested.

"And do what? I don't even see a restaurant in town. I don't have a car, there's no public transportation to take me to Hondo, and I'd never make enough money to pay a babysitter"—she stopped and inhaled deeply—"for even one baby, much less two."

"You can't raise a child—or children—in a shelter or on the streets," Sloan told her. "You know what will happen if you don't have a home to take the baby to when it's born. They'll put it in the system."

"Then I'll just deliver it on my own." Her tone went stone cold. "My child is never going in the system—not ever. The only way it will is over my dead body. I'm hoping to get a job where I can take the baby with me, maybe working at a day care center."

Sloan didn't know anything about those places, but he doubted that Ginger had the education or training for a job like that. She might have babysat for the kids in the foster homes where she had lived, but that wouldn't carry much weight in a licensed day care center.

"How many do you have?" Connie called over her shoulder toward Ginger. "Between us we've got one shy of three dozen. That means you have to have thirteen, or else there's still some out here to be found."

Ginger glanced down at her basket. "How did so many get in here? Did you cheat, Sloan?"

"No, ma'am. I only picked up the ones that you either had a toe against or else you pointed out to me," he answered with a shake of his head. "I'd never cheat at something with this much riding on the game."

What he didn't say was that while they were talking, he'd seen Betsy sneak up behind them and put a couple of eggs in Ginger's basket. Then Connie had done the same thing. Kate almost got caught giving one more to Ginger but had quickly run to the other side of the yard and picked up another egg.

"There's thirteen eggs in here." Ginger frowned. "But I only remember picking up about six or seven."

"Guess you was all involved with Sloan and didn't keep a good count. Looks like you win the contest and get the hundred dollars," Betsy said. "It's time for our last picture of the day. We all sit on the porch like we did when we were little girls with our baskets full of eggs on our knees."

They made their way to the porch, and Sloan took the picture, but he sure wished they hadn't cheated. A hundred dollars would take Ginger a long way from Rooster, and he didn't want her living on the streets with a new baby to take care of.

Why? What difference does it make to you? You vowed to never get close to anyone again after they sent you home to Texas. The pesky voice in his head was like a little kid with too many questions to answer.

Who says I'm close to her? he argued.

Time for a reality check, Cowboy. This time it was his buddy Wade's voice in his head. Wade, from down in southern Louisiana, had gone through basic with him. Wade—who'd been out on that detail with the team that morning that changed their world forever.

He hadn't heard that deep Southern accent since the night before Wade had died, and it jarred him to the very marrow of his bones. He took the final picture of the day and then followed the ladies into the house. When they'd agreed on what pictures they wanted, he'd be free to leave. His hands shook as he set the phone on the table and they gathered around to fuss over the photos.

Have you forgiven me? he almost said out loud.

Ain't nothing to forgive. It was a fluke. Wade was like that. Sloan had never heard him say a negative thing about anyone or anything. Once when they were out on a mission, they'd had a flat tire. It was at least a hundred and fifteen degrees, and the sun was beating down on them like it was trying to fry their brains right out of their heads. A wind had picked up and sand blew in their faces when they stepped out of their vehicle. He remembered thinking that not even Wade Beaudreaux could find something positive to say about that situation, but old Wade had just grinned and spit the sand out of his mouth. Then he had said, "Well, boys, at least it's on the shady side of the truck."

Sloan shook his head and came back to the present in the Banty House. Kate had just handed Ginger a hundred-dollar bill, and the woman was holding it like she'd won the lottery. He quickly snapped a picture of her and slid it over into his personal folder.

"So what are you going to do with it?" Betsy asked.

"That'll require more thinkin', but the first thing I'm buyin' is a cute little outfit for my baby to wear home from the hospital," she answered.

Sloan couldn't help but wonder just exactly where home would be when she delivered her child.

Chapter Seven

On Monday morning, Ginger awoke, went right to her suitcase and felt around in the pocket. She'd dreamed that the money they'd given her for finding the most eggs—even though she wondered how she'd managed to do that—had been stolen. Lucas had taken it to buy drugs and booze, and she'd awakened in a sweat, fearing that it was gone. He wasn't a mean drunk, but he could get mean if he didn't get his way. Alcohol didn't have anything to do with those times when they were low on money and he couldn't have what he wanted right that moment, like beer or joints or a new video game. At one time he had suggested that she take her skinny butt out on the street, saying she'd make more money than she could ever bring in as a waitress.

The first time he'd said that, she'd locked herself in the bedroom and cried herself to sleep. After the fiftieth time, it had rolled off her like water off a duck's back. By then she was wishing he would just leave. She was paying for everything anyway. He was always using his money to buy something to snort up his nose or to pour down his throat.

Everything came to a head the night she came home to find his worthless friends at the apartment with him. He told her that they were going to pay him fifty dollars each to get two hours with her in the bedroom. She'd told him to go to hell and stormed out of the apartment. She'd slept in a shelter that night, and when she got home from her job the next day, she'd learned that Lucas was dead. If he hadn't been, her plan was to gather up her things and move out of the apartment, even if she had to go back to the shelter.

She found the hundred-dollar bill and held it close to her chest for a few minutes, then put it back in the suitcase. It, along with what the Carson sisters would pay her on Thursday, would take her a long way toward California. She'd heard that there were lots of jobs there and that cafés were constantly needing waitresses. She slumped down in the rocking chair over beside the window and gave thanks that she hadn't let Lucas talk her into selling herself that night. Had she done that for him, she wouldn't know who the baby belonged to, and somehow that was important to her. Even if Lucas had been a lowdown bastard, at least she knew who her baby's father was.

Tears gathered at the corners of her eyes and ran down her cheeks. She'd just made a judgment that was unfair. The Carson sisters hadn't known for years who their father was, or even if they had the same one. They were all kindhearted and sweet ladies, and she hadn't meant to condemn them or their mother.

She was sleeping in a room where no telling how many men had paid for a woman's time and feeling all superior with a better-than-thou attitude because she hadn't taken those junkies to the bedroom. She could have been sleeping on a park bench or living in a box under a bridge if Connie hadn't sat down beside her a few days before.

As if on cue, Betsy knocked on her door and poked her head inside. When she realized that Ginger was crying, she hurried across the room and gathered her into her arms. "What's the matter, darlin'? Is it the baby?"

"No. I wasn't thinkin' nice thoughts," Ginger admitted, wiping her nose. "I've been blessed to get to spend time here and . . ." Her voice trailed off. She couldn't tell Betsy that she'd been patting herself on the back for being righteous when the sisters lived in a house that had been a brothel. It seemed so ungrateful for all the love and care she'd received since she'd been there.

"We're the blessed ones, my child," Betsy said softly. "And you are welcome to stay with us and help us out for as long as you like."

"Are you serious?" Ginger asked.

"Very much so." Betsy straightened up and patted Ginger on the shoulder. "We can use an extra set of hands, and we just love having you here with us. It's up to you to make the decision about when you want to leave. We don't want to pressure you in any way, and we'll take you to the bus station any day that you say you want to go, but we could sure use some help. We ain't none of us gettin' any younger."

Ginger pulled a tissue from a box on the table beside her and dried her eyes. "I can't believe you're sayin' that. What about Kate and Connie?"

"They agree with me," Betsy said. "I've already talked to them."

"I could be a scam person, just here to talk you out of your money, or even worse. How can you trust me like this?" Ginger asked.

"I'm a pretty damn fine judge of character." Betsy smiled. "Now, let's go downstairs and get breakfast on the table. Connie's got a full day planned for the two of you, and I don't want to hear her bitchin' about me hornin' in on her time. She gripes enough because you like to be with me in the kitchen."

Ginger couldn't ever remember anyone—not even Lucas—being jealous of someone else spending time with her. Maybe she would just stay a little while longer and get a nest egg built up for the baby.

❖ ❖ ❖

Later on that morning, Connie took her upstairs to the sewing room long before the first knock came to the door, but Ginger found out pretty quick that Connie would know exactly what all went on in the living room. She'd set up a baby monitor on the sewing table beside her, and when they heard the rap, she turned it on.

"Shhh . . ." She put a finger to her lips. "We'll just sit back here for a few minutes and listen."

"They can't hear you on the other end. The monitor picks up the sound down there and you get it up here," Ginger whispered. "One of my foster mothers had a setup like this."

"I know, darlin', but I don't want to miss a word." Connie grinned.

"Hello, Gladys," Betsy said. "Come right in. Can I get you a glass of sweet tea or lemonade? Both were made fresh this mornin'."

"I could sure use a glass of lemonade," Gladys answered.

Ginger closed her eyes and put a face with the high, whiny voice. Gladys was the last woman who'd asked Betsy about buying mint jelly at church the day before. She had a long, thin nose set in the middle of high, thin cheeks that looked skeletal. Her bright-red lipstick had run into the wrinkles around her mouth. Her icy-cold eyes had started at Ginger's feet and slowly made their way up to the little fascinator hat.

The sounds of someone bustling around came through the little white box on the sewing table, and then Betsy told Gladys to have a seat. "You mentioned that you wanted mint jelly. I've only got six jars left. The mint is beginning to spring up again out back of the house, but it'll be a while before it's ready to harvest for jelly."

"I'll take two of them," Gladys said. "This is sure some good lemonade. You still squeezin' your own? I've gone to that powder stuff that you just put in water."

"I like it made from fresh lemons best," Betsy told her. "I'll bring out that jelly so you don't forget to take it with you when you go."

Ginger and Connie heard more rustling, and then Gladys whispered, "I'm glad you answered on the first ring. I'm here at the house now. There's no sign of that girl they brought to church. Maybe it's one of their strays and she's already gone. Here she comes back. I'm hanging up now."

"I wonder who she was calling," Ginger said.

"Probably Edith Wilson," Connie said. "They've been inseparable since we were all in first grade."

"So you've known them that long? Were you friends?" Ginger asked.

"Until maybe third grade, when they found out what the Banty House used to be. Mama shut it down after I was born, so it hadn't been in operation for almost ten years by then. Mama's girls used to come back to see her real often—real refined ladies they were," Connie said.

"Two jars," Betsy said. "That'll be ten dollars. More lemonade?"

"No. I was just wonderin', though, who that pregnant girl was that came to church with y'all yesterday," Gladys said.

"Just a very good friend of ours," Betsy said.

"Someone I might know? One of your mama's old"—she cleared her throat—"acquaintances?"

"Nope. Don't reckon you've ever met any of her folks," Betsy answered.

Someone else rapped on the door, and Betsy excused herself for a minute. "Be right back now. I'm sure it's Flora Thompson. Only her truck rattles like that," Betsy said.

Kate's voice came through the monitor. "Well, hello, Gladys. I didn't know you were here. I just got a phone call from Flora, and she said she was on the way. I understand that she'd got a terrible sore throat and needs a little of my special apple pie to help her out."

"Damn drunk," Gladys muttered, but it came through the monitor loud and clear. "I must be going. Would it be all right if I leave by the kitchen door? I parked my car right up next to the garage doors."

"Why, sure, darlin'," Kate said.

"Who's Flora?" Ginger asked.

"She's one of Kate's best customers. She pays for her medicine with eggs and butter. She churns the best in Medina County, and her chickens are free range, so that helps with cholesterol problems. When you smoke as much as I do, you got to watch the other issues that could pop up. Don't pay no attention to Gladys," Connie said. "She's pretty close to Edith for bein' snobby and self-righteous."

Ginger gave a brief nod and leaned in closer to the monitor.

"I thought I saw that self-righteous Gladys in here. I expect she was trying to weasel something out of Betsy about that pregnant girl that y'all brought home from Hondo last week, wasn't she?" Flora's voice was as distinctive as Gladys's, but in a very different way—deep enough to be a guy's and as gravelly as if she smoked three packs of cigarettes a day.

"I feel kind of like we shouldn't be eavesdropping," Ginger said.

"Shhh . . . ," Connie said. "It's not listenin' in if Kate and Betsy know, and they do. I like Flora. She ain't never put us down for what our mama did. She even got to come to our house to spend the night when we were little girls."

"Yep, she was," Betsy said. "Want some lemonade or tea?"

"No, honey, but I wouldn't say no to half a glass of that new peach shine that Kate brews up," Flora said. "I'm so dry, I'm spittin' dust."

"I tried some strawberry this past week. Want to sample a little of it?" Kate asked. "And while I'm in the cellar, how much apple pie do you want?"

"Three pints," Flora answered. "And strawberry will be just fine. You offer Gladys any?" She burst out laughing.

"Nope. I don't waste good shine," Kate answered.

That brought out another bout of laughter. "She wouldn't have taken it anyway. She thinks if she takes one little sip, the devil will come up out of the ground and drag her kickin' and screamin' to hell. I've brought six dozen eggs and two pounds of butter. That sound fair?"

"More than," Kate said. "I'll bring up a half pint of my peach to go with the apple pie. I know that you like it pretty good, too."

"Thank you, darlin'. You always do right by your friends," Flora said.

"Do my best," Kate said, and then there was a lull.

"How's your mama doin'?" Betsy asked.

"Poorly," Flora said. "She's as stubborn as a constipated mule. Won't take medicine. Says the doctor is tryin' to poison her. Thank God she'll take a shot of shine every few hours. It helps with the pain and knocks her square on her ass for a little while so I can get some work done around the farm."

Ginger looked over at Connie and raised an eyebrow.

"Her mama is dyin' with the cancer," Connie said. "She's never been one much for doctorin'. She was a sweet old girl until she got that tumor in her brain. Now she's turned right the opposite way."

"Poor thing," Ginger said.

"Yep, and poor Flora," Connie said. "I hear another car arrivin'. I bet that's Edith. She's the one who's going to try to talk Betsy into sayin' we'll put floozies out on the porch. Here." Connie handed her the skirt of a long white dress and a seam ripper. "You ever use one of those things?"

"Yes, ma'am. I took home economics in a middle school down south of Harlan while I was there. I made an apron," Ginger answered.

"Well, you take the seams out down the sides. I think I can splice in about four inches from one of the other dresses that's fallin' apart, and it'll cover my chubby little body," Connie told her.

"Other dresses?" Ginger started the painstaking job of gently removing each stitch.

"We have the last six dresses that the working girls wore in the Banty House," Connie said. "On Rooster Romp day, we wear them and drink sweet tea on the porch. I hope the roses are in bloom so folks that stop to take a picture of our old whorehouse get a little color in their photos."

"These don't look like hooker clothes," Ginger said. "I was expecting something raunchy, like black lace teddies or maybe red silk with garter belts holding up fishnet hose."

"This wasn't a normal brothel." Connie set to work on taking the stitches out of the bodice of the white dress. "That's why we won't let Edith talk us into disgracing the name of the Banty House."

"Well, hello, Kate." A different voice came through the speaker. This one was soft as butter and sweet as honey.

"Edith," Kate said. "Come right on in. Flora and Betsy are in the living room."

"Oh dear, I didn't realize that you had company. I can come back another time. Maybe later this week," Edith said.

Ginger heard the door close and then footsteps.

"I guess Edith didn't want to sit in the same room with me, did she?" Flora laughed.

"Guess not," Kate said.

"I'd like to stay and visit and meet this girl you got hidin' away somewhere, but she's y'all's business and not mine. I reckon y'all will come clean about her if she stays much longer. You should hear the rumors. I done heard that she's the child of a daughter one of you gave away at birth. Another rumor has it that she's really Belle's granddaughter instead of one of y'all's. That your mama gave birth to a fourth child and the father took her away. Now, with all this technology, the girl has found y'all and is here to claim her share of the Banty House," Flora said. "Great strawberry shine. Needs just a little more sweet put in it. When you get it perfected, save me back a pint. I think Mama might like it."

"Sure thing, and don't believe everything you hear," Betsy said.

"Never do," Flora said.

The sound of people walking and then the front door shut. Connie leaned in closer to the monitor.

"Okay, you can turn it off now," Kate yelled.

"Damn, Sister, you almost deafened me," Connie hollered down the steps.

Ginger could hear Kate giggling even after she had reached over and switched off the monitor. She'd never felt as if she'd had roots no matter where she'd been sent, but in less than a week, she could almost feel a few growing around her heart.

❖   ❖   ❖

Tinker seemed to be as restless as Sloan that night. He'd whine at the door and then come back to the rug under the coffee table and flop down. Then in five minutes he paced around the room and barked. Sloan wasn't much better. He surfed through the channels on the television several times and found nothing that looked good enough to watch. He pushed the little red power button on the remote and picked up a book from the end table. He read five pages, laid it down, and went to the kitchen. When he opened the refrigerator, he found that the sweet tea jar was empty, so he got out a bottle of water and carried it back to the living room.

He remembered being restless and bored a lot of times when he and his team were on deployment. They'd play cards, tell tales about things they'd done back home, or watch movies and wait for the next moment when someone needed them to take care of a bomb. Ever since he'd come home, he'd tried to stay so busy that he didn't have time to be bored or to even think, but here lately things were changing. He wasn't sure just what to do about it. He couldn't get back in the army, but he'd begun to want a regular job.

"And just what would I do with my skill set?" he asked Tinker.

The dog ran to the door and whined.

"Okay, okay, we'll go for a walk, but only up to the old tree this time," Sloan said. "You were so worn out after we went all the way to the Banty House that I was afraid I'd find you dead the next morning."

Tinker wagged his tail and shot out the door the second Sloan opened it. The night air was warm, so Sloan left his jacket behind, but he carried the bottle of water with him. The dog was content to walk along beside him and didn't even chase a cottontail rabbit that ran across the road in front of them.

"Killing that snake took all your energy, didn't it?" Sloan asked him.

Tinker looked up at him and barked, but Sloan didn't know if he was saying yes or no. Sloan had been home for only a few weeks when his granny died, and so Tinker had been his only companion for the next months. Then Kate Carson had come to his house, given him a good talking to, and then asked him to work for them a day a week. She'd mentioned that she'd walked down to the cemetery that morning to check on her mother's grave and found it all grown in. When she left, Sloan had scaled the fence separating his house from the graveyard and was appalled at the condition it was in. His parents' and his grandparents' graves had sunk in and needed more dirt and some grass planted on them. Weeds covered the whole pitiful-looking place. That day had been a Monday, too, and he'd vowed that once a week he'd see to it that the cemetery was put to rights.

Tinker plopped down on his tummy at the edge of the old log. A turtle was slowly making its way across the road, and he kept an eye on it, but he didn't even give it so much as a growl.

Dark clouds drifted back and forth across the sun that evening. When the wind picked up, Sloan could smell a storm brewing off to the southwest. Maybe that's what had made him and Tinker both so restless. He opened his bottle of water and downed half of it, then held it down and let a slow stream flow out so that Tinker could have a drink.

"Hello again," Ginger said as she walked up and sat down on the other end of the log. "Do you think we're in for some bad weather?"

"Kinda looks that way," Sloan answered. "You take a walk every evening?"

"I didn't until I got here," she answered. "I was on my feet all day, running back and forth between the kitchen and the customers at the café where I worked. I was usually so tired when I climbed the steps up to my apartment that I only had enough energy to grab a quick shower and go to bed."

"What did the baby's daddy do?" Sloan asked.

"Not much, other than try to scam folks out of their money, sell drugs, and make my life miserable. I was a fool to ever move in with him," she replied.

"So y'all separated?" Sloan was prying, but he wanted to know more.

"No. He got killed, and his folks came and got his body to take home with them to bury, or maybe they cremated him. His mama was one of those hoity-toity women who looked down her nose at me. Her hair was all done up fancy, and the suit she wore probably cost more than I made in six months as a waitress," she said.

"I'm so sorry." Sloan knew what it was to lose friends and still grieved for those he'd lost in Kuwait. A wave of guilt washed over Sloan as he remembered all the friends he'd lost.

She shrugged. "I hate to say it, since he's the baby's daddy, but it was more of a relief than a grievin' burden. That was months ago, and I didn't even know I was pregnant at the time."

Some of the heavy chains surrounding Sloan's heart felt as if they'd been loosened. "Did you go to the funeral? I'm sorry if I'm prying into your business—you don't have to answer that."

"Don't mind answering at all," she said. "Matter of fact, since I got here, I've talked more about Lucas than I have since he was killed. It's helped to make me see that I don't have to feel guilty about the way I feel. He was a charmer who talked me into moving in with him and then treated me like crap. I was glad when his parents came to the apartment and told me I wouldn't be welcome at his funeral. I didn't have the money to travel from Lexington all the way to the western part of the state anyway."

"You're a good person, Ginger," Sloan said. "You deserve better than that kind of treatment. Are you going to tell them about their grandchild?"

"Nope," she said. "I've given it a lot of thought, and I figure it's best just to keep that to myself."

"What're you going to tell the baby when it's old enough to ask?" Sloan handed the water bottle to her. "Tinker and I both had a drink, but it didn't touch Tinker's mouth, only mine." He thought about all the times his grandmother told him stories about his own father. She'd stepped up and been a wonderful mother, but she never let him forget that he'd had parents who loved and adored him.

She twisted the lid off and finished what was left. "When my baby asks about his or her father, I'm going to tell them the truth, that he's been dead for a long time. What about you, Sloan? Did you always live with your granny?"

"My mama and daddy were big-rig truck drivers. They started that job when I was about two years old, and they'd leave me with Granny when they went on long hauls. We lived in a house in Hondo, but I stayed with her a lot. They were killed out in New Mexico when a gunman walked into a café and started firing a rifle. I was seven at the time, and I went to stay with Granny permanently," he answered.

A flash of lightning streaked through the sky, followed by a loud clap of thunder that seemed to be right above Sloan's and Ginger's heads. Tinker got up and started toward home in a trot.

"Guess that's our cue to get going toward home, too," Sloan said.

"I'd say so," Ginger agreed as she got to her feet.

"Want me to walk you home?" he asked.

"No. We'd better just go our separate ways, or we might get stuck at one place or the other when the rain starts," she said. "Besides, I won't melt."

"See you later, then." He stood up and waved.

"Maybe tomorrow night if the weather lets up," she yelled over her shoulder.

Sloan made it home moments before the first big drops of rain fell from the dark clouds. He went straight for the old wall phone in the kitchen and called the Banty House. Kate answered on the second ring and assured him that Ginger had gotten back to the house just fine.

He hung up the phone and slumped down on the sofa beside Tinker. The dog was already snoring, so evidently he was content to stay in the house now. Sloan leaned his head against the back of the sofa and thought about what Ginger had told him. They'd both been orphaned. The only difference was that he'd had a loving grandmother who was willing to raise him, and evidently Ginger hadn't had anyone to take care of her.

He didn't pity her. He applauded her for taking charge of her own life.

"I guess it's way past time for me to crawl up out of my own pity pool and do the same, ain't it?" he asked Tinker.

The dog barely opened one eye and thumped his tail once.

"You'd never pass the exam to be a full-fledged therapist." He scratched the dog's ears. "But I'm glad you're here to listen to me. There's just something about having someone trust me again, even with a little of her life's story, that sure feels good."

Tinker looked up at him and barked.

"Okay, okay. Yes, I know the Carson sisters trust me, and the folks trust me with the cemetery, and people around town trust me to do a good job when they hire me to do odd jobs, but this is different."

Tinker wagged his tail and licked Sloan's hand.

"I'm glad you can't talk and ask me why, because I couldn't answer that question."

Chapter Eight

Kate was in the basement working on a recipe for blackberry shine when someone knocked on the door at the top of the stairs. "Come on down," she called out.

She knew who it was the minute she heard combat boots on the old wooden steps. Someday, she kept telling herself, she was going to ask Sloan to replace the stairs and maybe paint them white, so as she got old they'd be easier for her to see.

"I'm glad you're here." She didn't even look up from her notebook. "That rain last night blew down all kinds of limbs. Reckon you could work a few hours?"

"Not today, but I'll sure get them on Friday," Sloan said when he reached the bottom of the stairs. "I'm on my way into town for supplies. Y'all need anything?"

"Nothing I know of, but you might check with Betsy," Kate replied.

"Maybe some cat food?" He pulled a kitten from behind him and held it out to her.

Kate dropped the pencil on her worktable and reached out with both hands. "Where'd you get it? Can we keep it?" She held it close to her chest like a baby and swayed back and forth. The kitten snuggled down into her arms and began to purr.

"I guess so. It showed up on my porch this morning. Poor little thing was havin' a fit for something to eat. I fed her a scrambled egg and some milk, but she'll probably do better on her own kind of food. Y'all said something a while back about lookin' for another cat, so I thought maybe you'd want her," Sloan said.

"We've never had a girl cat in the house," Kate said. "When we were kids, we had a big old gray fluffy boy named Dutch."

"Why'd your mama name him that?" Sloan sat down on the bottom step.

"Dutch is a breed of Bantam chickens, so it seemed appropriate, and the cat was colored up like a banty rooster that had been on the property when she was a little girl." Kate eased down into an oak rocking chair and started it in motion with her foot.

"That little girl is solid black, so I'll be interested in what name y'all come up with. I'll be going now. See you in a couple of days," he said.

"Thank you," Kate said. "This will help Betsy so much if Ginger decides to leave."

"How about you and Connie? Think it will help y'all if Ginger leaves?" he asked.

Kate swallowed a lump in her throat. "I'm sure it will, but honestly, Sloan, I want her to stay as much as Betsy does. Things were gettin' so routine and old around here. She's spiced things up for us."

"Kate Carson, are you about to cry?" he asked as he got to his feet.

"How can a person get attached to someone in only five days?" She wiped her eyes with her shirtsleeve.

"Looks like you already fell in love with that cat in only five minutes," he said. "Ginger is a sweet woman. It wouldn't be hard to get attached to her, especially knowing what all she's been through. I don't think she'd want your pity, though."

"You're right," Kate said. "She needs a friend, not pity."

"My granny used to tell me that friends were better than gold," Sloan said.

"Your granny was one of the wisest women I ever knew," Kate told him.

"Yep." He nodded. "See you later."

She sat there for several minutes, just simply enjoying holding the baby kitten in her arms. Then the door at the top of the stairs opened and Connie's voice echoed off the walls. "Kate, you got to come up here and see what Ginger found on the back porch."

"I'm on the way." She pushed up out of the rocking chair and headed up the steps with the baby kitten still in her arms. She'd wanted a while longer to savor having it all to herself, but it was only fair to share with her sisters.

Betsy held out something as Kate emerged from the doorway and said, "Look!"

Connie, Betsy, and Ginger all seemed like they might break into a jig any minute.

Two little white ears popped up out of the towel that Betsy was holding, and two blue eyes stared right at her. "Ginger found it on the back porch, half-drowned and cryin' for someone to rescue it." She opened up the towel and showed Kate the all-white kitten.

Too bad, Kate thought, *she didn't find two out there, and then each of us could have our very own.* "Well, look what Sloan just brought us." She held up the black kitten.

"It's a beautiful day." Connie rubbed her hands together. "We've got a black one and a white one living in a brothel. Couldn't be better. We'll have to have a meeting after supper tonight to talk about names. The white one is a girl."

"So's this one," Kate said.

"Just gets better and better," Betsy said. "The symbolism is fantastic. Mama would have just loved it. Remember how she used to say that Dutch was gray because it was a mixture of black and white?"

"Want to hold this one?" Kate held her kitten out to Ginger.

93

"I've always wanted a cat, but . . ." She let the sentence trail off as she took the kitten. "Oh, my goodness! It's so soft. The white one was wet and didn't feel like this."

"You've never held a kitten before?" Betsy asked.

"Yes, but not one this soft," Ginger admitted as she held it up close to her face and kissed it on the nose. "I can't imagine anyone throwing such sweet creatures out in the rain."

Kate considered herself a strong, independent woman. She'd endured a lot in her lifetime and had overcome even more, so why in the devil was she choking up for the second time that day? Three old women stood there in the kitchen, with a young woman who definitely needed help and two stray cats. What was so emotional about that?

❖ ❖ ❖

"Are you going to keep them?" Ginger glanced out the kitchen window and caught a glimpse of Sloan picking up a few sticks as he made his way to his truck. He tossed them into the bed, then got into the vehicle and drove away.

"Oh, yes, we are," Connie answered. "We've been talkin' about gettin' another cat ever since the old tomcat that came begging for scraps at our back door up and died. That was over three years ago, and we just never got around to it." She reached for the black kitten, and Ginger handed it over to her. "I decided last week to put a river rock in my bag of stones." She pulled a velvet bag from her pocket. "Mama said it signifies water and will bring your wishes to you."

"I don't believe in all that crap, but I got to admit that the rain was probably what brought these babies to us. Someone most likely dumped them out in Rooster, and they were looking for shelter when the rain started last night," Kate said.

If these three ladies were this excited over a couple of kittens, Ginger couldn't begin to imagine how they'd react to a baby. She probably should leave before she gave birth, just so her child wouldn't be spoiled rotten.

Housework, making another batch of jam, and even the moonshine business got put on hold the rest of the afternoon while they all sat in the parlor and laughed at the two kittens' antics. The sisters named the black one Hetty after the lady that had helped their mother in the house when they were little girls. She'd been a short, gray-haired woman with a ruddy complexion, which she said came from her Irish ancestors, and the girls had loved her. The white one got tagged with Magic because Connie declared that it was pure magic that they'd gotten two in one day and that they were the same size and got along so well. Maybe they were littermates and Hetty had just gone farther on down the road than Magic had.

Ginger watched the kittens romping around and then falling flat on their stomachs and sleeping, usually at the same time. *Would it be so bad to have twins who could grow up together?* she asked herself. She hadn't even thought of having more than one baby until Sloan brought up the possibility. Now she began to yearn for two, even though she had no idea how she'd even support one.

❖　❖　❖

Rain had brought a whole new scent to the land that evening when she took her walk. The city, or even the suburban areas where she'd lived, hadn't smelled like the wet dirt surrounding her as she set her sights on a different walk. She turned to the right and walked toward what was left of the town of Rooster, only a block or two up the road. She made it to the old post office and sat down on the bench out front.

She'd heard about towns so small that they rolled up the sidewalks at five o'clock. She believed it that day, because not one person was out and about and not a single car passed by on the street. Maybe they all went to bed with the chickens, too—whatever that meant.

"Just what time do chickens go to bed anyway?" she wondered out loud.

"As soon as it gets dusky dark," Flora answered.

Ginger would have recognized that voice anywhere, but it still startled her. "Hello. I'm Ginger."

"I know who you are." Flora sat down beside her. "And I know you're living at the Banty House. I live back behind the old post office with my mother, and I usually get out for a little fresh air in the evenings. This is my spot."

"Oh—I'm so sorry . . . ," Ginger stammered. "I should be going anyway."

"I'll share with you," Flora laughed. "Stick around a little while and visit. As you can see, not much happens around here, so we all get excited when someone new comes to town. When's that baby due?"

"Not real sure. I think about the first of June, but I could be wrong," Ginger answered.

"Well, the Carson sisters will take good care of you." Flora sniffed the air. "There's another storm brewin' off to the southwest. The television weatherman says it's going to bring some hail, so we might not oughta sit out here very long. I do love the smell of a good cleansing rain, though, don't you?"

"Yes, ma'am," Ginger agreed. "The city don't ever smell like this when it rains. Just gives off the scent of wet sidewalks."

"Ain't that the truth." Flora smiled. "Well, I'd best get on back, as much as I hate to. Mama gets restless when there's a storm comin'. Maybe I'll meet up with you again on this bench sometime soon."

"Maybe so." Ginger stood up and started back toward the house.

She'd gone only to the corner when she heard a vehicle and looked over her shoulder to find Sloan pulling up to the curb.

"Need a ride?" he asked.

"Love one." She rounded the front of the truck.

He bailed out and went around the back side to open the door for her. The long bench seat was covered with a blanket and the carpet was gone, leaving only bare metal on the floor, but she felt like Cinderella again as he helped her into the truck.

"I was in town getting some weed killer for the cemetery, and I picked up some cat food for the new kitten. Did you see it?" he asked.

"Yep, but there's two of them now. Hetty is the black one you brought in. But I found Magic on the back porch. She's white and pretty close to the same size, and they seem to get along real well. Thank you for bringing food," she said.

"No problem," he said as he put the truck in gear and headed on down the street. "So, what made you decide to walk to town rather than to the log this evening?"

"It's a little shorter distance, and it's gettin' harder to carry all this." She pointed to her stomach. "If I keep getting bigger, the sisters can just roll me into the doctor's office on Thursday. I feel like I'm filled up with concrete."

For some odd reason, Sloan looked relieved. Did he think she was avoiding the log because of him?

He parked in the driveway at the Banty House just as the rain started to dot the windshield. He got out, ran around the truck, opened the door, and scooped her up in his arms. He took off in a dead run toward the porch while hail beat down on them. She wrapped her arms around her belly to protect the baby, even though it was only a few yards from the truck to the shelter of the porch.

She'd never been carried by a strong man—or any man, for that matter—before in her life. She could feel his heart racing in her ear and her own pulse rising. The experience took her breath away, even if hailstones were falling on them.

Betsy threw the door open and motioned them inside. "Did she faint again?"

"No, but I heard the hail hitting the top of the truck and didn't want her to slip and fall on it," he explained.

"That's good." Betsy slammed the door behind them. "Let's get a good pot of hot chocolate going. You sure ain't leavin' until this stops, Sloan."

"Thank you." He set Ginger down. She started to lean in and hug him, but quickly stopped herself. Someone as good looking as Sloan Baker would never have a romantic interest in a woman like her, she thought. Besides, she was pregnant, and she would never settle down in a place like Rooster. Her child needed to be raised in a place that had ballet lessons and maybe soccer or T-ball for little kids. Ginger wanted it—boy or girl—to have all the things she'd never gotten to experience, and it dang sure wasn't in Rooster.

Suddenly, Sloan jumped and then chuckled. "I guess they think I'm a tree." He pointed to both kittens, who had their claws sunk into the legs of his camouflage pants.

Betsy laughed out loud and pulled them free, carried them to the parlor, and put them on the floor. "They'll have to learn manners, and I'm just the one to teach them. Y'all come on into the kitchen with me. Connie and Kate will be here soon. They're down in the basement checkin' on the new batch of shine that Kate's been workin' on." She went to the basement door and yelled, "Sloan and Ginger are here. I'm making hot chocolate, and it's hailing cats and dogs and baby elephants."

Both of the sisters appeared at the top of the steps within a minute or two, and Connie immediately looked around for Hetty and Magic. "The babies were right here under the table when I went down to the basement. Did you hide them so you can keep them in your room tonight?" She eyed Betsy suspiciously.

Betsy shook a wooden spoon at her. "I most certainly did not. They were being bad, so I banished them to the parlor."

"Tough love, huh?" Sloan chuckled.

Both kittens slid around the doorjamb, with Hetty in the lead. They stopped long enough to have a squabble under the table and then took off like lightning streaks back to the living room.

The thought of having twins danced through Ginger's mind again. The best thing she could ever do for her baby was give it a sibling—something she had never had. Sure, she had lots of foster siblings, all ages even. But a blood-kin sister or brother was something she'd always coveted.

"Guess hailstorms and thunder don't bother them so much," Kate said.

"I just hope that we don't have to put a new roof on the house because of this," Connie sighed.

"It sounds worse than it really is since y'all got a metal roof a couple of years ago," Sloan reassured her.

Ginger couldn't imagine Lucas saying something like that to Connie. He'd be too busy figuring out how much he could get for the silverware at the pawnshop, or how he could get them to give him a $1,000 down payment for a new roof. Then they'd never see him again.

The lucky woman who wound up with Sloan would sure enough get her Prince Charming. Ginger was surprised that he hadn't already been snagged, but then the Carson sisters had hinted that he'd been sent home from the military with some kind of problem. Maybe that's what kept the women from lining up at his front door.

Chapter Nine

*K*ate said the rain that fell all day on Wednesday was a bless-ing from heaven. According to her, it was just what the corn needed to sprout and grow. Ginger wasn't so sure she agreed with her when it was still coming down in a slow, steady drizzle and she couldn't take her walk after supper. She went to her room and took a book that looked interesting from the shelf. She stretched out on the chaise lounge. Normally, a story would have taken her to another world. Not so that rainy evening. Minutes ticked away slowly as she stared out the window at the falling rain.

"Hey." Betsy poked her head in the door. "We was wonderin' if you'd like to watch our programs with us?"

"What?" Ginger hadn't seen a television in the house, and she'd been in every room.

"We have three shows we watch on Wednesday nights," Betsy said. "Well, they're not really on television right now, but we buy the DVDs when they come out and we watch them. I make popcorn. We have cold soda pop so we can pretend we've gone to the show in Hondo like we did once in a while when we were kids."

"I'd love to." Ginger closed the book and laid it aside. "I'll make a bathroom stop and then be right down."

"The lights go out at seven o'clock, and the shows start right after that. I'm going to make the popcorn right now. See you in the parlor." Betsy waved and then disappeared.

Ginger was baffled. She'd just dusted the parlor the day before, and she hadn't seen a television. Maybe, she thought, they hung a sheet up over the fireplace and showed old home movies on it. "No, that can't be right," she muttered. "Betsy said DVDs."

The buttery aroma of popcorn floated up the stairs as she started down. Sometimes she'd keep back a few dollars of her tip money and sneak off to watch a movie when Lucas was drinking and playing his fantasy games on the television in their apartment.

She shouldn't have spent the money for a movie since they slept on a mattress on the floor and she cooked in pots that she'd gotten from a junk shop. They couldn't afford cable and the only station that was clear had been one that showed nothing but news, but Lucas had his games, his DVDs, and enough joysticks so that four people could play. When he was killed, she had sold the whole lot to one of his friends and paid a month's rent with the money.

Only one lamp was burning when she reached the parlor. Kate motioned her into the room, pointed toward one of the crimson recliners, and said, "That's your seat right there. Betsy and I sit on the sofa, and Connie has the other chair. Tonight we are watching two episodes of *The Golden Girls*, two of *Designing Women*, and one of *NCIS*. We will start the evening with *NCIS*."

"I thought maybe Wednesday night would be church night." Ginger eased down into the chair and threw the lever to prop her feet up.

Connie did the same thing in the matching chair. "Nope. God can forgive all our sins on Sunday morning. We never have gone for the midweek service."

Kate sat down on the end of the sofa and propped her feet on the coffee table. Betsy brought in four brown paper bags of popcorn and four candy bars. She passed them out and then went back to the kitchen and returned with a bottle of root beer for each of them.

She took her place on the sofa, picked up the remote, and pushed a button. To Ginger's surprise, a panel on the wall above the fireplace slid back to reveal a big-screen television.

"That's pretty cool," she muttered.

"Mama didn't believe in modern things," Betsy explained. "She thought we were all better off without. We had the television put in about thirty years ago, but we made a vow that we'd only watch it once a week. We hate commercials, so we buy whatever shows we like and watch them over and over. Sometimes we get a season and hate it. When that happens, we give it to the library in Hondo."

Ginger had seen reruns of the three shows they mentioned at the shelter, so she was familiar with them. "Do you ever watch movies?"

"Oh, yes," Connie answered. "When it's my turn to choose, I usually pick two movies. I love Western movies like *Quigley Down Under*."

"And when it's my turn," Betsy said, "I like *Justified* and *Longmire*. You'll have to look through everything we have when it's your turn here in about four weeks. We just started all over this evening. Kate got to choose tonight. Next week is my turn. Then Connie's and then yours."

Ginger wasn't even sure that she'd be in Rooster in a month. Since the ladies had been so kind as to offer to let her stay, she'd given it some thought. She hadn't settled on a definite yes or no, not by any means. If she did stick around, though, she wondered if they had seasons of *Friends* in their collection. She'd watched reruns of that show in the last foster home she'd stayed in.

"We're watching *NCIS* first because sometimes it shows dead bodies and autopsies and such," Betsy explained. "Kate loves it, but then she needs to see something funny to get the images out of her mind."

"I understand that very well." Ginger opened her candy bar and took a bite.

Betsy turned off the lamp, and when the room went dark, a nightlight came on out in the foyer.

"Here we go." Kate started the show with the touch of a button on one of the remotes on the sofa between her and Betsy.

Ginger had never seen the episode that started on the screen. It had to do with a woman in the military having a baby that belonged to some big shot over in one of those foreign countries. The baby's father's people wanted to kidnap the child as soon as it was born, since it would be heir to a big oil business.

Ginger's hands shook when she thought about what could happen if Lucas's folks ever found out about her child. Of course, everything turned out well at the end of the show, but life wasn't always like that. Maybe it would be best if she told the sisters that she'd be moving on west after tomorrow.

She needed to get settled, and the sooner the better. A permanent home was important. Her baby needed to go to the same school from kindergarten all the way to graduation. It needed to make friends that would last longer than the few weeks or months that the two of them might live in one spot if she decided to keep moving on toward the west.

Betsy sniffled at the end of the show. "We've watched this episode dozens of times, but I always hold my breath during the gunfight when Gibbs is delivering that baby girl."

Kate handed her a tissue. "And she always cries at the ending."

"Well, I did always want a daughter." Betsy blew her nose loudly, then tossed the tissue into a small trash can beside the sofa.

Both Magic and Hetty ran into the room, did some wrestling and growling under the coffee table, then crawled up on the sofa to settle down in Betsy's lap. "Look at you sweet babies," she crooned. "Y'all have come to comfort me when I'm sad."

"You can't have both of them." Kate held out her hands. "I get to hold one."

"And I get one when this show is over. You have to share," Connie piped up from her chair.

"I love animals more than both of y'all, and the kittens know it," Betsy said.

"Maybe you do," Kate agreed. "But that don't mean we don't love them at all, and they belong to the whole bunch of us, not just to you."

Betsy handed over Magic, and Kate laid the kitten on her shoulder like she would a baby. The comment Betsy made about wanting a daughter resonated so much with Ginger that she crossed her fingers and sent up a silent prayer asking God, if she was carrying twins, to make one of them a girl.

"And now we have an hour's worth of *Designing Women*," Kate announced as she picked up a second remote and hit a button.

As luck would have it, the first episode had to do with Annie Potts's character having trouble with her ex-husband's new girlfriend. Ginger had threatened to go back to the shelter once when she found out that Lucas had brought another woman to their apartment. He'd sworn that his three friends, Chip, Lil' Dan, and Tat, had been there the whole time, and she'd come around to buy some product from him. The next night when she'd come home from work, she'd smelled expensive perfume on her pillow, and Lucas hadn't come back for three days. By the time he appeared again—with his friends in tow—she hadn't even cared enough to argue with him.

My life would make a television series, she thought, then changed her mind. Folks would say that there was too much drama and way too few funny moments in her story, but then, the truth was always much weirder than fiction.

It seemed only fitting that they ended the evening with *The Golden Girls*. From Gibbs delivering a new baby, to women running a design shop, to senior citizens—life was pretty well covered right there. Ginger put each of the ladies into the roles played out by the older ladies in the show. Kate became Dorothy, because she was tall. Betsy was Blanche, all spicy and with a deeper Southern accent than her two sisters. That left Connie as Rose, which wasn't an exact match. Connie wasn't ditzy, but she was shorter and a little rounder than her sisters.

When the credits began to roll, Kate shut the power off to the television, hit the right button to slide the doors shut, and put the remote control devices into the end-table drawer. "Well, that's it until next week."

"Why do you have two controls?" Ginger finished off the last handful of popcorn in her bag, then wadded it up and tossed it into the trash.

"One for the DVD player and the television, and one to close the doors." Kate yawned. "I love Wednesday nights. You know, we really should start inviting Sloan to movie night. I bet he'd enjoy it. Next time you see him, Ginger, ask him if he'd like to join us."

"Yes, ma'am." Ginger popped the footrest down and stood up. "Thank you for the entertainment. I hate to run, but all that root beer has hit bottom." Were the ladies trying to play matchmaker between her and Sloan? If so, they were going to be disappointed, because Ginger wasn't sure she could ever trust a guy again—not even one as sweet as Sloan.

"Go right on. We're all going up to our rooms, anyway. We'll see you in the morning," Betsy said.

"We'll be leaving right after breakfast," Kate called out. "Your doctor's appointment is at nine o'clock and then we go to the beauty shop, and after that we do our grocery shopping."

"I'll be ready when I come downstairs in the morning," Ginger yelled as she hurried up the steps and practically jogged to the bathroom. When she finished using the toilet, she took a bath and brushed her teeth, then padded across the hallway barefoot to the bedroom she'd been using.

She stretched out on the comfortable bed and laid a hand on her stomach. "Tomorrow we find out just when you'll be here and maybe if you are a girl or a boy—or twins. I love you, baby, whatever you are and however many there are of you. We're going to figure out our lives together and do the best we can to be happy in whatever lot we get thrown at us."

❖ ❖ ❖

Ginger didn't know who was more nervous at the doctor's office the next morning. The nurse took her back to a room, where she told her to take off her top, put on the gown to open in the front, and lie on her back on the bed. Getting comfortable on such a narrow bed was no easy feat, and Ginger feared that she'd fall off until all the Carson sisters trooped right into the room with her.

When Betsy took Ginger's hand in hers, Ginger's fears floated away. If she fell, someone would catch her for sure. Connie laced her plump little fingers into Ginger's left hand, giving her even more support. Kate took a place at the head of the bed and kept a hand on her shoulder. When Dr. Emerson came into the room, Ginger wasn't a bit surprised to see that he was gray-haired and wore wire-rimmed glasses. That was exactly how she pictured a doctor who would have treated the ladies for most of their lives.

"Well, good mornin' to all y'all. Looks like there's going to be a baby at the Banty House pretty soon. Let's take a listen to your tummy and then measure you," he said. "Is it a boy or a girl?"

"She hasn't been to the doctor yet," Betsy answered. "This is her first visit."

"Good Lord, child!" Dr. Emerson jerked the end of the stethoscope away from her stomach. "Why didn't you go get proper prenatal care?"

"I couldn't afford it," Ginger answered honestly.

"Well, you're in my hands now, and we'll do our best to see to it that everything goes smoothly from here on. We'll definitely need an ultrasound today and blood work, and I'll send you home with a bottle of vitamins. Do you have any idea how much you weighed before you got pregnant?" He repositioned the scope on her stomach.

"One twenty," Ginger said.

"Well, you're at one forty today, so that's good," he told her. "Healthy heartbeat. Sounds like a girl to me, and I'm not often wrong, but we'll see what the ultrasound says. I'm going to send Linda Sue in to draw some blood and take care of that business, and then we'll talk again about a due date."

Ginger had had a few shots in her life, but it seemed more than a little strange to think of her life's blood flowing into that tube. To think that so much could be learned by testing only a few drops was baffling to her. When the nurse finished, she put a cotton ball on the puncture site and covered that with a Band-Aid. "I'll run this down to our lab. We may have some results by the time you ladies get done with your errands today. I'll give you a call if we do. You can get up off that bed and go through the door right there." Linda Sue pointed. "That's the ultrasound room. Keep your gown on and lay down on the bed in there. I shouldn't be more than five minutes."

Betsy kept a hand on Ginger's shoulder as she went from one bed to the other. "I can't wait to see what it is. It would sure be nice if you stayed with us until the baby gets here."

"We promise not to fight over it like we do the kittens," Connie said.

Ginger took a deep breath and let it out slowly. "I'd love to stay until the baby is born, but when the baby and I are able to travel, I still want to see the ocean." She was so afraid that she'd disappoint Betsy that she couldn't raise her eyes to look at her. "I want my child to do all the things I never got to do, like ballet lessons if it's a girl and baseball if it's a boy, or being in band in high school."

"Honey, she could do all those things in Hondo," Betsy said. "You don't have to live in Los Angeles for your daughter to do that kind of stuff."

"I hadn't thought of Hondo being so close," Ginger said. "But I've always wanted to see the ocean."

"Maybe we'll go with you. We could take the car and talk Sloan into driving, or we could just fly out there, spend a week, and then fly home. We ain't never been on a vacation, and it's one of the things on my bucket list." Kate muttered the last part.

Ginger could hardly believe her ears. "For real? I've never been on a vacation, either. Folks who came into the café always talked about things like going to California to Disneyland or to walk on the beach. It sounded like so much fun."

"It's something to think about, but the next thing on our long-term agenda is the Rooster Romp and then getting a room ready for the baby since you've agreed to stay," Betsy said.

"That's long term?" Ginger asked.

"Honey, at our age, we don't put much on the calendar past two months down the road," Connie told her.

Linda Sue came into the room and peeled back the gown. "This is going to be cold." She squirted some sort of clear jelly on Ginger's tummy and ran a wand over it. Immediately, Ginger could hear the heartbeat, and then a picture of her baby appeared on the screen to the side.

"It's a pretty good-sized baby," Linda Sue said. "From what I see, you're pretty close to right on that due date. I'm going to call it at May 22. We'll need to see you every week from now until then. And would you look at that—she's got hair."

"She?" Ginger and all the ladies said at once.

"It's definitely a girl." Linda Sue moved the wand to show them a picture of her lower parts.

"That amazes me," Kate said. "Look at her little toes and her cute button nose."

"She's lookin' at me," Betsy said. "I'm going to be her favorite. She's going to call me Nana."

Tears rolled down Ginger's cheeks. Love poured from her heart like nothing she'd ever felt before, and yet mixed in with all the other emotions was just a little bit of sorrow. She'd hoped for twins, and there was definitely only one baby. She hadn't started off by giving her child a brother or sister. Maybe someday, later on down the road, she'd have one more baby, so this one would have a playmate. Perhaps her second one would even have a full-time father who would love both the children.

"Why are you crying?" Connie wiped away her tears with a tissue.

"This is the mo-most emotional moment of my life," Ginger sobbed. "That's my daughter right there, and she's beautiful, and I love her so much."

Betsy put her head in her hands and cried right along with Ginger until she got hiccups. "I'm so glad you're letting us share all this with you," she said.

Linda Sue removed the wand, wiped off the jelly, and held out a hand to help Ginger sit up. "Our little lab is backed up, so I'll have to call y'all this evening with the results of that blood work. I've made you an appointment for next Thursday at the same time. Oh, and here comes your pictures."

"What?" Ginger asked.

"The printout of your ultrasounds." Linda Sue handed the black-and-white photos of the baby to Ginger.

The ladies all gathered around to stare at the pictures. Kate reached out with her forefinger to touch the image. "It's amazing what they can do these days. Mama didn't know what we were until we were born. She said once that she was glad we were girls, because she'd have no idea what to do with a boy child."

"I wonder if my mother ever saw something like this when she was carrying me," Ginger whispered. "I can't imagine having to give my baby up only an hour or two after she's born. It would tear my heart right out of my chest."

Betsy's chin quivered. "Once a mother, always a mother. I'm sure she thought of you often, darlin', and maybe even had hopes of gettin' you back when she got out of prison."

"Or maybe of you going to visit her when you got old enough to look her up," Kate said.

"Let's buy a picture album today," Connie suggested. "We'll put one of the Easter pictures of all of us in it and then this photo, and you can keep adding to it as the baby grows."

"That would be so special," Ginger said. "I never had any childhood pictures that I could keep. Some of my foster parents took photos of us kids, but I never got to take them with me when I left."

❖ ❖ ❖

Sloan was caught up on everything that afternoon, so he went over to the cemetery and pulled the weeds that had popped up around his grandparents' graves after the rain. When he finished, he sat down on the weathered bench he'd moved from the front porch of his house and stared at their tombstone. Ernest Dale Baker, July 4, 1933–October 31, 1999. Martha Jane Baker, August 1, 1935–April 1, 2018.

He'd only been two years old when his grandpa died, so he didn't remember much about him. According to the pictures that were still scattered about the house, Ernest had been a tall, lanky man with a thin face who wore a smile all the time. Sloan glanced over to the tombstone on the other side of his grandparents, where his parents had been laid to rest. Richard and Sarah were their names, and he remembered them, but what came to mind more than their physical appearance was the love and happiness they shared when they would come home from a trip and scoop him up in their arms and hug him.

Tinker jumped up on the bench beside him and laid his head in Sloan's lap.

"Thank you for not peeing on the spot set aside for me," Sloan said as he scratched the dog's ears. "It's nice to sit here and let the good memories wash over me. That's something Ginger can never do. She probably doesn't know where her father is buried or her mother either, or even where her baby's father has been put in the ground. She can't even go sit and have good thoughts like I can."

He thought of his teammates who'd been killed that horrible day. Their families had probably had memorial services, but there hadn't been much to ship home after the bomb exploded. Maybe they at least had gravesites where their loved ones could go visit them. Someday maybe he'd look them up on the internet and see if he could find the places where they'd been laid. He should visit the places and apologize to each of them. That might bring him closure.

Tinker yipped once, but Sloan figured he was telling a squirrel or a rabbit to get out of his sight. Then a movement to his left took his attention away from the dog and his own thoughts, and there was Ginger not six feet away, walking right toward him.

"Hey, mind if I join you?" Ginger asked.

He picked up the dog and held him in his lap. "Have a seat."

"Your folks?" she asked.

"Yep." He nodded.

"Must be nice."

"It is," he said. "I was just thinkin' about you."

"Really?" she asked. "What about me?"

"When I come here, I think about the good times I had with my parents and my grandparents. You don't get to do that, so I should be thankful that I can," he explained.

"I intend to make those kinds of memories you're talkin' about with my daughter," she said.

"So it's a girl for sure?" he asked.

She pulled something from her pocket and handed it to him. "There's my baby. She's due earlier than I thought. The doctor says

May 22. I told the sisters that I'd stay at the Banty House until after she's born."

Another one of the chains around Sloan's heart loosened up a notch or two. "It's great that you are staying. The sisters have gotten attached to you in a big way. Looks like a big baby to me." He handed the pictures back to her. "I've seen a couple of those in the military from the guys who had pregnant wives. I can tell that's a baby. Some of the ones they showed me looked more like goldfish or sea monkeys. Are you happy that you're having a daughter?"

"Very," Ginger said. "I wouldn't know what to do with a boy, and besides, I kind of feel like a boy needs a father even worse than a girl does. Role model and all that."

"All children do better with both parents, but lots of kids only get one these days. I only had my granny from the time I was seven years old, and she did a good job of being mama, daddy, and granny to me," Sloan said.

They sat in silence for a few minutes before Ginger said, "I should be starting back."

"Why don't you come on in the house with me and Tinker? I've got iced tea already made up," he offered.

"I'd love to." She took another look at the picture and put it back in her pocket. "Kate bought an album to put my pictures in, but I wasn't ready to let go of this one just yet."

"I can understand that. If I was going to be a father, I'd probably be the same way with the pictures." He offered her his arm. "The ground is pretty uneven and there's mud puddles."

She looped her arm in his. He shortened his stride and slowed his pace to match hers. When they reached his porch, she removed her arm and held on to the banister. "Your yard and home look like something straight out of a magazine," she said. "A pretty little white house with a picket fence, flowers beds everywhere, and even a porch swing. It's so beautiful that it doesn't look real."

"Thank you." He felt like a king sitting on a golden throne at her words. "Granny liked for the place to look nice, and I've kept it up in her memory." He opened the door and stood to the side. "Welcome to the Baker house. It's not as big or fancy as the Banty House, but it's comfortable."

"It's so cozy," she said, looking around. "You must be related to Connie. She can scare dust right out the door."

"Granny's training and then the military added more training on top of that." He grinned. "I'll pour us a glass of tea. Sit anywhere and make yourself at home."

Ginger stood in front of the sofa for several minutes, staring at all the pictures arranged on the wall behind it. "I can't imagine having relatives like this. Is this your granny and grandpa in the middle?"

"That was taken on the day they got married. She was eighteen and he was nineteen." Sloan filled two glasses with ice and then poured sweet tea into them. "He was in the army and got deployed right after they married. They didn't have my dad until a couple of years after he got home. The one on your right is my dad when he graduated from high school. On your left is my mama. They dated from the time they were fourteen, and married about a year after they graduated. All the rest are pictures of me as I grew up." He carried the tea to the living room and set both glasses on the coffee table. "That one right there"— he pointed—"is when I won grand champion on my steer at the state fair, and that one is my army picture when I graduated from basic training."

"What'd you do in the army?" She eased down onto the sofa and picked up her glass of tea.

"I was sent to school and trained to defuse bombs." His mouth went dry when he uttered the words.

"Do you ever get called on to do that now?" she asked. "It sounds pretty dangerous."

"No. I've been declared a washup." He drank down half of his tea. "There was a big problem in Kuwait, and . . ." The words trailed off as he stared into space.

Had she pressured him to go on, he might have dug his heels in and clammed up, but she just looked into his eyes and waited, giving him time to collect his thoughts. "We weren't supposed to have liquor or even real beer over there. The country was primarily Muslim and they don't allow liquor or beer, and when Granny sent jerky to me, it couldn't be pork. We had to go through classes before we went to be sure we didn't cause an international incident," he finally said. "But sometimes the guys would get it in a care package disguised as mouthwash. Put it in a Listerine bottle and no one even thinks to open it and check. Or they could put a few drops of blue food coloring in a bottle of vodka and it'll pass as Scope."

"So y'all got drunk when you weren't on duty?" she asked.

He shrugged, not sure if he wanted to go on but wanting to get it off his chest. The therapist had wanted him to talk about it, but he'd just sat through those sessions with the guilt lying heavy on his shoulders—not saying a single word.

"Hey, if you don't want to talk about it, then tell me a story about your granny instead." Ginger laid a hand on his bare arm.

Her touch gave him the courage to go on. "I was the only one who got drunk that night. The rest of the guys weren't drinking. I'd just gotten a phone call from my granny telling me that my dog, a big old red-boned hound that she got for me when my folks were killed, had gotten hit on the road and killed. I'd had him since I was seven years old. Granny thought that it might help me when my folks died to have a puppy."

"I'm sorry." Ginger gave his arm a gentle squeeze. "I can't imagine having a pet and then losing it. But you still had Tinker, right?"

"Tinker showed up after I graduated from high school and left home," he said. "He was an old dog when he arrived on Granny's porch step, and she took him in. He's been a lot of company to me since she passed away."

"So you got drunk," she said. "Is that the reason they sent you home? Over one night of drinking?"

"No." He cleared his throat and went on to say, "I was hungover the next morning when my team got a call to go out to one of the far buildings on the base. Someone had called in a bomb threat. They left me on my bunk with a trash can beside me and told my commander that I had the flu." His voice sounded hollow in his own ears. "They took another bomb tech along, and . . ." He stopped to swallow the lump in his throat. "And, well"—he took a deep breath—"to make a long story short, it wasn't just a threat, and the guy they took with them had evidently never dealt with a device like that."

"What happened?" she asked.

"My entire team, plus a 'cruit that had just arrived the day before, were killed," he whispered. "John Matthews," he said, and tears began to flow down his cheeks. "Chris Jones." The first sob caught in his throat. "Creed Dawson." He grabbed a tissue. "Bobby Joe Daniels and Wade Beaudreaux. I didn't even know the new guy's name until later, when I read about the private memorial that was held on the base."

"And you blame yourself?" Ginger took the tissue from him and wiped his face with it. Then she tilted up his chin and looked him right in the eyes. "Don't punish yourself."

"Who else is there to blame or to punish?" he asked.

"Way I look at things is that everything happens for a reason. Evidently God has a purpose for you to fulfill on this earth before He takes you on to heaven to be with your granny. He's not obligated to tell us His plans, but we should respect them." She didn't blink or look away.

"You really believe that?" he asked.

"I went to church with the cook sometimes, or to just whichever one was open when I left work." She gave a brief nod. "I kind of lost my faith for a while, and I'm still not real sure what God's plan is for me, but I do know that it wasn't your fault that all your buddies were killed. Did you go to any of the memorials?"

He shut his eyes. "I was in the hospital at the time with what they said was the worst case of depression they'd ever seen. I was almost catatonic. I remember wishing that I could just stop breathing, but my body wouldn't let me. I killed those men, Ginger, just as surely as if I'd executed them one by one with my rifle."

She slapped him on the thigh. "No, you did not. Whoever the hell that terrorist was that planted that bomb killed them. You've got to get that shit out of your head, Sloan. Work it out with sweat. Cry it out with tears. But get it out however you can, because it's going to wind up eating away at you if you don't."

"How'd you get to be so smart?" he asked.

"Hard living," she answered without hesitation. "At least you had someone here to take you in and love you when they sent you home. When I finished high school two years ago this month, I had no one and no place, except a shelter that the social worker recommended."

"But you never killed your best friends, did you?" he asked.

"No, but if I'd had a shotgun, I might have blown holes in three guys one night when Lucas wanted me to take two of his buddies to the bedroom. They offered to give him fifty bucks if he'd make me have sex with them. They even offered to let him join in the fun," she said.

"Holy shit," Sloan said. "What did you do?"

"I left the apartment and didn't come home until the next day. That's when I found out that Lucas was dead, and I didn't even care. I felt guilty for not having any emotion other than relief, but it was what it was. I had no idea that I was probably six weeks pregnant when that happened," she said.

Sloan took her small hand in his. "I guess we've both lived through some rough times."

"Yes, we have, and it's made us tough enough to face whatever lies ahead of us," she said. "Maybe God or Fate or Destiny put us here in this place at this time so we could help each other make peace with the past."

"I like that idea." He smiled.

"Me too," she said. "Now I reckon I should be goin' on back to the Banty House. The sisters will be gettin' worried."

Thunder sounded like it rolled right over the top of the house.

"Let me drive you home," Sloan said. "You're liable to get wet if you walk."

"Thank you." Her smile lit up the whole room. "I will surely take you up on that."

He pulled her up by the hand and kept it in his the whole way outside and across the yard to his truck. She didn't resist, and that simple little fact, and knowing that she was going to stay in Rooster for a little longer, brought him so much comfort that mere words couldn't have begun to describe the feeling.

Chapter Ten

There was an envelope lying on Ginger's plate at the breakfast table on Friday morning. "What's this?" she asked.

"Your paycheck for the past week," Betsy said. "We all get paid on Friday. Our CPA takes care of the payroll and puts ours directly into our individual bank accounts. If you want, we can have Sloan drive you into town this afternoon, and you can start a bank account with yours. After you do that, we can have Suzanne do a direct deposit for you, too."

"Are you serious?" Ginger asked when she peeked inside the envelope. "This is more money than I made in two weeks at the café, and I had to pay rent and utilities and buy groceries." She had always held her breath and hoped that she could stretch each check from one payday to the next. There had certainly never been enough money to even think about starting a bank account.

"Well, do you want to start an account?" Connie asked.

"Yes," Ginger said, nodding her head the whole time. "Yes, I do. I wouldn't even know what to do with all this money except to save it up so I can buy what the baby needs."

"All right, then. As soon as Sloan gets through taking care of the car, he can drive you into Hondo to our bank and help you get things done. And while you're in town you can run by the store and pick up a few things that I forgot yesterday," Betsy said. "I was so excited about seeing the baby like we got to do that I plumb forgot to get some vanilla extract, and I need another twenty pounds of sugar for blackberry jam this week."

"Just make a list, and I'll be glad to get whatever you need." The thought that went through Ginger's mind was that she could pack her bag and get all the way to California with the money she already had and there would be enough left to stay in a cheap motel until she could find a job. She thought about it for a split second before she shook the crazy notion from her head. Next week, she'd have a paycheck just like this one, and by the time the baby came, she'd have even more. For the first time in her life, she'd have money in the bank. She couldn't leave behind a deal like this, not even to dip her toes in the ocean.

When breakfast was over, the table cleared, and the dishes done, she and Betsy put a turkey in the oven for the noon meal. In this part of Texas, that was dinner and the evening meal was called supper. Ginger had been in one upscale foster home where the meals were called lunch and dinner and some not nearly as fancy where they were dinner and supper. Lucas used the terms "lunch" and "dinner" and looked down his nose on anyone who did differently.

"What on earth are four people going to do with a whole turkey?" Ginger shook her head to get rid of the vision of Lucas's face when he made snide remarks about the people he considered beneath him and his family.

"We eat what we want, and then, when you get back from town, we'll pick all the meat off the bones, make a couple of turkey potpies for the freezer, and maybe if there's enough left, we'll have turkey-salad sandwiches for supper tonight," Betsy said. "That way if we get a call that someone in Rooster is sick or has died, all we have to do is pop a potpie in the oven and we're good to go."

"To go where?" Ginger started taking the leaves off the ends of strawberries.

"Honey, if someone dies, we take food to the house where the family is gathering. If someone is sick, then they probably ain't feelin' like cookin' for the family, so we do the same," Betsy explained.

"That's so sweet." Ginger thought she might never leave this place if all the folks were that kind. She cocked her head to one side. "Who's whistling?"

Betsy cupped a hand around her ear and slowly made her way to the door leading out to the garage. "That's not Kate's whistling. Hers is higher pitched and not nearly as happy." She picked up a glass from the counter, put the top of it against the door, and placed her ear against the bottom.

"What the hell are you doin'?" Kate asked as she opened the basement doors. Alcohol fumes mixed with a faint hint of something minty followed her into the kitchen.

"Shhh . . ." Betsy put a finger over her lips. "Sloan is whistling."

"You're kiddin' me." Kate jerked the glass out of Betsy's hand and listened for herself. "You are so right. Sloan is whistling. I ain't seen him happy enough to whistle since before he left to go to the service." She handed the glass back to Betsy and turned to Ginger. "What'd y'all talk about last night?"

Ginger raised one shoulder. "Just life in general. How it ain't fair, or at least that's the way it seems until we done lived through it and got on down the road a few years. Then we look back and figure out that maybe things worked out the way they were supposed to."

"That's pretty deep for a girl your age," Betsy said.

"It's just the way I see it, I guess." She went back to washing the berries and getting them ready for Betsy.

"Well, whatever you did, do some more of it." Betsy crossed the room and got out the big pot that she used to make jam.

If Ginger could whistle, she might have been doing the same thing as Sloan, because her heart felt lighter that morning—even before she found her paycheck on her plate—than it had ever been.

❖   ❖   ❖

Folks at the bank knew Sloan, and several of the tellers either waved or else spoke to him when he and Ginger came in the front door. Some even raised their eyebrows at him coming in with a pregnant woman, but he was long past the time when he cared what people thought or even what they might say when he was gone. He showed Ginger into the office, where a girl he'd graduated from high school with took care of new accounts, and then he went to one of the teller's windows to transfer some of his money from checking to savings.

"Hey, is that the woman I've been hearing about?" The teller was a girl who lived in Rooster, named Samantha. She was a few years older than Sloan and was a daughter to the preacher at the Rooster church.

"What woman and what's been said?" he asked.

"That you met her when she came to the cemetery looking for her relatives' graves and y'all had a fling. Now she's come back and says she's pregnant with your baby. The Banty House ladies are letting her stay with them while y'all sort this crap out and you can get a DNA done when the baby is born." She made out a slip and handed it to him. "All done with your transaction. Need anything else?"

"Not today." He knew that gossip was crazy in small towns like Hondo, but holy smokin' hell. How had the rumormongers ever come up with a story like that?

"Are you goin' to tell me if the story goin' around is anywhere near right?" she asked.

"Not today," he said, repeating his previous words, and walked over to the office where Ginger was signing papers.

She glanced up and saw him standing in the open doorway and held up a finger. "Just a few more minutes. They're making me a debit card right now."

"Take your time." He stopped just short of saying "darling" just to keep the rumors going. What kind of wild stories would folks tell when Ginger left Texas—would he be the son-of-a-bitch, deadbeat father who didn't even acknowledge his own child?

That got him to thinking about what it would be like if the rumors were true. Would the news that he was about to have a daughter make him happy? His grandmother would probably shout so loud in heaven that he could hear her right there beside the Cottonwood Cemetery. One of the last things she had told him before she died was that someday she wanted him to find someone who'd make him as happy as his grandpa had made her.

He was deep in thought when Ginger touched him on the arm. "I'm all done, now."

He tucked her arm into his, and they walked out of the bank together into a fierce wind that whipped Ginger's hair around in her face and sent Sloan's cap tumbling down the sidewalk right beside a big tumbleweed. He chased after it while Ginger stood on the sidewalk and laughed. Finally, after several tries, he caught the blasted thing and shoved it in the hip pocket of his camouflage pants.

"Good thing your hair is attached to your head," he teased when he came back to her.

"And that I've got the extra weight of this little girl in my tummy to anchor me," she said. "I'll treat you to an ice cream at that store over there, if you'll go with me."

"I'd love a hot fudge sundae," he said. "But are you sure you want to be seen with a man like me?"

"What's that supposed to mean?" she asked.

He told her what the gossips were saying about them, and she threw back her head and laughed. If the wind could have carried the sound of her laughter across the whole eastern half of Texas, it would have put a smile on lots of folks' faces.

"I've never mattered enough for anyone to spread gossip about me," she said. "I think that's pretty funny. Anyone who knows you should know that you are the kindest, most honorable man in the whole state."

"Didn't you hear a word I said the other night about my buddies?" He took her hand in his, and they bent forward against the wind as they crossed the street. No one could ever understand what he was going through, not even a woman with a hard-luck past.

"Yes, I did, but you need to let that go and move on with your life. You're not dead for a reason," she shot back.

The business of going forward was tough when he carried the guilt of not being there for his team on his shoulders. He couldn't just throw off the weight like a bag of topsoil or fertilizer. If he was alive for a reason, he damn sure wished he could figure out what it was.

"I try, but it's easier said than done." He took a deep breath and let it out slowly. After all, it wasn't Ginger's fault that he was the cause of his team's death. "Let's go get ice cream now, but before we go into the ice cream shop, let me tell you, I can't let you treat me. My granny would rise up out of her grave and use a pecan-tree switch on me if I let a lady pay when I'm with her. Besides, it'll show everyone that I do have a little decency left in me." He opened the door for her and had to fight it to keep the wind from slamming it shut.

"All right," she agreed as she crossed the floor and looked at the menu up above the counter. "But if you pay, then you have to stay and play dominoes with us tonight, and you have to come to movie night next Wednesday."

"I've played dominoes with the ladies a few times, and beware, darlin', those old gals take their games very serious. But I didn't know about movie night. They don't even have a television, do they?"

"I want a caramel sundae," she said.

"I'll take a hot fudge sundae with chocolate ice cream," he said.

"Oh, do we get to pick the ice cream? If so I want butter pecan under my caramel," she told the young lady behind the counter.

"Have it right out to you," the girl said as she made change from the bill that Sloan handed her. "Y'all sit wherever you want."

Ginger slid into a booth beside the window. "Their television is behind the wall above the fireplace." She went on to describe the whole thing to him and then to tell him about the shows they'd watched.

"What time does it begin?" Sloan asked.

"Seven on the dot. Betsy makes popcorn and puts it in bags for each of us and brings us each a candy bar and a bottle of root beer. I could ask them if they'd mind if you had a real beer. I don't think they'd mind since Kate makes moonshine," she said.

"I haven't had a drink . . ." His voice trailed off.

She laid a hand over his. "Then root beer it is."

The girl brought their sundaes, and they both set about eating. To Sloan, even in the midst of a busy ice cream shop, there was no one else but the two of them in the world right at that moment, and he rather liked the feeling.

❖ ❖ ❖

So this is what it feels like to have real friends, Ginger thought that evening as they sat around the dining room table and played dominoes. Connie won the first hand of a game called Shoot the Moon, and Betsy won the second. Sloan whipped them all in the third hand, and Kate declared that Connie hadn't shuffled the pieces well enough when she lost the next round.

Betsy excused herself to go get the snacks after the fourth round, and Ginger followed her into the kitchen to help.

"What can I do to help?" Ginger asked.

"Get out the cheese tray from the refrigerator and fill the center part with black olives," Betsy said. "I'll slice up some apples. Didn't want to do them too early or they turn dark, but Sloan likes them with my special cream-cheese dip."

"How often do y'all have a domino night?" Ginger went to work following Betsy's orders.

"About once a month," Betsy answered. "Mama said if you play something too often it'll get boring, so we vary things. We didn't play last week because you needed to get settled in a little. It was Kate's turn to choose our Friday game that time, and she always picks dominoes. Next week it'll be my turn, and we're playing Scrabble. That's good for the mind. Keeps it active. Connie changes her mind and goes back and forth between Monopoly and Yahtzee."

"I like playing games with y'all and Sloan." Ginger finished arranging the olives in the center section of the crystal plate. She didn't say it out loud, but she also liked helping make pretty food with Betsy in the kitchen.

"Did you remember to ask him to movie night?" Betsy asked.

"Yes, I did, and he said he'd come next Wednesday," Ginger answered.

They took the food plates to the dining room and set them on the buffet.

"Whoever isn't playing at the time can help themselves," Betsy said. "Plates and napkins are right here. Don't get anything greasy on Kate's dominoes or she'll throw a fit."

"You bet I will. There's no telling how many games have been played with these little ivory darlin's." Kate shuffled them well, and then everyone slid their own share over to set them up. "Mama kept really good records about who played dominoes and who got baths."

"What do dominoes and baths have to do with each other?" Ginger asked.

"Honey, this wasn't a regular old whorehouse where men came and went all night long," Connie explained as she started out the game by laying down a double six. "This was a special brothel. Only six men, one to each of her girls, were allowed through the doors each evening, and they had to make an appointment. Mama had senators and doctors and lawyers comin' to the Banty House and we have all her records to prove it."

"But what about baths?" Ginger asked.

"It was like this." Kate talked as she studied her dominoes. "Each man got special treatment the night he came to the Banty House. To start with, whichever girl he had an appointment with gave him a bath and then a massage."

"Why?" Ginger asked.

"Honey, this is Texas," Connie whispered. "After a hard week's work, Mama's customers smelled pretty bad."

Kate giggled and went on. "After that, she served him a good meal of his choosing—fried chicken, roast beef, steak—Mama's menu usually offered their choice of one of several meats and sides, right along with dessert, coffee, and a cigar if he wanted one afterwards. The meal was served in his girl's bedroom so the two of them could have conversation and visit."

"That must've been very expensive," Ginger said.

"It was." Kate laid out a domino with a sharp click. "The clients had to pay up front, and they had to be gone by seven o'clock in the morning. Mama ran a strict house. Straight-up sex if the guys wanted it—no whips or cuffs and nothing demeaning to her girls."

"The girls got one-third of what they made, but Mama made them save part of it. The house got one-third, and the other part of the money they collected each evening went into a general fund. When a girl had worked a year, Mama gave them a severance package and put them on the train to wherever they wanted to go so they could get a fresh start in a new place," Connie said.

"Why?" Sloan asked.

"Mama said that it was good marketing to keep fresh faces in the house," Betsy said. "And she never let her girls look like anything but angels. They wore white dresses every night. That way the menfolk thought they'd made a trip to heaven when they left in the morning."

"Did she ever have trouble keeping help?" Sloan played a domino.

"She had a waiting list of girls who wanted to work when she closed down the place right after I was born," Connie replied. "And from what she said, she hurt a lot of guys' feelings when she had to tell them that she wouldn't be doing business anymore."

"I betcha there's a whole list of folks who would kill to get their hands on those records your mother kept." Sloan chuckled.

"They're in a really good safe at our bank," Kate said. "Mama didn't believe in blackmail, but she did believe in protection."

Kate finally won the last round of the evening. "Aha," she said, "the ivories didn't totally forsake me."

Sloan covered a yawn with his hand. "Thanks for the evening and for the food, ladies. I'll be here soon as the dew dries tomorrow to mow the lawn and spruce up the flower beds."

"I need you to take half a dozen jars of jam to Joy Goodman over in Hondo right after lunch. She's havin' some kind of fancy whoop-de-do with her book club and wants to give them away as door prizes," Betsy said.

"Sure thing." Sloan tipped his cap toward them and started for the door. "Want to walk me out, Ginger? You didn't get your evening stroll. It'll just be across the yard to my truck, but you can get a nice breath of fresh air."

"I should stay and help Betsy clean up." She glanced around at the dirty plates.

"I'll help her," Connie said. "You kids go on. It's a lovely night to sit on the porch swing."

"Are you sure?" Ginger asked. "I was gone part of the afternoon already today."

"You'll make it up later. We don't punch a time clock around here. If we did, you would have already been working overtime, since you played dominoes with us all evening."

Ginger grabbed a hooded sweatshirt from the coatrack in the foyer and slipped it on before she went outside with Sloan. He waited until she was settled on the swing and then sat down beside her.

"I'd never heard that story about the way the brothel was run," he said. "Granny always said that Belle Carson had good business sense and knew when to shut the place down."

"I wouldn't have thought she'd tell her daughters all about it," Ginger said.

"Maybe she was hoping they'd understand why she did what she did, or maybe she was trying to help them realize if times got really tough again after she was dead, they could always get creative in ways to make money." Sloan kept the swing going with his foot.

"I want to be that honest with my daughter," Ginger said. "I want to be a mama like theirs was."

"She must've been one special lady," Sloan said. "But then so are you."

"I don't know about that, but I sure intend to try." Ginger sucked in a lungful of fresh air. "I smell honeysuckle."

"It's blooming on fences everywhere around here," Sloan said. "The wind is bringing the scent right to you."

"I'm worried, Sloan," she whispered.

"About what?"

"Leaving," she admitted. "I've only been here a week and a day. Walking away would break my heart. I've never had friends like you and the sisters."

"It's sure something to think about." He leaned over and kissed her on the forehead. "I really should be going. It smells like we might be in for more rain, and I left my truck windows down."

"Have a good rest of the night." The touch of his lips on her skin sent tingles dancing down her spine.

She sat on the swing and watched him cross the yard and get into his truck, continuing to keep an eye on the red taillights until they disappeared into the darkness, and then she touched her forehead to see if it was as hot as it felt.

Finally, she placed a hand on her stomach and said, "Baby girl, how about the name Belle. Does that suit you?"

The baby kicked her hand hard enough that Ginger giggled. "I'm not sure if that was a yes or a no, but you sure had an opinion about it."

Chapter Eleven

On Saturday morning the sun came out, bringing heat and humidity with it. Betsy said the weather was like sending her flower beds to a spa all day. Sloan showed up right after breakfast, made a trip into Hondo to deliver jam to Joy Goodman, and then worked in the garden most of the morning. In the afternoon, Connie claimed Sloan and Ginger to help deep clean the two spare bedrooms.

"This is Mama's room," Connie explained as she opened the door. "I clean it every spring from top to bottom. I come in here and sit in her rockin' chair when I'm having a hard day, and after a few minutes, everything is peaceful inside my heart again."

"I'm not against anything that brings about peace. I'll get the bed dismantled and put out in the hallway," Sloan said.

Ginger had thought they'd wash the baseboards and clean any dust that might have collected off the ceiling fan. Evidently, Connie's idea of deep cleaning and hers were two very different notions.

"And then the dresser and the rest of the furniture. Mama hated spiders, so we'll be sure there's not even a teensy one hiding anywhere in her room." Connie went to work cleaning off every flat surface. "Ginger, you can clean off the top of her dresser. Just lay whatever is there in the drawers. It's on casters, so it won't be hard for Sloan to push out of the room," Connie said.

While Sloan took all the covers from the bed and tossed them into a pile out in the hallway, then started tearing down the four-poster bed, Ginger opened a drawer to find nightgowns and underwear still folded neatly in it. Pictures of all sizes, some in black and white, a few in color, gave testimony that Belle's girls had been her life. Ginger had already put her ultrasound picture of the baby into her album, but someday she was going to have pictures of her family scattered about like this—and like what she'd seen in Sloan's house. History was something a child could hang on to, could talk about. Sloan could say that his granny told him this or that. The Carson sisters knew all about their mother and their grandparents and could remember their sayings. Ginger had none of that, but by golly, her child was going to at least have a mother who'd provide her with memories.

She looked down at the neatly folded white silk underpants in the drawer where she'd laid several framed photos. "How long has your mother been gone, Connie?"

"Well, let's see." Connie held up her fingers. "I guess it must be sixty years this summer. Kate was twenty the year she died and she's eighty now." She carried knickknacks from the nightstands and the table beside the rocking chair out into the hallway and lined them up against the far wall. "We had good intentions of giving all her things away when she'd been gone a year, but we just couldn't do it. Then one year turned into two and then it was ten years, and we decided having her room as it was when she was with us brought us comfort. We had a little family meeting and decided that we'd probably never use the room anyway, so I just clean it every year and we leave it alone." She raised her voice as she carried another armload of things out into the hallway. "Besides, when I clean, it brings back good times."

"Such as?" Sloan carried out the rocking chair.

"I bought her this little ceramic bunny for Mother's Day the year before she died. Since Easter was her favorite holiday, we often bought her little gifts that would remind her of that day. I can still see her face when she opened her present." Connie smiled.

"Granny liked Thanksgiving, so there's still a whole collection of little turkeys in her bedroom," Sloan said.

"Your grandmother's name was Martha Jane, right?" Ginger remembered the tombstone he'd been sitting in front of that evening.

"Yep." He nodded.

Martha Belle, she thought. *That would be a good solid name for my daughter.*

Sloan's muscles strained the sleeves of his T-shirt as he moved the dresser from the room. The old wooden casters hardly worked at all anymore, so finally he just picked it up and carried it out of the room. Lucas had needed the help of all three of his friends just to move a flat-screen television up two flights of stairs. Granted, all four of them combined wouldn't have a single bulging muscle like Sloan.

You shouldn't compare people. Everyone has weaknesses and strengths. A school lesson on judging came back to haunt her as she stood in the middle of a totally empty room.

"All right, now we wash the walls," Connie said. "Sloan, will you go in the bathroom and fill the bucket with warm water? Well, rats! I forgot to get the bucket and the spray to take the dark spots off the walls. I'll be right back." She headed out the door.

"I can get those for you," Sloan said.

"It'd take more time to tell you what I want than to just go get it myself. I'll pick up three bottles of water while I'm in the kitchen," Connie said.

"Are you really okay with washing ceilings and doin' this kind of work?" Ginger asked him when Connie was out of hearing distance.

"It all pays the same, but I'd do it for free," he answered. "And besides, none of the sisters should be on a ladder at their age. If they fall, they could break a hip or an arm. They've been so good to me my whole life that it would break my heart if one of them got hurt doing something that I could've done for them."

Lucas had never helped with one thing in the apartment. His theory was that men didn't do housework of any kind. They didn't even pick up their dirty dishes and cups and take them to the kitchen sink. He wouldn't even have understood why a person might wash walls.

Stop comparing, that pesky voice in her head reminded her again.

She couldn't help it. Lucas was the male in her past life. Sloan was the one in her present. They held different roles. Lucas had been her escape from the shelter. Sloan was her friend. Maybe what she was experiencing was what she'd heard called pregnancy brain, but lately it seemed like she was analyzing every little emotion and event that came into her life.

"Here's what we need." Connie brought a blue plastic bucket into the room and began to unload it. "Water and some cookies in case we need a snack, cleaner to put in the water, and some stronger stuff to spray on the walls."

"What do I do?" Ginger pulled a rubber band from the pocket of her jeans and twisted her hair up into a ponytail.

"You are going to wash the middle third of the walls. I'll do the bottom third, and Sloan will do what we couldn't get when he gets finished." Connie tied a bandanna around her head and knotted it in the middle of her forehead. If she'd put on the same red lipstick she'd worn to the hairdresser, she'd have looked a lot like Lucille Ball.

"Your walls are papered instead of painted," Ginger commented. "How do you wash them?"

"I have them repapered every fifth year and dust them well every spring in the years in between," Connie said. "This little job will be done in an hour. We probably wouldn't need to do them every year, but I like to keep Mama's room all fresh and pretty."

Sloan set up the ladder, finished the ceiling and the fan, and then got down and started helping the ladies with the walls. "Was that fan put in before y'all had the air conditioners installed?"

"Yes, it was," Connie said. "Mama still had girls when she had the fans put in each room. It could get pretty warm in the summer without them. We didn't get air-conditioning until several years after Mama died, so she never got to see how wonderful it is."

Just as they finished putting the room back to rights that evening, Betsy yelled that supper would be on the table in fifteen minutes. Connie stopped at the dresser and eyed the pictures that Ginger had set up again on the top, and then she took an old Polaroid picture from her pocket and cocked her head to one side. Then she switched two of the small frames and moved one on the end slightly to the left.

"You did good remembering which ones went where, but . . ." Connie patted Ginger on the shoulder. "Now it's just like Mama had it fixed." She picked up the bucket and headed downstairs, leaving Sloan and Ginger alone.

"No spiders, no dust, and everything in its right place." Sloan turned out the light and ushered Ginger out with a hand on her lower back. There were those same sparks that she'd felt when he kissed her forehead.

"I don't think I've ever seen such a clean house," Ginger said.

"'Cleanliness is next to godliness,'" Sloan quoted Scripture. "That's what Granny always quoted on cleaning day."

"Speaking of that, why don't you go to church with us tomorrow?"

"I told you that me and God got some things to sort out before . . . ," he started, but she put her finger over his lips.

"God might meet you in the middle if you show Him you're serious about doin' that heart cleanin'. Maybe He don't like spiders and dust, either. And all you're doin' is lettin' your heart gather up dirt and varmints," Ginger said.

"So you *are* religious?" Sloan said.

"As I told you before, I'm not religious, but I have faith," she replied. "I think there's a difference, but I haven't quite got it put into words yet. I like going to church, even though my mind wanders from the sermon sometimes. I love the singing, so when I go, I pay attention to the words of the hymns. It didn't matter which church I went to when I was off work on Sunday, just so long as I could hear the songs."

"Did you ever sing all by yourself in the empty church?" he asked.

"Nah, I don't have much of a voice for singin'," she said when they reached the bottom of the steps. "We should've washed up for supper while we were upstairs."

Betsy poked her head around the dining room door. "It's all right if you wash up in the kitchen sink. Ain't no need to make another trip up the steps."

"So?" Ginger looked up into his face.

"So what?" Betsy asked.

"I asked him to go to church with us tomorrow mornin'. There's room on the pew where y'all sit for him, isn't there?" Ginger asked.

"Of course, and you know you're welcome anytime." Betsy smiled. "But you don't have to decide right now. Just show up and then come to Sunday dinner with us afterwards. Right now you kids need to wash your hands. Supper is on the table, and I know you're hungry after all that work that Connie made you do. Downright crazy to tear a room to pieces like that, if you ask me, but did anyone ask me? Oh, no!" She muttered all the way back to the kitchen.

When they were gathered around the table, sitting in their normal spots, Connie said a short prayer, and then Betsy ladled up homemade chicken noodle soup in all their bowls. Kate passed a plate of grilled cheese sandwiches that had been cut diagonally around the table and then a relish tray.

"Save room for strawberry shortcakes," Betsy said. "I had too many berries for the batch of jam I made today, so I whipped up a sponge cake to use for the bottom layer."

"There goes my idea for taking all you ladies up to the snow cone stand this evening," Sloan said. "We'll all be too full for that."

"Can we have a rain check and go after dinner tomorrow?" Kate asked.

"I've got a better idea," Sloan said. "If I go to church with y'all, would you let me drive you into Hondo and take y'all out to Sunday dinner? You've been so good to feed me extra meals this week, and I'd sure like to repay you."

"If . . . ," Kate said, "you promise to sit with us tomorrow, we would be honored to go to that pizza place in Hondo that has a big buffet dinner, and you can drive for us."

What changed his mind about church? Ginger wondered. Could it be that he was finally realizing a terrorist had killed his friends, and that neither he, nor God, could have stopped it from happening?

"Why that place? We could go to a nice steak house," Sloan asked.

"Because Betsy can't make pizza worth eating," Connie answered. "Anything else she can cook for us right here. Pizza is a treat."

"I've been craving pizza ever since I got pregnant," Ginger said when she felt all their eyes on her. "I've never tried to make it myself, but I sure do love it."

"Okay, then." Sloan nodded. "I'll be here at a quarter to eleven to drive you ladies to church."

Ginger wondered what the folks who were already spreading gossip would make of them all arriving together. Lord have mercy! If she and Sloan even sat beside each other, the cell towers between Rooster and Hondo might flat-out explode.

Chapter Twelve

*G*inger tried to concentrate on the short shopping list she'd made, but it was nearly an impossibility with Sloan sitting right next to her on the church pew. His shaving lotion—something woodsy and wonderful smelling—wafted over to her every time he moved even the slightest bit. With a sigh she forced herself to look straight ahead and not at him. That didn't last more than a minute, and she went back to stealing sideways glances at him. To everyone else, it looked like he was paying attention to the preacher's words, but he didn't fool Ginger one bit. His mind was wandering just like hers—only she'd bet that he wasn't thinking about her like she was him.

She forced herself to make a mental shopping list for when they went back to Hondo. She needed a dress that she could wear now, but also after the baby came—maybe one of those new little knit numbers that skimmed the knees. She had one suitable outfit for church other than her Easter dress from last week. If she was going to attend every week, she should have at least four so that she wouldn't wear the same thing all the time. She also wanted to get a cell phone. It didn't have to be fancy and have all the smart features on it, but it did need to be better than the one that she had to pay to add minutes to.

Then she should probably get a few things for the baby. If she spit up like that little guy did in her last foster home, it would take several gowns or outfits each day. Thank goodness there was a washer and dryer at the Banty House.

That worked for maybe three or four minutes, and then she went right back to thinking about Sloan. He sat so close to her that light couldn't make its way between their bodies. He'd dressed in starched jeans, a blue plaid shirt the color of his eyes, and tan cowboy boots that morning. Ginger had visions of women gathering around him like flies on an open sugar bowl as soon as services were over.

Did other people have wandering thoughts like she did? She glanced to her left, where Kate sat at the end of the pew. Was she thinking about loving her neighbor, or was she figuring out how to make adjustments to her recipe for blackberry moonshine? Connie was next in the lineup. While Ginger was watching, she removed a tissue from her purse and dusted the tops of the hymnals. Betsy's expression left no doubt that she wasn't hearing a word the preacher was saying, and Ginger would have bet dollars to doughnuts that she was devising a new way to make her pizza as good as what they'd eat after church.

"Penny for your thoughts," Sloan whispered softly in her ear.

"It would take more than that to get me to talk, especially in church," she answered.

He smiled and put his arm around her on the back of the pew and let his hand fall onto her shoulder. She heard a few buzzes behind them, but when the preacher cleared his throat, they ceased pretty dang quickly.

❖ ❖ ❖

The aroma of pepperoni, sausage, cheese, and hot marinara sauce made Kate's mouth water when she got out of the back seat of the car with her two sisters. The place had been in business since she was thirty, and she'd loved it from the first time she and Max had met there. The place had changed hands a dozen or more times in the past fifty years, but it still held the honor of being the first pizza place in Medina County, Texas.

They wound up sitting at a round table for five next to the booth where she and Max had sat that Sunday evening. Their first date—and their last—had been in the same place, but she wasn't going to think about him. Today was all about Ginger and Sloan. There was definitely a spark between them, and she intended to fan it as much as possible.

"Granny loved to come here," Sloan said.

"It was a treat for us when it first went into business," Kate said. "The first owners had a picture of me and your granny sitting beside the cash register. We were the first customers who pushed the doors open."

"I don't remember that." Betsy took a bite of a wedge of meat lover's pizza.

"You were at Woodstock, and Connie was helping with a funeral dinner at the church that day," Kate reminded them.

"Oh, that's right. That's when Theo Williams died. Poor guy was only twenty-eight when he fell off that horse and hit his head on a rock. You know, I had a crush on him when we were younger," Connie admitted. "He kissed me behind the schoolhouse when I was thirteen, and I liked it."

"Why didn't y'all ever get married?" Sloan asked.

"Just never happened," Kate answered. "Maybe we were all too picky." She thought about Max—but that was in the past, and should be left there.

"We were too sheltered," Betsy said. "Mama kept us close to her, and we were kind of socially backward. None of us had much outside social interest except for Sunday-morning church."

"Besides, just exactly who'd want to marry someone who lived in the Banty House?" Connie asked. "Personally, I have no regrets about my past. We might have had our sorrows, but for the most part, we've been happy."

"I'm going to do that," Ginger declared.

"Do what?" Kate asked.

"Be happy instead of dwelling on all the hard times," she answered. "Sloan?"

"I'm not there yet, but I'm workin' on it," he said.

Kate smiled and nodded in agreement. "We've all been blessed."

"Amen," Connie and Betsy said at the same time.

But there is a bittersweet part of my heart that wishes I was the one Max chose, Kate found herself thinking. *I could have had kids, grandkids, and maybe even great-grandchildren at this time in my life. Maybe if I'd been his wife, he wouldn't have passed away before he was seventy, and we'd be making moonshine together.*

"You look sad, Kate," Ginger said.

"Just woolgathering." Kate smiled, and wondered what it was about Ginger that seemed to bring out the past. Neither of her sisters had any idea about Max. It was the one secret that she might even take to her grave. Surprisingly enough, not even the seasoned gossipers knew that she'd dated him all those years ago.

Betsy pushed her empty plate to the middle of the table. "I'm ready for my Sunday-afternoon nap. You kids are going to have to go get snow cones without me."

"Me too," Connie said. "You can drop us at the house."

"If you'd take the car out for a drive and maybe get it up over fifty-five miles an hour, that would be nice," Kate told Sloan. "It's been months since it's had the cobwebs blown out."

"Miz Kate, I make sure every Friday that there's no dust or cobwebs, but I'll be glad to take it out on a good straight stretch and wind it up to about eighty for you." Sloan pushed back his chair. "This has been fun. I suppose it could turn into a regular date if y'all were willin'."

"All except for Easter," Betsy said. "Mama wouldn't like it if we didn't keep up with our traditions."

Kate shook her finger at Sloan. "And only if you go to church with us."

"Yes, ma'am." He smiled. "It's pretty special for this rough old soldier to be escortin' four lovely ladies around in a vintage car."

Back at the Banty House, Sloan parked at the curb and opened the back doors for the ladies, then made sure they were in the house before he and Ginger drove away. Kate kicked off her shoes and peeled off her pantyhose right there in the foyer before she headed to the living room to stretch out in one of the recliners.

"I can't believe you let Sloan take our car out for a drive," Betsy fussed. "Are you losin' your mind? Mama would be furious. She never let anyone but us three drive the Lincoln."

"Oh, don't get your panties in a twist." Connie flopped down on the sofa, removed her shoes, and stretched out for a nap. "Are you blind? You said you wanted Ginger to stay, didn't you? Well, if she and Sloan are given a chance, they might find that they like each other. Why do you think I had them clean Mama's room with me yesterday? I don't usually do her room until the very last when I start spring cleaning."

"What's your cleaning got to do with Sloan and Ginger?" Betsy grabbed a fluffy throw and sat down in the second recliner.

"Do you want Sloan in your bedroom?" Connie asked. "When I do spring cleaning in y'all's rooms, I don't move furniture because there might be something he don't need to see. Like your weed, Betsy, or your dirty books, Kate. I figure if I throw them together enough, maybe some sparks will start to fly. I'd be willin' to bet she's the reason he went to church, and if she stays, he'll start going all the time. We've got to encourage them a little by insisting they go for a drive like they're doin' right now."

"I don't have dirty books," Kate protested.

"Don't tell me that." Connie giggled. "I've opened those romance books in your room and read a few pages. Honey, most of them would make a sailor blush with shame by page one hundred and forty."

"How do you know that if you've only read a few pages?" Betsy asked.

"I may have borrowed them on occasion, but I haven't gotten into Kate's bottom drawer, where she keeps all her private toys." Connie winked across the distance at her older sister.

"I haven't used those in years," Kate declared.

"Well, if you don't want them, I'll take 'em," Betsy said.

"You touch anything in my room, and I'll break your arm," Kate told her. "Just go to sleep and stop talking. I know what I'm doing."

"Evidently you do from what I saw in that drawer when I was cleaning your room last year," Connie said.

"Why were you snoopin' in my stuff anyway? How would you like it if I got into your things?" Kate asked.

"I wasn't snooping. I was trying to get all the dust bunnies from under the dresser and the drawer just slid open when I pulled the dust mop out. If you touch anything in my room, I won't break your arm. I'll drown you in your moonshine," Connie told her.

"What a way to go," Kate muttered and pretended to be asleep for about three seconds until the doorbell rang.

"Dammit!" she muttered as she padded barefoot across the room. "We've got to get Ginger a key made so she can come and go as she pleases." She slung open the door, kicking aside her pantyhose in the meantime, but it was Edith Wilson standing on the porch, not Ginger.

Of all the people in the whole county, Edith was the last one she would've given up her Sunday nap to see that afternoon. Since she'd been taught not to be rude, she took a step back and said, "Come right in, Edith. I figured you'd be home taking a nap like all the rest of us old ladies."

Edith opened the screen door, entered the foyer, and just stood there like a statue in her cute little black-and-white polka-dotted suit and black nylons that had to be making her thighs sweat in all the humidity. "I need to visit with you and your sisters."

"They're asleep, but we can talk in the kitchen." Kate headed that way. "Can I get you a glass of lemonade or maybe a nip of apple pie? Either one is chilled and will cool you right down."

"Liquor has never touched these lips"—Edith pointed to her mouth—"but I'd gladly take a glass of lemonade. I should've driven up here, but it's only three blocks. I didn't realize how hot it was."

You might be a more pleasant person if a drop of my apple pie got past those lips, Kate thought as she poured lemonade into two glasses. "Please have a seat at the table. Kick off your shoes and cool your toes."

"My toes are fine." Edith threw a go-to-hell look at Kate. "You know my poor Max has been gone for years, but I'm just now gettin' around to takin' care of his things. I just couldn't bear to give them away at first."

Kate sat down with a bit of a thud. Surely Max hadn't saved anything from their days together. She had burned all his letters and pictures and had always figured he'd done the same.

"I came across these hidden in an old cigar box out in the garage." Edith pulled a small bundle of letters from her purse. "From the dates on them, I've figured out that you two were having some kind of fling when I was engaged to him."

"We saw each other a few times, but . . ." Kate shrugged.

"For the whole six months that we were engaged." Edith's voice went all high and squeaky. "My daddy would have killed the both of you if he'd known. He always held Max in the highest esteem, and . . ."

"What's going on in here?" Connie and Betsy came into the room at the same time.

Edith raised her voice a little higher. "Your sister had an affair with my husband."

"Bullshit," Betsy said.

"You weren't married to him at the time." For more than fifty years, Kate had kept her secret, but now a few letters that Max probably thought he'd thrown away had floated to the top of the stream of life.

142

"You were only engaged, and, honey, I was the one that broke it off. He wanted to be a preacher like your father, whom he admired very much. He couldn't have done that with me as his wife. I gave him his dream rather than preventing him from having it."

"Why couldn't he . . .?" Connie slapped a hand over her mouth. "The Banty House?"

Kate nodded.

"I hate you," Edith said. "You've marred what I thought was a perfect relationship between me and Max. From what I read in these letters, you were sleeping with him while I was saving myself for our wedding night."

"That was your choice," Kate said. "But don't give me that bullshit, Edith. You had your first child seven months after y'all married, and he weighed well over six pounds. No one thinks he was premature."

Edith popped up like a little banty rooster, but then that was only fitting considering the place she was in. "I did not . . ." She snapped her mouth shut and blushed.

"Aha!" Betsy grinned. "So if you weren't having sex with Max, then who does your oldest son, James, belong to anyway?"

"Looks like we both have some skeletons in our closet," Kate said.

"Y'all are crude, but then given what your mama did for a living . . ." Edith didn't get out another word.

Betsy doubled up her fist and slung a mean right hook into the woman's face. Edith reached out and got a fistful of Betsy's dyed hair with one hand and slapped her across the face with the other.

Connie wrapped her arms around Edith from behind and tried her best to pull them apart. Kate did the same with Betsy, but good Lord, her little sister was strong. She kept kicking and screaming that Edith better watch her tongue when it came to Belle Carson or Betsy would cut it out and feed the damn thing to her kittens.

As if on cue, both cats came running into the room, and all four of the women got tangled up with one another's feet as they tried not to step on the kittens. They went down in a pile of flying elbows and swearing that could have blistered the paint on the kitchen cabinets.

When Kate and Connie finally untangled them, Betsy glared at Edith. "Don't you ever set foot in the Banty House again, not for any reason. You aren't one bit better than my sister, so don't judge her—or my mama."

"Your mama was a hooker." Edith spewed out the words.

"Our mama was a saint," Kate said. "The only difference in what she did and what both of us did was that she got paid for it."

Edith took a step forward and kicked at Kate's leg, but Betsy stepped in front of her sister and the blow landed on *her* shinbone. Hetty and Magic chose that moment to head back to the living room, so when Betsy took a step back, she stepped on Hetty's tail. The cat let out a squeal and became little more than a blur as she left the kitchen.

Kate tried to catch Betsy as she fell backward, but all she grabbed was air. Betsy threw one hand behind her and went down hard on the kitchen floor. Her head bounced off the floor like a basketball. Blood spewed out from her head wound, but she was holding her arm when she sat up.

"That bitch broke my arm. Kill her, Kate," Betsy said.

The only thing that saved Edith Wilson's life that Sunday afternoon was that Sloan and Ginger rushed into the kitchen at that very moment.

"What's going on in here?" Ginger gasped.

"Is Betsy all right?" Sloan asked.

Kate wanted to finish the job her sister had started, but she couldn't kill Edith with Ginger there. The poor child had been through enough, and it might cause the baby to come early if she murdered that bitch right in front of her.

Edith's hands went to her hair, but no amount of patting would take care of the mess it was in right then. Kate was pretty sure the woman would have to see Lucy at the Hondo Cut and Curl the next day to get it under control.

"I'm bleeding," Betsy said, and then fainted dead away.

Ginger left Sloan's side and went to Betsy. "Don't be dead," she kept whispering over and over.

"She's not dead, darlin'. She's just fainted. She never could look at blood," Connie said. "Don't know how she handles raw meat."

That seemed to be a strange thing for Connie to say during a crisis, but it was the truth. Betsy came to herself before Kate could get the smelling salts and glared at Edith again. "You've got until I get up off of this floor to get off my property, or I'm going to get Mama's shotgun and shoot you myself. I won't mind spending my last days in prison if I get to see you in a casket."

"You'd better go on now, Mrs. Wilson." Sloan tried to guide her to the door by laying a hand on her shoulder.

Edith jerked away from him and glared at Kate. "I'll have you all in jail for this. And, young man, don't you ever touch me again. I don't need your help."

Ginger grabbed a tea towel from the countertop and went straight to Betsy. She applied pressure to the head wound at the back of Betsy's head and said, "We should get you to a hospital."

"You'll stay with me, won't you? You won't leave me," Betsy whined. "And you'll tell Mama that Edith started it."

"She's got a concussion," Ginger whispered. "She don't have any idea what she's sayin'."

"I know I'm disappointed in Kate for not killing Edith." Betsy's eyes rolled back in her head and she was out again, though she regained consciousness a few moments later.

Kate went straight for the wall-hung phone and dialed nine-one-one. While she waited for them to answer, she said, "We're not moving her. I'm getting an ambulance to come get her. We'll follow it to the hospital. I'm too nervous to drive. You'll have to do it for me, Sloan."

"While we're there, we better have you two checked out, too," Sloan said. "Kate, you're bleeding from a long scratch on your arm, and,

Connie, you've got bloody knuckles. What in the hell happened here, anyway?"

"History surfaced," Connie told him. "You can't hold it down forever."

"Testify, Sister." Betsy tried to raise her arm and cried out in pain.

As she was giving the operator the address, Kate noticed a look that passed between Sloan and Ginger. If everything happened for a reason, she sure hoped the result of four old women acting out like teenage drama queens had something to do with that.

Chapter Thirteen

*G*inger loved all the sisters, but she'd spent so much time in the kitchen with Betsy that she'd become her favorite. She sat on the floor beside her, holding her good hand and reassuring her every few minutes that everything would be all right.

"You won't leave me," Betsy kept saying. "You left me once, and I never got over it. I can't lose you again."

"I'll stay right with you the whole time you're in the hospital, no matter how long it takes," Ginger assured her each time.

"Kate's in love with Max Wilson." Betsy giggled like a second grader. "I went to Woodstock and slept around, but Kate did, too. Connie, did you have sex, or did you just get into Kate's special toy drawer?"

"She's delusional." Connie cocked her head to the side. "I hear the sirens. They'll be here any minute."

Sloan had just gotten back from seeing Edith to the door and said, "I'll let them in." He headed back to the living room.

Seconds later, two EMTs were hovering around Betsy, trying to figure out how to get her on a board and get a neck brace on her. Sloan began moving chairs to the living room, then picked up the kitchen table and set it off to one side to give them more room.

"Thanks," the one with DYLAN embroidered on his shirt said. "That makes it easier."

They got Betsy onto the board and then shifted her onto the gurney, popped it up, and rolled her toward the door, and not one time did she let go of Ginger's hand. "Am I going to die?"

"No, ma'am, not if we can help it," Dylan answered. "Me and Sammy here ain't lost a patient yet, and we don't intend to start with you. But you got to let go of the lady's hand so we can get you in the ambulance."

"She's going with me," Betsy said. "She promised."

"And I promise she'll be there when we roll you into the hospital, but, honey, there's not room for her to ride with us," Sammy said.

"It's only ten minutes," Sloan assured Betsy. "We're all getting into the car right now, and we'll follow right behind you."

"If you don't keep your word, as much as I love you, Sloan Baker, I will punish you." Betsy gave him an evil look.

"I always keep my word." He stepped back so Dylan and Sammy could get her into the ambulance.

Ginger hurried over to the car and got into the passenger's seat. When they were all strapped in, Sloan started up the car, and they were soon right behind the ambulance.

"Why'd y'all come back so soon?" Kate asked.

"I forgot my purse, and Sloan said we could go to Walmart so I could shop for a few baby things," Ginger answered, then let out a loud whoosh of air. "One of y'all want to tell me what Betsy was talking about when she said she'd lost me?"

"I expect she'll tell you that when she's ready. It ain't our story to tell," Connie said. "But we will tell you what happened with that bitch Edith."

"I better own up to the background first." Kate gave them a short version of her involvement with Max Wilson fifty years before. "All this time, I figured he was sleeping with both of us, but I guess old Edith has some skeletons in her closet, too."

"Who threw the first punch?" Sloan parked behind the ambulance at the emergency-room entrance.

"Betsy did when Edith said bad things about Mama." Connie got out of the car and slammed the door. "You take this to a place in the parking lot where it won't get scratched, Sloan. Then you can come on inside with us."

A random thought chased through Ginger's head. Sloan had been used to taking orders in the military, so it didn't bother him so much for Connie to boss him around. It seemed like she'd been listening to people tell her what to do and how to do it for so long that it didn't faze her either.

"Gin . . . ger . . . ," Betsy called out. "Where are you?"

"I'm right here," she said as she ran from the car to the ambulance and laid a hand on Betsy's shoulder. They wheeled the gurney through the doors and straight on back to a cubicle. Two nurses and a doctor rushed into the area, and pretty soon an IV was in Betsy's arm, oxygen tubes were in her nose, and her arm was stabilized on a different board.

"Get an X-ray machine in here and get some blood work down to the lab." The doctor barked more orders and then looked over at Ginger. "Are you a relative?"

"She's my granddaughter," Betsy answered.

"What happened?" the doctor asked.

"I tried to kill Edith Wilson, but I didn't have a stake to run through her heart." Betsy giggled.

"Four senior women got into a fight, and Betsy wound up on the floor. She's got a concussion," Ginger told him.

"Are you a doctor? If not, then keep your medical opinions to yourself," he said sternly.

Betsy let go of Ginger's hand and shook her good fist at the doctor. "Don't you ever use that tone with my child again. I'm payin' you to treat me, and I don't even like you, so you can have some manners."

The doctor chuckled. "Yes, ma'am!"

"And we won't talk about my age or my weight, or you'll feel that right hook again," Betsy told him.

"Yes, ma'am." The doctor nodded. "Now, let's get a film of that head and the arm. Does anything else hurt, Miz Carson?"

"Just my pride," Betsy answered. "I'm bigger'n Edith, so it's not right that she's not in this place with me."

"I understand that Edith kicked her pretty hard on the shinbone, and that's what made her fall," Ginger offered.

"Then we'll get an X-ray of that, too. Do you want to see the police to file an assault charge?" the doctor asked.

"Hell no! I hit her first," Betsy said. "I meant to knock her dentures down her throat, but I got her on the chin instead of the mouth. Now, fix me up and send me home or else send someone to get my weed stash. I always have a little joint before I go to bed at night."

"Jesus!" the doctor muttered.

"Hell no again. Don't be sending Him after my weed." Betsy groaned. "He'll throw it all away, and this is the best I've ever grown. Did you already treat my sisters? Are they all right?"

"I took a look at them on the way here. They've got some scratches, so I prescribed an ointment," the doctor said, departing with visible relief.

It was almost time for supper when they finally made a diagnosis and got Betsy into a room. Just a day or two for observation and to be sure that the concussion wasn't any worse than the doctor thought— that's what the nurse said when she told Ginger they were admitting Betsy and taking her to a private room.

When they rolled her out of the cubicle, Ginger made her way to the waiting room. Kate, Sloan, and Connie all stood up. "She's going to be all right. Are y'all okay? The doctor said he'd looked at your scratches. Good Lord, what were all y'all thinkin' fightin' like that?"

"That bitch Edith was bad-mouthin' our mama. She's worse off than me and Connie. If Betsy hadn't slipped and fallen, we'd be buryin' a body right now instead of sittin' in this hospital. Tell us more about Betsy," Kate said.

"She's bein' real sassy." Ginger couldn't keep the grin off her face. "She's a scrapper, and she really hopes that Edith is dead by mornin'. Y'all need some help making that happen, just let me in on the deal."

"Does she get to go home today?" Connie asked.

Ginger shook her head. "They're going to admit her a couple of days so they can keep a check on her. Her arm is sprained, but it's not broken. Her shin will be bruised, but it's not broken, either. They had to shave a patch of hair from the back of her head about the size of my palm and put ten stitches in it."

"We'll have to watch her," Kate sighed, "or she'll go after Edith for sure. Betsy's hair is her pride and joy. When can we see her?"

"I came out here to get you. They told me what room they're putting her in," Ginger said. "And I promised to stay the night with her."

Sloan slipped an arm around Ginger's shoulders. "Let me take you somewhere and get you a burger for supper, and then I'll take you home to get whatever you need to spend the night here."

"That's a good idea." Kate nodded. "We can all stay if she wants us to. Sloan can taxi us one at a time back to the Banty House for what we need."

Ginger was afraid to let both of them go at one time. They might stop by Edith's and finish off the job they'd started. Was the woman batshit crazy? Ginger knew from day one that Belle was the queen of the Banty House and no one had better say a word against her. Just thinking about someone hurting her new family in any way—with words or punches—filled Ginger with anger.

"Maybe you could just pick out a pair of shorts and a top for me and bring my toothbrush when one of you go." Ginger frowned. "I gave her my word that I wouldn't leave the hospital until she does."

Sloan kept his arm around her as they all went up the hall toward Betsy's room. When they walked in, she was arguing with the nurse, saying, "I don't give a damn what your policy is. My granddaughter is going to sleep on that bed over there tonight, or else I'm going home. Just charge it to my account and I'll pay the damned bill, or else my sister Kate will bring you a case of her moonshine and we'll call it even."

"We have to keep that bed ready in case someone else needs it." The nurse tried to reason with her. "But I can bring your granddaughter a pillow and a blanket and she can sleep in the recliner right here. It goes all the way back and makes a nice little bed."

Ginger went right to Betsy and laid a hand on her good arm. "I really like the chair better. That one is way too high." She leaned down and whispered, "You know I have to get up all through the night to go to the bathroom."

"If you're sure," Betsy said.

"Absolutely," Ginger reassured her. "And look who's here to see you."

Betsy looked right at Kate. "Did that bitch hurt you and Connie?"

"Just some scratches," Kate answered. "We're all right. You just need to get well. You know neither of us can cook worth a dang."

Betsy realized that she was wearing a hospital gown and narrowed her eyes. "My head hurts. Someone stole my clothes just like they did at Woodstock. I'm not young anymore. A lady needs her bra."

Jesus, Mary, and all the angels. Betsy must've been a rounder in her day. Ginger wished that she *had* been her daughter, or even her granddaughter.

"*You* need to rest," Ginger told her. "Just lay back and be very still. Close your eyes and . . ."

Betsy shook her finger at Ginger and then waved it around to include all of them. "Don't you let them put Edith in that other bed. I never did like that woman. She was too goody-two-shoes for me, wantin' us to dress up like whores so she could look down on us, and then we find out she ain't no better." Her eyes snapped shut and she started to snore.

Ginger giggled under her breath. "I've heard about ladies from the South wearin' sassy britches, but I don't think Betsy ever takes them off."

"You got that right. She's always been the one with more spunk than me and Connie put together. She might sleep for a little while," Kate whispered, glancing over toward Sloan. "If you'll take me and Connie home, we'll get what we need and come on back."

"Why don't y'all just sleep in your own beds tonight," Ginger told them. "I promised I'd stay, and they might let her go home after twenty-four hours if her mind clears up. I promise I'll call if she asks for you."

"Okay," Kate agreed. "I'm sure not lookin' forward to sleepin' on one of those straight-backed chairs. Just give us a call, and we'll be here as fast as I can drive us."

They filed out of the room, but Sloan stayed behind. "I'm going to drive them home, get my truck, and come back. What do you want me to bring you to eat?"

"Apples, peanut butter, and dill pickles," she said.

He didn't even blink or hesitate. "You got it. I'll sit here with you until bedtime so you won't be alone."

"Thanks, Sloan." She smiled up at him. "That is so sweet of you."

❖ ❖ ❖

Sloan took the ladies home and waited while they gathered up what they thought Ginger might need. Then he drove his truck down to his house, made sure Tinker had water and food, and packed a small bag for himself. No way was he letting Ginger stay by herself all night. What if Betsy got a brain bleed and died? Ginger could stress out and wind up losing the baby. He brushed away a tear. The ladies had always been a force, and he couldn't imagine one of them gone.

"See you later," he told Tinker as he headed outside. "Hold down the fort while I'm gone."

Tinker hopped up on his favorite end of the sofa, curled up, and shut his eyes.

Sloan stopped by the grocery store and picked up four different kinds of apples, a jar of peanut butter and one of dill pickles. Then he went by a drive-through and got two burger baskets and a couple of milkshakes. When he reached the hospital room, Ginger had stretched out on the chair and was sound asleep. Betsy was still snoring and the other bed wasn't being used yet. It still surprised him that Betsy hadn't bullied the nurse into letting Ginger sleep on it.

"Are you staying for a while?" a nurse whispered from behind him.

"Yes, ma'am," he answered.

"Then"—she pulled the recliner that belonged to the other bed around for him—"use this. I can't let anyone sleep on the bed, but you can use this chair."

"Thank you very much," he said, repositioning the chair so he could sit right beside Ginger.

She opened her eyes. "I smell food."

"Burgers and fries and milkshakes if you're hungry," he whispered.

"Starving." She popped the chair back into a sitting position.

"Has she been awake any at all?" Sloan asked.

"Only when the nurse comes in and wakes her up. Then she cusses about Edith and goes right back to sleep," Ginger answered. "I guess that's normal. I've been too afraid to even ask."

"I've seen my fair share of concussions." Sloan opened the brown paper bag of food and set a burger, an order of fries, and one of the milkshakes on the bedside table that Betsy wasn't using. "I got chocolate. Hope that's all right."

"It's great." Ginger bit into the burger. "Going out to eat twice in one day is a big thing. Thank you."

Someday, if she stuck around long enough, Sloan was going to really take her out for dinner and maybe a movie. He'd show her what a real date was supposed to be. He squeezed out ketchup into the paper boat the burger and fries came in and dipped a french fry in it. She reached across from her chair and dipped one of her fries in his ketchup. If one of his buddies had done that, the fight would have been on, because Sloan had a thing about sharing any portion of his food. Strangely enough, it seemed perfectly all right to share with Ginger.

"I wonder why Betsy thinks I'm her granddaughter and why the other sisters won't talk about it. As far as I can understand, none of them ever had a child," Ginger said between bites. Poor old darlings only had each other. Connie and Kate would be devastated if something happened to Betsy. "I wish I was her daughter," Ginger muttered. "Growing up in that house with them would have been like growing up in heaven."

"I guess it kind of was. Granny was their friend, so I could go up there and visit them anytime I wanted. I've always taken it for granted until today when I saw Betsy on the floor. I guess it never dawned on me that someday they'd be gone," Sloan said. "In some ways, I guess I was their child as well as Granny's. I always wished I'd had a brother or a sister, but who can complain with neighbors like I've got."

"I wanted a sibling, too. I'll probably only ever just get to have one child because I'll be trying to raise her all alone, but if things were different, I'd want at least four." She spoke in low tones so she wouldn't wake Betsy. "I never knew anything but foster homes, so that was life, but I always wanted a brother or a sister that was all mine. If I had a choice, I'd want my child to have brothers and sisters. If"—she paused—"I had a sister, I could support her, and she could do the same for me. We'd have each other, kind of like the ladies have had all this time."

"There were other kids in the homes, right?" Sloan asked.

"Oh, yeah, and most of the time I was the oldest and had to take care of them, but I never had a real sibling. Someday, maybe I can give my daughter one," she said. "But if things don't work out that way, I'll just give her all the love I can and make sure she knows she's special."

"What was your mama and daddy's names?" Sloan asked.

She whipped around to look him in the eye. "That question came out of the clear blue."

"I was just wonderin' if it would help if you could go visit their graves. Family seems pretty special to you, so maybe if you could see where they're buried, it might bring you some closure," he said.

"Do you think it would bring you closure to go see where your buddies' graves are?" she asked.

Her question hit him square in the chest, and he felt as if an elephant had plopped down on him. Thinking of that again made it hard for him to breathe. He couldn't even imagine what he might feel if he stood beside where they'd buried what was left of Creed or Bobby Joe, or his other three friends.

"According to my birth certificate, my biological parents were Brenda and Larry Andrews," she finally answered.

"Ever look them up?"

She shook her head. "Why would I? My mother killed my father in a bad drug deal, and then she died in prison. I would assume both of them are buried somewhere in Kentucky, or maybe they were cremated. I have no idea."

"What about grandparents?"

"When I got old enough to ask the social worker about them, she told me that my mother and father were both raised up in the system. There was no family to take me when I was born, so that's exactly where I went, too." She finished off her burger and fries and then went to work on the milkshake.

Sloan didn't feel pity for her. Instead he felt even more pride than ever in the fact that she was so strong and independent, coming from that kind of background. He also felt just a little ashamed that he hadn't gotten closure for what had happened in Kuwait. Maybe in the near future, he'd do just what she suggested—go and visit all the graves of his fallen buddies. All of them were buried in Oklahoma or in Texas. They had always said that's why they made such an amazing team—they'd been raised in adjoining states, liked and had respect for the same things. Well, other than the weekend of the OU–Texas game. Then all claims to friendship were off.

"Hey, you two, what's . . . ?" Betsy sat up in bed and grabbed her forehead with both hands. "Where am I? What kind of weed did I get into that would give me this kind of a headache?"

"Do you remember Edith coming to the Banty House?" Sloan asked.

Betsy shook her head. "Did Kate tell her that I got my dress fixed just fine and we refuse to hire girls to act like hookers?"

"No. I don't think that's why she was there," Ginger answered. "She was bad-mouthing your mother."

"My head hurts. I can't think or talk about that now. Why am I in the hospital? Dear Lord," she gasped when she noticed her arm. "Did I break it?"

"Yes, you're in the hospital, and your arm is only sprained. You'll have to keep it in a sling for a few weeks." Ginger continued to answer questions. "You fell in the kitchen, hit your head on the floor, and hurt your arm. You have a concussion and several stitches in the back of your head, and you've got a big bruise on your shinbone."

Betsy's hand went to the bandage on the back of her head. "Did they shave my hair off?"

"Just a little bit. You can wear a hat to church and no one will even notice," Ginger assured her. "Right now, you just have to rest and get better so you can go home."

"Why did I fall?" Betsy looked up at Ginger.

"Seems you and Edith had a fight, and you stumbled and fell backwards," Ginger explained.

"She pushed me, didn't she?" Betsy closed her eyes and the snoring began again.

"I'm kind of surprised that she even said that," Sloan said. "Sometimes folks with concussions can't recall things that happened twenty-four hours before."

A couple of minutes later she opened her eyes, scanned the room until she found Ginger, and asked, "Did we go to church this morning?"

"Yes, we did," Ginger answered.

"Good, then God will forgive me for tryin' to kill Edith," she said, and then her eyes closed again.

"We never got a chance to talk about church this morning. Did it make you uncomfortable to be there?" Ginger asked Sloan.

He shook his head slowly from side to side. "I dreaded going in those doors, Ginger." He felt as if he could bare his very soul to her, almost as if God, Himself, had sent an angel to Hondo for the Carson sisters to discover. Other than his team members, who were like brothers to him, he'd never felt so comfortable with anyone. "The last time I was in church was for my granny's funeral. God took her away from me when I had already lost all my buddies. God was too unfair. But today, right on that pew, it was almost like she was right there with me. I liked the feeling. I don't know why I've stayed away so long."

"Did you pay attention to the hymns?" she asked. "The first one we sang said to simply trust every day and to trust all through the storm."

"Trust is a bit of an issue for me," he said.

"Me too, as you can imagine, but whether you call it destiny, God, or Fate, I think I was brought to Rooster for a reason. I got to be friends with a woman in the last café where I worked. I've never met a person with stronger faith. She was always telling me that destiny would not take me anywhere where the hand of God would not protect me," Ginger said.

"Do you ever intend to go back and see her?" Sloan asked.

"No, she died and the owners closed it down soon afterwards. Customers expected food like she made, and well, she was gone. I would go see her if she was alive, though. I really loved her." Ginger wiped a tear from the corner of her eye. "She reminded me of Betsy. She loved to cook and was kind of round." She clamped a hand over her mouth. "That was rude. I'm sorry. I didn't mean that Betsy was ugly. I love her so much that I don't care what size"—she shook her head—"I'm just diggin' myself deeper into a hole."

"Did I hear my name?" Betsy roused again and looked out the window. "It's dark. How many days have I been in this place?"

"You just got here this afternoon," Sloan answered.

"And you might get out tomorrow," Ginger said.

"Where's Kate and Connie? Did Edith hurt them, too? Are they in another room? Dammit to hell, Sloan! Go tell the doctor to put them in here with me. I don't even care if Connie smokes in here. Just bring them in here with me."

"They are fine," Ginger said in a soothing voice, patting her arm.

"They were here until just a little while ago. They went home to get some rest. Do you want me to call them?" Sloan took his phone from his pocket.

"Lord, no!" Betsy moaned. "They need their rest. Oh. My. Goodness." She gasped. "Neither of them can cook. They'll burn down my kitchen if they try."

"Don't you worry." Sloan got up and stood beside the bed. "I'll go get them in the morning and take them out to breakfast before I bring them to see you."

"And I'll cook when we get home," Ginger said.

"I'm only half a mile down the road, and I can be there in two minutes anytime you need me," Sloan offered.

Home had been many different places to Ginger—last count maybe as many as twenty—but the word had never really felt right coming out of her mouth until that moment. Maybe going to California wasn't such a big deal after all. She felt like she was needed right there in Medina County, Texas, and it was pretty nice to have that kind of feeling.

She glanced at Sloan, who smiled at her and nodded. The warm feeling that wrapped itself around her heart was far more than friendship. Who would have thought she'd find family and possibly love right here in Rooster?

Chapter Fourteen

Betsy awoke with a headache the next morning, but other than that she seemed to be feeling okay and thinking clearly. When Ginger questioned her, she even remembered the fight with Edith. Ginger started to ask her what she meant when she said she'd lost her once and didn't want to lose her again, but on second thought, she decided it would be better to wait until they were alone in the kitchen together.

Just as Ginger had said, when Connie and Kate arrived that morning, the three of them were still talking about the confrontation with Edith—only this time in even more detail. Getting all the spotty parts of Betsy's memory filled in took almost an hour, and then they moved on to the subject of how they'd manage the next few weeks.

"There's nothin' sayin' that I can't sit in the kitchen and supervise Ginger. She's picked up a lot this past week, and she's already better at cookin' than either one of y'all," Betsy said.

"What about your jam business?" Sloan got up from a chair and stretched. "I've helped you with that so much, I could probably take care of it with a little help from Ginger."

Ginger could only imagine how many kinks he might have in his back and neck after sleeping on the other chair all night. Her body ached in places she hadn't even been aware that she had.

"It will be put on hold. Cooking is enough for Ginger in her condition, and you've got other things to do. There's a supply built up already down in the basement," Betsy said.

Ginger was elated that Betsy could make decisions and remember what had happened. She'd seen a few folks that were younger than Betsy who hadn't popped back as fast.

"Thank you," Connie and Kate said at the same time.

Dr. Emerson poked his head in the room in the middle of the morning and said, "I hear you had quite a dustup yesterday. Did you know that Edith has filed a restraining order against you? The sheriff's deputy will probably bring it to you when you go home later today."

"Well, if that ain't good news," Betsy said. "Now she'll stay away from the Banty House, and, Doc, that was just round one. When the fight's over, I'll bet you a pint of Kate's apple pie and a nickel bag of my best product I'll be the winner."

"I wouldn't bet against you for anything," Doc said with a laugh and came on into the room. "I looked at your X-rays and everything looks good. I will want to see you in my office in a week to check on your arm and leg. Stay off the leg and keep it propped. Don't try to lift anything with the arm. I'll probably take the stitches out of your head when I see you again."

"That mean I can go home?" Betsy asked.

"After two o'clock," Doc said. "I want you to be here a full twenty-four hours."

"You just want to charge me for another day in this bed," Betsy accused him.

He threw up his hands. "Busted! See you in a week, but I'll see *you* on Thursday." He pointed at Ginger. "Why don't you bring old cranky pants here with you, and I'll change that bandage then?"

"We'll be there." Ginger smiled. "But after calling her that, I'd run real fast if I was you."

"Good advice." Doc started toward the door and then turned around to say, "I'll let the nurse know to discharge you after two o'clock."

He stopped at the door and winked at Ginger. "I was so worried about her when she got here. I've treated all of the sisters for years. They remind me of my old aunts, who I don't get to see very often but who would probably take a switch to me for talking about them like this to strangers." He waved and left the room.

"If he'd been here last night, he would've let me go home," Betsy complained.

"Then thank God he wasn't," Kate argued, "because me and Connie wouldn't have slept a wink for worrying about you."

Connie put in her two cents. "You caused us to miss our Sunday-afternoon nap, and now I'm a day behind with my cleaning."

"I didn't cause jack crap." Betsy glared at her sister through the rails on the side of the hospital bed. "Blame Edith, not me. If she'd kept her skinny butt at home where she belonged, then I wouldn't be here."

Kate flashed a grin, deepening the crow's-feet around her eyes. "Oh, but if she hadn't brought those old love letters, we wouldn't know her secret, now, would we? I just wonder what our own Preacher James would think if he found out his biological father wasn't Max Wilson."

Connie pursed her lips and narrowed her eyes. "You know very well that we'll never tell him or anyone else. Mama didn't believe in spreading gossip."

Betsy held up a finger to get their attention. "But Edith doesn't know that, does she?"

"You got that right, Sister." Kate nodded.

"She won't be coming to your house anymore, sure, but y'all do realize that if she really did file a restraining order against you, then you can't be in the any of the same buildings with her," Sloan said. "How's that going to affect you going to church on Sunday?"

Kate gasped. "Well, I'll be damned. She filed that so we wouldn't be around James. She thinks we're as petty as she is when it comes to rumors. Now what are we goin' to do about church? I promised Mama that we'd always go on Sunday morning."

Ginger stood to her feet and wiggled her head from side to side to get the stiffness from her neck. "When I decided to go to church, I didn't go to just one—churches are pretty much all alike anyway but for the singin', Kate. Next Sunday, let's just get in the car and pick out one here in Hondo. We passed at least a dozen coming to the hospital. That way, you won't break your promise to your mama."

"Or get thrown in jail for violating a restraining order," Sloan told her.

"You really are an angel," Betsy whispered. "God sent you to us for sure, and she's right, Kate. We can drive into town and pick out a different one every week."

Connie chuckled.

"What's so funny?" Ginger asked.

"Number one." Connie held up a finger. "We'll never be able to agree on which one, so we better all decide right now that we take turns on choosing. Number two"—another finger shot up—"do you think for one minute that James is going to let us take the money we put in the offering plate on Sunday elsewhere? He'll be around to the Banty House to talk to us if we stop giving our dues. Y'all do know that what we give the church at the end of each year pays his salary and what we donate on Sunday keeps the electricity bill paid."

❖ ❖ ❖

Sloan started to say something, but he changed his mind and walked over to the doorway. His grandmother had been a big contributor to the church when she was alive, and Preacher James had come to talk to him when he stopped attending services. He remembered the day well. The preacher had told him he shouldn't blame himself for what had happened. Sloan had listened to him talk for a while, and then he'd simply walked out of the house. Rude or not, he couldn't listen to the man trying to talk him back into church—not when the hurt was still so raw.

"Do we go from oldest to youngest like we always have?" Kate was saying.

"For what?" Ginger asked.

"For choosing a church house each Sunday morning," Kate explained.

"Since it's Ginger's idea, I vote that we reverse the order. She chooses the first week and then we go from the youngest of us to the oldest," Betsy said.

Sloan didn't care where they went to church or even if they went. He could be close to God sitting on his front porch with Tinker.

"I agree." Connie covered a yawn with her hand. "I need caffeine. I'm going out to find a coffee machine. Anyone else want a cup?"

"I'll go get all of us a cup," Ginger offered. "Anything else y'all want? I've got peanut butter, apples, and pickles in the bag over there." She pointed toward the small vanity between the two closets.

"A candy bar for each of us." Kate handed her several dollar bills. "Coffee is free in the lobby, and there's a little gift store right there where you can get candy bars for a lot less than the vending machine charges."

Ginger shook her head. "I've got a debit card now, so I'll get them." She hurried past Sloan and started down the hallway. As he leaned to watch her go, he noticed a suspicious-looking man carrying a duffel bag down the hall. The guy turned his head away from every camera in the hallway. He wore a baseball cap and sunglasses, even though he was in the building.

Terrorist! Sloan thought and then scolded himself for even thinking such a thing. But he trailed the guy all the same—just to be sure.

Every nerve ending in Sloan's body was on full alert. The last time he'd felt like that was when he'd gone into a burned-out building to disarm a bomb. Fear, anxiety, and nerves all balled up together inside him, and when he had that feeling, something was terribly wrong.

Then the guy tucked the duffel bag inside a janitor's closet and took off running toward the other end of the hall. Sloan eased the door open and carefully unzipped the bag to find a bomb inside it. He shut the door behind him and then started jogging down the hallway to report it to the nearest nurse, doctor, or even janitor.

The few times that he had left the room earlier, the nurses seemed to be pretty calm and collected. Now they were hurrying down the long hall, stopping at each room just long enough in each to say a few words and then closing the door. He was trying to track a nurse down when he noticed one talking to Ginger.

"Get back to whatever room you were in," she said.

"Why?" Ginger asked.

"For your own protection," she said and kept going.

"Did someone already report something?" he asked the nurse.

"Someone called in a threat," she answered with a nod.

"It's more than a threat. I just now found a bag in the janitor's closet right down there." He turned to Ginger. "We've got to get you out of this hall and into Betsy's room. They're going to have to evacuate the hospital, and it's easier room by room."

"Why?" she asked again. "And what's in the closet?"

"A bomb," he whispered.

"Did you check the bag?" she asked.

"There's a bomb in it. Not big enough to level the hospital, but it could do some serious damage to this floor and especially to the rooms on either side of that closet," he said.

"Go dismantle it," she said.

"That's not my job." He guided her toward Betsy's room.

A man in a three-piece suit passed them, and Ginger grabbed his arm. "Do you work at this hospital?" she asked.

"Yes, I do," he said. "I'm Warren, and I'm the head of security. You two need to be out of this hallway."

"Did someone call in a bomb threat?" she asked.

"How did you know that, and who are you?" Warren narrowed his eyes at her.

"Because this man is my . . . my . . . ," she stammered.

"I'm former military and I saw a man put a bag in the closet down at the end of this hallway. I checked it and there is definitely a bomb in there, sir," Sloan said.

"He defused bombs in the military. He can help you if you'll trust him. How long will it take to get a bomb squad in here?" she asked.

"They're in San Antonio right now, so maybe thirty to forty-five minutes," he answered and looked right at Sloan. "You really qualified to do that?"

"Maybe . . . I don't know . . . but I'll be glad to look at it closer." Sloan wasn't sure that he could control his shaking hands enough to disarm even the simplest bomb. He hadn't even looked at one since the day before he'd lost his buddies.

"Okay, son, let's go take a look at it," he said. "I don't know why they'd call in the threat if they really wanted to harm anyone."

"Maybe it's someone that knows what's going on and why, and can't live with their conscience if they let it happen." Sloan led the way down the hall to the closet. He opened the door and dropped to his knees. "It's enough to take out three or four rooms of this place, and it's on a timer. If your people can't get here in about"—Sloan looked at the bomb's timer—"fifteen minutes, it will explode. Who's in those two rooms on either side of the closet?"

"A judge who's scheduled for surgery later today is in one, and the room on the other side is empty," Warren told him.

"Then I'd guess this isn't terrorism, but someone who's got a beef with the judge. You probably need to move him to another room or out."

Ginger laced her fingers in Sloan's and looked up at Warren's worried face. "Listen to him. He spent time in Kuwait taking care of situations worse than this." Then she turned to focus on him. "You can do this. I have faith in you," she whispered.

"All right," Warren said. "I may have the legal department down on me later today, but I'm going to believe you and your wife. What do you need from me?"

Ginger opened her mouth to say that they weren't married, but she clamped it shut without saying a word.

"Nothing but permission." Sloan wiped his clammy hands on the legs of his jeans and then took out his pocketknife. "And your promise that you won't tell anyone that I did this. When it's over, just let everyone think it was a drill. I'll be glad to give the police a description of the guy, but . . ."

"No notoriety. I get it," Warren said.

Sloan nodded and looked up at Ginger, who was standing right beside him. "Go on back to Betsy's room. Wait for me, and in case I'm wrong, do me a favor."

"You won't be wrong, and I'm not going anywhere," she told him.

No pressure now. He didn't have time to argue with her, and he'd never live with the guilt if she was hurt in the blast.

"If . . ." He stopped. "Just promise me that if I'm killed doing this, you will put my name on the birth certificate as the baby's father. You can't put Lucas on it because his parents could find out later and cause trouble. A little girl doesn't need to look at her birth certificate and see 'unknown' in the space for a father's name."

"I'm not talking about this right now, because we're going to walk away from this—together." Ginger sure had more confidence in him than he had in himself. "Let's get to it and not waste any more time."

"Betsy will kill me if anything happens to you," he whispered as he started following the colored wires back to the detonator.

"Then don't let it," Ginger told him.

"Whoever built this thing is an amateur, but he's got plenty of explosives wired to the timer."

"Is that a pipe bomb?" she whispered.

"No, darlin'. It's more sophisticated than that, but still not professional grade like a terrorist would use. But it's plenty good enough to take out the judge."

You can do this, Tex. Chris Jones's voice was so real in his head that he almost believed his old teammate was right there beside him. Sloan had been all jittery inside since he first realized there was a bomb in the bag, but just hearing Chris in his head calmed him. Suddenly, he felt like he was in Kuwait and all his team was right there with him and had taken positions to protect him as he did his job. His hands steadied, and he could concentrate wholly on what was in front of him without glancing at the timer every second.

The person who made this particular bomb might not be professional, but he'd sure put together a confusing piece of art. Every single wire was the same shade of gray, making it hard to keep track of which ones he'd already traced and which ones he hadn't. He'd seen something like this once before. He closed his eyes for ten seconds to recall exactly what that one had looked like. He could hear Bobby Joe chuckling behind him. "I'll buy you a drink if you'll hurry up. I've got a date tonight with a cute little filly over in the ladies' barracks."

Sloan opened his eyes, found the right gray wire, and cut it. The timer stopped at three minutes and five seconds remaining.

"We did it, Ginger," he whispered as he stood up, and the two of them stepped out of the closet.

❖ ❖ ❖

"*You* did it. You just saved a lot of lives," she told him.

He wrapped his arms around her, hugged her tightly, and felt the baby kick against his belly. He took a step back, grinned, and said, "She just said 'thank you' by kicking me."

"I believe she did." Ginger locked eyes with him.

He leaned in just as she moistened her lips with the tip of her tongue, but before he could kiss her Warren turned the corner in the hallway and was right in front of them. "How much time do we have?" he asked.

"All the time in the world," Ginger answered.

"It's disarmed," Sloan said. "What about the person I saw trying to escape on the elevator?"

"Our security caught her on the third floor. They're holding her until the police get here. From what information I've got, she was mad at the judge for his ruling on a divorce last week." Warren chuckled. "I guess it's right what they say about hell having no fury like a woman scorned."

"Her? I could've sworn I saw a man running away," Sloan said.

"She's tall and pretty good sized. I can see where you might think that." Warren nodded.

"I'm glad it's all under control," Sloan said.

"Me too, and anytime you want a job working for me, you just say the word." Warren wiped sweat from his brow with a white handkerchief.

"Thanks, but I reckon I've got enough to keep me busy." Sloan took Ginger's hand in his and started back down the hallway toward Betsy's room.

"Hey, I didn't even get your name!" Warren called out.

"Sloan Baker," Ginger threw over her shoulder.

"That job offer still stands anytime, Sloan," he said.

"Thanks, but no thanks." Sloan waved over his shoulder.

"Why'd you go and do that?" Sloan groaned.

"Because you wouldn't. Let's go get coffee and candy bars for the sisters. They all need a little snack," she told him.

"How can you be so calm?" he asked. "Until I felt my old team around me back there, I didn't know if I could get my hands to stop shaking."

She stopped and tiptoed so she could brush a soft kiss across his lips and then took a step back. "They wouldn't have come to help you if they blamed you for what happened over there. They were tellin' you that it's time to let all the guilt go."

"Maybe so." He finally smiled.

A deep voice Ginger recognized as that of Mr. Warren filled the hospital from the PA system. "Good evening, folks. We have just completed a safety drill. It's now all right to open your doors if you wish to do so. Have a great rest of the day."

"They'll never know how close a call that was," Ginger said.

"How'd you stay so calm during those minutes?" Sloan led her into the small gift shop and stopped at the selection of baby things.

"I wasn't calm," she told him. "My stomach was threatening to give back that bacon, egg, and cheese biscuit you brought me. My hands were sweating, and a couple of times the whole hospital swayed to one side. I found out that I'm not ready to die, but I couldn't run or even walk because my feet wouldn't move," she answered honestly. "I was glad that you hugged me, because I was on the verge of passin' out stone cold."

"And here I thought you were a rock." He grinned.

"Had you fooled, didn't I?" She let go of his hand and picked up five candy bars.

He laid a cute little bow for a baby girl's hair and a bill on the counter. "That's a prize for the baby and to pay for the candy."

The clerk rang up their purchases and put them into a bag. "There you go. Y'all make a cute couple." She smiled.

"Thank you." Sloan flashed a wide grin.

"I was going to get that," Ginger said. "I have my Easter egg money. And why did you let her think we're a couple?"

"Next time you can buy something for the baby. This is just a small token of thanks for giving me courage." Sloan handed her the bag. "You take this, and I'll carry the coffee. And, honey, it would have embarrassed her if I'd said we weren't together. Besides, today I kind of like the idea." Sloan tucked her free hand in his.

Ginger smiled up at him. "Me too."

She'd helped him. She'd given him courage—he said so himself. A warm feeling wrapped itself around her like a fuzzy blanket on a cold night. He'd let someone think they were a couple, and that made her feel like she was floating two feet off the floor.

They were halfway to Betsy's room when Sloan asked, "Are we going to tell the sisters that this wasn't a safety drill?"

"Oh, yeah," Ginger answered. "It's way too good of a story *not* to tell them. They can keep a secret. And it will stop them from asking us all kinds of questions about why it took us so long to get back with the coffee and candy."

"I think I asked before, but I'll do it again. How did you get to be so smart?" Sloan followed her into Betsy's room.

"I'll have to blame anything I know on life," she said as she showed the sisters the cute pink bow with feathers all around it.

"Did you go to Dallas to get the coffee?" Connie asked.

"Nope." Ginger passed out the candy bars.

Sloan gave everyone a cup of coffee, then sat down. "We got sidetracked."

"Doing what?" Betsy tore the wrapper from her candy bar and took a bite.

"Sloan is going to tell you the story, but it can't leave this room," Ginger said. "And you ain't goin' to believe it."

Chapter Fifteen

"I want you to think about what I asked you to do at the hospital," Sloan said when Ginger walked him out to his truck a couple of days later. He'd stopped by to say goodbye to Ginger and the ladies before he left on a three- or four-day trip that he should've taken when he first got back to the States.

"You mean about listing you as the father? That's a lie that could come back and bite you on the butt, Sloan," she said.

"I'll take that chance, so promise you'll give it some serious thought, please," he said.

"You said that when we thought one or both of us would be killed," she told him.

"But I meant it." He tipped her chin up with his fist and gave her a sweet kiss.

"You think about it while you're gone," she said. "We'll talk when you get back."

"Will you think about it?" he asked.

"I will," she promised. "Be safe and call me. Now that I've got a smarty-pants phone, I can even get texts and pictures and we can FaceTime."

"That's why I talked you into it." He gave her a quick hug and got into his truck before he changed his mind about the trip. "See you in a few days. I expect to be back for church on Sunday. I want to see which one you choose."

He watched her in the rearview mirror as he pulled away. She stood on the side of the road in her faded skinny jeans and a T-shirt that was stretched out as far as it would go over her belly. She was still waving when he made the slight curve into town and lost sight of her.

According to the map he'd pulled up on his phone, the first leg of the trip would take four hours. That would put him there by midafternoon and give him all the time he needed in the Crawford Cemetery to find Bobby Joe Daniels's grave.

"Well, Tinker." He reached over with his right hand and rubbed the dog's ears. "You'll be able to say that you've been outside Medina County after this trip."

Tinker didn't even open one eye; he just kept sleeping on his favorite throw from the house. Sloan had thought about asking Ginger if she'd go down to the house and check on Tinker every day, but she had her hands full with Betsy. The old gal had been cranky with everyone except Ginger since she'd gotten home from the hospital. Ginger did a fine job of keeping the peace, but Kate and Connie were about at their wits' end with their middle sister.

He turned on the radio and kept time to the music with his thumb on the steering wheel. One song that played reminded him of Bobby Joe's sense of humor, and the next one made him think about the way the two kisses he'd shared with Ginger had affected him.

"Putting those two together in my head is downright weird." He chuckled. "But, Bobby Joe, you would have liked Ginger. You might have even fussed at me for not asking her out already, but she's pregnant and she's only nineteen, and it would be awkward if things went south between us. The Carson sisters would come gunnin' for me if I made her cry, but I do like her a lot."

He remembered the first time he'd met the team. They'd been thrown together after he'd finished with his training after basic. He and Bobby Joe hated each other at first sight. Sloan never could put his finger on it, but there was something about that guy that just rubbed him wrong. Finally, he went to his commander and told him to either put him with another team or else get rid of Bobby Joe.

The commander called them both into his office and asked Bobby Joe if he had a problem with Sloan Baker.

"Yes, sir, I surely do," Bobby Joe admitted.

"What is the trouble?" the commander asked.

"I just flat-out don't like him," Bobby Joe said.

"And you can't give me a reason why?" The commander stood up from behind his desk.

"He's always judging me," Bobby Joe answered.

"And you have the same problem with this soldier?" the commander asked Sloan.

"Yes, sir. I don't judge him, but I just don't like him."

"Well, then, here's the solution we're going to apply to this problem. You two don't have to like each other, but it might be best if you did, because I'm not splitting up this team. You are the cream of the crop, and you'll learn to get along. From right now and for the next six weeks, while y'all are getting ready for your first deployment to Afghanistan, the two of you will not ever be more than thirty feet from each other. No, make that twenty feet. If this man"—he pointed to Bobby Joe—"goes to the latrine, you go with him. If this one"—he turned toward Sloan—"goes outside to sit in the sun, you go with him. You are to sit together during classes and eat beside each other in the mess hall. Is that clear?"

"Yes, sir." They had both saluted.

"Dismissed," the commander had said.

"I'll always hate you," Bobby Joe had smarted off the minute they were outside.

"I don't reckon I'll shed too many tears over that," Sloan had told him.

Tinker brought Sloan back to the present when he reared up on his hind feet, looked out the window, and barked.

"There's a rest stop a mile up the road, so hold it until then," Sloan told him. "Did I ever tell you about Bobby Joe? Well, I woke up in the middle of the night to find Bobby Joe was gone from our twenty-foot limit. I panicked. If the commander found out he'd gotten away from me, I could get a dishonorable discharge, so I went huntin' for him."

Tinker looked up at him and whined.

"Yep, I had to find him in a hurry, and since I know why you're whimpering, the rest is kind of fitting. I found my friend in the latrine, curled up in a ball in the corner. He was holding his phone to his chest and bawlin' like a baby. His girlfriend had broken up with him in a text, and he threatened to go AWOL. I talked to him all night long, and come morning, we were best friends."

He pulled into the parking lot of the rest stop, snapped a leash on to Tinker's collar, and took him over to the doggy section. Tinker hiked his leg on a small bush and then pawed the earth. Sloan made a few laps around the park area with him, just to give them both some exercise, then took him back to the truck and gave him some water.

Sloan got back behind the wheel and opened a bag of beef jerky. He gave Tinker a nice big piece and then bit off a chunk to chew on while he continued on up the road. He didn't stop for lunch but drove straight to Hillsboro, Texas. He stopped at a convenience store for a cold soda on his way to the cemetery.

"Would you know anything about a Bobby Joe Daniels?" Sloan asked.

"Yep, that'd be my cousin. He got blowed up over in Kuwait a couple of years ago. He's buried up in Crawford Cemetery. Grave is on the first road to the left after you go through the gates, down toward the end. Can't miss it because there's a big old granite stone that says Daniels on it. It's where the whole family is buried," the young man said. "Why'd you ask?"

"I was a friend of his in the military," Sloan said. "Thanks for the directions."

"Sure thing. What'd you say your name was?" the guy yelled.

"I didn't, but it's Sloan Baker." Guilt went with him as he left the place. He felt like he should have told the fellow that he'd served with Daniels, or that he'd been on the same team with him—or better yet, that he'd been responsible for his death.

He drove to the cemetery, followed the directions he'd been given, and found the Daniels stone in the middle of a large section of ground. Headstones dating back to the 1800s were lined up all around the huge chunk of granite that had green moss growing on it. He found one with Robert Joseph Daniels at the back side of the group. A small American flag flapped in the wind above the grave, and a red rosebush was in full bloom at one end.

"Hello, Bobby Joe." Sloan whipped off his cap and knelt in front of the grave. The breeze shifted and brought a strong scent of roses with it. He inhaled deeply and tried to say something, but words wouldn't come out past the lump in his throat. He felt a presence near him and figured it was his imagination, but then a shadow fell over his shoulder.

"Good afternoon, Sloan," a very familiar deep voice said.

Sloan stood up and turned around slowly, half expecting to see Bobby Joe and find out that he had survived the blast after all, but the man leaning on a cane not five feet from him was an older guy.

"I'm Teddy Joe Baker, Bobby Joe's grandpa." The man before him was exactly what Sloan would have thought his friend would look like in fifty years. "One of my grandsons works down at the convenience store. He called me soon as you left. I wanted to meet you since Bobby Joe talked about you so much when he called home."

"Pleased to meet you, sir." Sloan extended a hand.

They shook, and then Teddy sat down on a nearby bench. "I've been expectin' you for more'n two years now. I keep in touch with y'all's commander, and I been prayin' for you every day since all this happened."

"I figured you'd rather shoot me as pray for me," Sloan said. "If I'd been there, I could have defused the bomb."

"Son, didn't they tell you?" The old man frowned. "It wouldn't have mattered if Jesus Himself had walked into that place. It went off before they were halfway across the tent. They never even got to it."

"What?" Sloan's knees went weak, and he had to sit down.

"The commander said that it took months for them to get the scene re-created, but that's what happened. The thing wasn't on a timer. It was detonated remotely, maybe by a cell phone. Didn't the commander call and tell you?"

"Maybe. I quit taking his calls because I . . ." He let the sentence hang.

"I can't even think about what kind of hell you been goin' through all this time. I sure wish you'd have come around sooner, so you could get over it," Teddy said. "Since you're here, you want to come home with me for supper? Bobby Joe's granny is cookin' up a pot of chicken and dumplin's."

"Thank you, but I've got a few more miles to go before I stop today, and I've got a dog in the truck," Sloan answered.

"Well, anytime you're in this area, feel free to stop by. We'd love to hear stories about Bobby Joe. We still got all his letters. Maybe someday we'll get them out and laugh about all the things he wrote about you boys." Teddy stood up and started back to his truck, which was parked out near a big pecan tree.

"I'll sure keep that in mind, and thank you, sir," Sloan called out.

Teddy threw up a hand, but he didn't look back.

"Is he tellin' me the truth, Bobby Joe, or just feedin' me a line of crap so I'll feel better?" Sloan muttered to himself. He sat there for a while longer, letting one memory after another of the good times with the team wash over him, and then he knelt again and touched Bobby Joe's stone. "Goodbye, my friend. Maybe I'll see you again in eternity."

He and Tinker drove on that evening to Paris, Texas. It was near dark when they got there, and he didn't find a hotel that allowed pets until the third try. Once he was settled in, he ordered a pizza delivered to the room. Tomorrow, he would go visit Creed Dawson's grave. While he waited on the pizza he found the commander's phone number in his contacts.

He hit the call button but hung up before it could even ring. If the military folks had just told Teddy that so there could be no blame issued, then did Sloan really want to know? Or would he rather just believe the fairy tale to assuage himself of the guilt he'd been carrying around all this time?

Tinker hopped onto the bed and curled up on Sloan's pillow, then growled at him.

"So you think I should call no matter what?"

Tinker growled again.

"All right, but I might be an old bear to live with when I do," Sloan told the dog as he found the contact and hit the call button again.

"Sloan Baker, is this really you?" the man asked.

"It is really me," Sloan said.

"How're you doin', son? I've called at least a dozen times," Commander Watterson said.

"It's been tough," Sloan admitted.

"I imagine it has. You've got PTSD and we sent you home riding a guilt trip that you couldn't shake. We were wrong in thinking that you could have defused that bomb in time, but we didn't know it then. And I was afraid to put you anywhere near an explosive again," he said.

"I defused one in the local hospital two days ago. It helped." Sloan wandered around the room as he talked, picking up the HBO guide from in front of the television and the little coffee pods by the sink, then putting them back where they had been.

"Good for you," Commander Watterson said.

"Today I visited Bobby Joe's grave and met his grandpa." He poured a cup of water into the one-cup machine and slid a pod into the right place.

"Nice old guy. I visit with him about every six months. Did he tell you what the reconstruction crew said about the bomb?" Commander Watterson asked.

"Is that the truth or just some bullshit to cover up for me?" Sloan pushed the button to start making a cup of coffee.

"Pure truth. I can even send you the report if you want," Commander Watterson said. "I hated to lose your team. Y'all were so good at what you did that we still haven't found another bunch like you. But if you ever want to go back to work in a civilian training capacity, I could sure use you to train new teams. I've never had a soldier learn as fast as you did. You'd make an excellent instructor. It would pay well, and you'd still keep your disability benefits."

"Thank you, sir, and I *would* like to see the report, and I'll think about that job offer," Sloan said. "Did y'all catch the guy who planted the bomb?"

"We did, but he escaped after he confessed. The story I got out of him was that Chris Jones had slept with his sister, Basima, and then dumped her. That had made her unfit for marriage in that culture. The young man was simply avenging his sister's honor," the commander said. "If you hadn't gotten drunk, you'd be dead right along with them."

"I told him that seeing Basima was asking for trouble." Sloan groaned.

"You were right," the commander said.

Sloan carried the phone with him when he heard a knock on the door. "I should go," he said. "My pizza is here, and I've taken enough of your time. Thanks for talking to me."

"Anytime, son. I'm just glad we got to the bottom of this. Keep in touch, and if you're ever in Atlanta, look me up. Bye, now," the commander said.

Sloan touched the "End" button, opened the door, accepted the pizza and handed the kid a bill. "Thank you. Keep the change."

"Thank you," the kid said and whistled down the hall toward the elevator.

He'd just taken the first slice out of the box when his phone rang. The picture that popped up on the screen was one he'd taken of Ginger on Easter Sunday. He laid the pizza back in the box and answered on the second ring.

"Hey, how's things in the Banty House?" he asked.

"Betsy is cranky, but then she's in a lot of pain. She still has headaches and her arm and leg hurt. I'd be in a pissy mood, too, if I was in her shoes," Ginger answered. "So where are you tonight?"

"Paris." He chuckled.

"I would've hitched a ride with you if I'd known you were going to France," she said.

"Paris, Texas." He laughed out loud. "I had a great day, and I just hung up from a wonderful phone call." He told her all about Teddy, and Chris and Basima, and that he'd found out the truth behind the whole story.

"Feel better?" she asked.

"I really do, and I've got you to thank for it. If you hadn't made me defuse that bomb, I would have never taken the first step to recover from all this guilt I've been carrying around. Now I really believe that it wasn't my fault. There wasn't anything I could have done if I'd been there." Just talking to Ginger made even more of the heaviness leave his heart.

"So what do you do tomorrow?" she asked.

"I'm going to see Creed's grave, and then I'll go on up to Hugo, Oklahoma, and find Chris. I imagine Tinker and I'll stay there tomorrow night and then go on over to Randlett and finish up our circle in John and Wade's town. Then we'll come home on Saturday. Seems like we should go get that snow cone we were going for last Sunday as soon as I get home," he said.

"I'd like that," Ginger agreed. "Hey, I'm going to put this on speakerphone so the ladies can talk to you, too."

"Is Tinker doin' okay?" Betsy asked.

"He's lovin' to travel. He's liable to want to go every time the truck moves from now on," Sloan answered.

"And how about you?" Kate asked.

"It was tough, but I got through it, and . . ." He went on to tell them about talking to his commander. Talking around the huge lump in his throat wasn't easy, but he finally got the shortened form of the story out. "I hope he's telling me the truth."

"Why wouldn't he tell you that before they sent you home?" Kate asked.

"They didn't have all the details, and then I wouldn't answer his calls," Sloan admitted honestly, and his heart felt lighter for doing so.

"And your old truck is running fine?" Kate asked. "Too bad the law wouldn't let me send some shine for you to sell along the way."

"If I could have, I would." He realized that she was changing the subject since no doubt she could tell just how emotional he was right then.

"It's been great to hear your voice," Connie said. "But we're going to let you two kids talk now, and we'll go on out to the parlor and get our movie night ready to go. Safe travels, and it's good to hear your voice."

"Y'all enjoy your movies," Sloan said.

"I'm back, and we're alone now," Ginger said. "I miss you, and you've only been gone a day. The crazy thing is that I've only been here for two weeks, but it seems like I've known you and the ladies for years."

"A wise young lady told me once that everything happens for a reason," he said. "It's helped to talk about today, Ginger. And that wise lady was right."

"Oh, really!" From her tone, he knew that Ginger was smiling. "How could anyone have wisdom when they aren't even twenty years old yet?"

"Guess they're born with it," he told her, "and when will this lady be twenty, anyway?"

"June first," Ginger answered. "How old are you?"

"Twenty-four last January."

"Oh, my! You *are* an old man." She laughed out loud. "I should be going. I think they're waiting for me to start the movie night. Will you join us next week?"

"Sure thing, and I'll bring the candy bars," he offered. "Good night, Ginger, and thanks again for telling me that I needed to do this."

"You are so very welcome. Bye now."

He hit the "End" button and laid the phone to the side. He wished that he was home so he could kiss her good night, but all he had was a box of semi-warm pizza. He got out a slice and sat down in a chair in the corner. Being there kind of reminded him of when he and his buddies would order pizza from the little shop on base and watch a movie. For the first time, he didn't feel like crawling into a dark hole when he thought of those guys.

❖　❖　❖

Ginger wished that her old friend at the café hadn't died so she could call her and tell her everything that had happened in the past two weeks. But then, if she hadn't passed away, Ginger wouldn't have left and wouldn't be where she was right then. She would still be working for tips at the café and wondering how on earth she was going to pay the hospital bill when her baby was delivered.

She wasn't sleepy that evening, and she was a little worried about taking Betsy to the doctor the next day, so when the movie ended, she slipped outside to sit on the porch swing. Crickets and tree frogs were having a competition to see which one of them could make the most noise, and a gentle breeze brought the smell of honeysuckle right up to her.

"Mind if I sit with you a spell?" Flora didn't wait for an answer but sat down on the other end of the swing.

"Be glad for the company." Ginger was startled but quickly regained her composure, "Are you out for your evening walk?"

"Yep, and I've wandered a little farther than usual. Sometimes when I come this far, I just borrow the swing without asking. I just sit here and swing and try to think about things other than a mother that drives me crazy. I know Betsy and her sisters won't mind because we've been friends since we were kids. We were kind of the misfits around these parts," Flora said.

"I always made up stories in my mind about my mama," Ginger told her. "In my stories, she wasn't anything like the foster mothers, and she always made cookies and had them ready for me when I came home from school. I hope someday I can be a mother like that."

"Belle Carson was that kind of mama." Flora pulled a knee up and retied her shoe. "My mama was the opposite. She's always been self-centered and never had any time for me. I always envied the Carson girls, and anytime they invited me to their house, I was delighted."

Ginger wondered which kind of mother hers would've been if she hadn't died in prison. She and Ginger's dad had both been into drugs, either using them, selling them, or maybe both, so it wasn't probable that she would have been a cookie-baking mama. *Would her mother have reformed and really cared about Ginger and the baby?* she wondered.

"So your mama didn't care that you came to the Banty House?" Ginger asked.

"She didn't even know where I was most of the time." Flora shrugged. "She had her television programs that she watched all afternoon and into the night, so I was a bit of a bother."

Ginger laid a hand on Flora's shoulder. "I'm sorry."

"Honey, I'm sure I didn't have it as bad as you. At least I wasn't being shifted around in foster care," Flora said. "Now, let's talk about something else. I heard that Edith took out a restraining order on every person in the Banty House. She says that she came here to visit and the Carson sisters tried to kill her. I also heard that Betsy had to spend a night in the hospital over it."

"Yep." Ginger nodded, not really knowing how much to tell. "They got into it when Edith bad-mouthed Belle. Betsy hit her and she kicked Betsy. Seems our new cats got in the way somehow, and anyway, Betsy fell and sprained her arm. She also got stitches in her head."

"Dear Lord, what are they going to do about church?" Flora asked.

"We're going to go to some over in Hondo starting this Sunday. I don't want to see Betsy in jail." Ginger figured saying that much wouldn't be overstepping her boundaries.

Flora threw back her head and guffawed. Her laughter was high pitched and so infectious that Ginger couldn't help but join her, even though she had no idea what was so funny.

When Flora got herself under control, she raised up her shirt and wiped the tears from her eyes. "Edith has done crapped in her little nest."

"What does that mean?" Ginger asked.

"When we were kids, her daddy was the preacher, and she always said she would marry a man like him, and she did. Then, when her son James came along, she said from the day he was born that he would be the third-generation preacher, and he was. She's built this nest of preacher men in her family. It takes money to run a church and pay James's salary, and Belle was the lifeblood of the Rooster church when it came to donations. Her daughters continued what their mother started.

Now that Edith has made it so they can't go to James's church, they'll take their money and go elsewhere," Flora explained.

"Honey, that air-conditioning and those lights and the maintenance on the building isn't free. Edith just crapped in her nest, like I said," she repeated. "Tell Betsy tomorrow that I'd appreciate it if y'all would pick me up on Sunday morning. I'd rather go with you as sit with Edith. I'll be waitin' on the bench in front of the old post office."

"All right." Ginger nodded.

"On that note, I'm going home now. You have a good night." Flora left as quickly as she had appeared.

Ginger let the swing stop moving and stood up. She heard a ping on her new phone and pulled it out of her hip pocket to find a text from Sloan: Thinking of you as I fall asleep.

She sent back a smiley face with hearts where the eyes should be, and went inside and up to her bed with a smile that not even sucking on a lemon could have erased.

Chapter Sixteen

e still and stop wiggling," Dr. Emerson told Betsy. "I swear to
God Himself, you are worse than a kid."

"You're yankin' me bald-headed," Betsy told him.

He lifted the bandage and leaned in close to her. "It's lookin' good,
and you're only bald in one little spot. It does look a little like you have
the mange, so you would be wise to wear this." He handed her hat back
to her and then looked at her leg and arm.

"So, can I get rid of this sling and start cooking tomorrow?" she
asked.

"No, you cannot. No lifting for at least two more weeks, and then
we'll take some more X-rays to see how your arm is healing. Old people
don't mend as fast as the young'uns," he said.

Ginger patted Betsy on the shoulder. "It's all right. I'll be there to
do whatever you want."

"What I want is a joint," Betsy sighed. "It helps me sleep. I didn't
realize how much it helped my arthritis until I couldn't have it."

So that's why she was so cranky, Ginger thought. *She's having with-
drawal symptoms. For almost sixty years, she'd been growing and smoking
the stuff.*

"Who told you that you couldn't have it?" Ginger asked.

"I asked a nurse in the ER when they brought me in, and she said definitely not," Betsy said.

Doc patted her on the knee. "Honey, if you want a joint before you go to bed each night, then you have one. Just don't go down stairs or—"

Betsy reached up and hugged him before he could finish the sentence. "I'll see to it that Kate tucks in a pint of her strawberry shine next week Monday when I come to get the stitches out."

"That will be great," Doc Emerson said as he took a step back and pulled Ginger's chart up on his tablet. "Now, young lady, let's listen to your baby's heartbeat. Looks like you gained two pounds this week, which is about normal at this point in your pregnancy. We want to keep it below thirty pounds overall if possible."

"Yes, sir." Ginger felt like a cow when she got onto the table and lay back. "I read that walking helps, so I've been doing that most evenings."

"Good girl." He put the stethoscope on her tummy and listened for a while, then extended a hand to help her sit up. "Everything looks great. We'll see you next week. Make an appointment when you leave. And Betsy can have her wacky weed, but you'd best leave it alone."

Ginger gave him her best smile. "I quit that and alcohol of any kind when I found out I was pregnant."

"That's great. Liquor and smoking make for underweight babies," Doc Emerson told her. "Looks to me like you got a good healthy one on the way."

"I hope so," Ginger said.

"Okay, then I'll see y'all on Monday for Betsy and then on Thursday for you," Doc said as he left the room.

Betsy stood up and moved her hips from side to side. "I get a little taste of weed tonight. Life is good."

"I've got a good-sized baby." Ginger mimicked Connie's head wiggle.

"Good doctor's visit. Let's go home and make a chocolate pie for dessert tonight," Betsy said, and then her eyes got big. "Better idea! I'm in the mood for some double-layer cheesecake brownies, so we'll stir up a batch of those."

Ginger was elated to see Betsy in better spirits. "Those do sound good, but no funny grass in them, right? Or I can't have them."

Betsy raised her good arm. "Hand to God. I would never jeopardize our baby, darlin' girl. But I just might make up a little batch of double chocolate, or I should say I'll show you how to make them, to put in the freezer. Never know when I might need some of them for a special occasion."

"Betsy?" Ginger lowered her head and raised her brows.

"I make a little pan for Flora every so often," Betsy told her. "Purely medicinal purposes. She's given them to her mother to help her."

Betsy had always been truthful about everything, from the reputation of the Banty House to her little patch of weed in the flower garden out back, and even what was drying in the garage, so Ginger had no reason to doubt her. But there was something in the glint of Betsy's eyes that caused her to smell a rat.

When they got home, both Connie and Kate were waiting in the kitchen. Connie had a glass of sweet tea. Kate had a glass of shine at least as big as a glass of tea and was sipping on it. The two of them looked more like sisters with their gray hair and cute little red sweat suits that day than Betsy did with her dyed hair. She'd dressed in her Easter dress and hat to go to the doctor's office, and she came in with a limping spry step in her walk.

"Doc says I can have my little smoke before bed, so I'm happy." She threw her hat at a chair and missed. Both Hetty and Magic made a dive for the hat and started clawing and kicking at it like they were trying to kill the strange thing.

"Praise God." Connie threw both hands into the air. "If I'd known that abstaining from your weed was what was making you so bitchy, I'd have rolled one for you myself."

Kate just smiled and held up her glass. "I've got the blackberry perfected. Want a sip?"

"You know I don't drink," Betsy said. "That stuff ain't good for you. And for God's sake, Kate, get my hat off the floor before those cats . . . No, leave it there. Let them have their fun. Y'all get on out of our kitchen. Me and Ginger is going to do some baking."

"You sure you didn't let her roll one on the way home?" Kate whispered to Ginger.

Ginger just grinned and shook her head.

❖   ❖   ❖

Sloan made the drive to Grant, Texas, on Thursday morning. When he and Tinker reached the cemetery, he gave the dog the full length of his leash so he could run and play. Then he sat down in front of Creed's grave. He closed his eyes for a minute and let his mind go back to the two years he had had with the team. Creed had been the quietest one of all of them. He had a wife back here in Texas, and a couple of kids—rug rats he called the twin boys.

Thinking of babies sent Sloan's thoughts to Ginger. The way she'd reacted to only one baby made him think she was disappointed, but he hadn't asked her outright about it. Maybe he'd do that tonight when they talked. He blinked a couple of times, and a wave of guilt washed over him. He'd come to make peace with Creed, not think about Ginger.

Don't waste your time thinkin' about me, Creed's voice popped into his head.

"Hello," a female voice said behind him.

He was losing his touch for sure. Two people in as many days had snuck up on him. No wonder they'd sent him home to Texas with a disability discharge. If he couldn't even hear someone coming up behind him in a quiet cemetery in broad daylight, he sure wouldn't have lasted long in the field.

"Hello," he said.

"Are you a friend of Creed's?" she asked.

"Was at one time," Sloan said. "How about you?"

"I knew him, but not well. He went to school with my younger brother. I just come by when I visit my mother's grave, since it's close to hers. I'm Gloria Tisdale, and you are?" she said.

"Pleased to meet you. I'm Sloan Baker." At first it seemed strange that someone who knew Creed would be in the cemetery, especially after the day before, when Teddy had shown up. "Do you know his wife and kids?"

"I did, but only because they attended the same church as I do," Gloria answered. "She's remarried now and living out in California somewhere. She doesn't get back here very often."

"Creed would have wanted her to move on," Sloan said.

"He was a good guy, so you're probably right. I should go. My husband is waiting for me in the car. Nice talking to you, Sloan."

"Same here." Sloan turned back to the tombstone and did the math. Creed had been twenty-five when he died, and he had already gotten married and had two little kids. Suddenly Sloan felt as if he was dragging his feet.

He and Tinker drove on up to Hugo that evening, and checked into a hotel right close to a Mexican restaurant. He made sure the dog had plenty of water and food before he walked next door to have supper. If he struck up a conversation with someone, maybe they could tell him where the cemetery was.

An hour later, he was back at the hotel. The folks at the restaurant had come from Oaxaca, barely spoke English, and he had spent the time looking up cemeteries on his phone while he waited for his order. In the morning he planned to go see Chris's grave and then get on over to Randlett for John's and Wade's gravesites. They'd come from Randlett and a little town called Chattanooga, or Chatty, as the locals called it according to Wade. Even though the towns were close together, they hadn't known each other until they enlisted. Could be that he'd be home by dark tomorrow evening after all.

He fell back on the bed and sent a text to Ginger asking her if she was free to talk for a while. The phone rang within a few seconds.

"How are things going?" she asked.

"I couldn't ask for them to be better," Sloan answered, "and I feel like I've lost about a ton of weight off my shoulders. How'd the doctor visit go? Is the baby all right? How about Betsy? Stitches weren't infected, were they? And are those scratches on Kate and Connie healing up?"

"Whoa," she said. "One question at a time. Let's see . . ." She went on to tell him all about her day, ending by telling him about talking to Flora the night before.

"You need to watch Betsy like a hawk," he warned.

"Why?" Ginger asked.

"She's sly as a fox, and believe me, she and Flora are good friends. I'll just bet she's got something up her sleeve that she plans to do with those brownies," Sloan said.

"You mean with Edith?" Ginger gasped.

"I wouldn't put it past her. She'll work her way around that restraining order somehow. She's pretty mad at Edith over whatever she said about Belle," Sloan said. "But I didn't call to talk about our children."

"Children?" Ginger almost shrieked.

"Don't you feel a little like a parent raising rebellious kids? We've got one making moonshine in the basement, one growin' pot in the flower beds, and God only knows what Connie is doing that we don't even know about. She's the sneakiest one for sure." Sloan laughed. "And you just came into the parenting business a couple of weeks ago. I've been at it for more than two years now."

"I never thought of it like that," she said. "It's one of those role-reversal things, isn't it? I should be in the *Guinness World Records* if this is true. I'll have a new baby and three daughters who are all nearly eighty."

"You are so funny," Sloan said. "You put sunshine in my life."

"Now, that's a fine pickup line," she told him.

"What do you know about pickup lines?" he asked.

"Honey, I've been on my own for almost two years. You think I never used a fake ID to get into a bar?" she fired right back.

"It would take a lifetime to hear all of your stories, wouldn't it?" he asked.

"Yep, and another one to hear all of yours," she agreed.

❖ ❖ ❖

By the time they said good night and hung up, Ginger was restless. She wanted what he already had—parents and grandparents. Even though they had passed on, he could go sit in front of their tombstones and think about them.

She pulled out her phone and followed thread after thread until she found the funeral homes that had cremated her parents. She didn't expect anyone to answer, but she made the call anyway to the one that took care of prisoners when no one claimed their bodies.

"Solid Rock Funeral Services," a man answered.

Ginger waited for the rest of the message so she could leave her phone number.

"Hello, hello, is anyone there?" the deep voice asked.

"I'm so sorry. I thought you were an answering machine." The words tumbled out so fast that she had to stop and catch her breath. "My name is Ginger Andrews. My mother died in prison about nineteen years ago. I'm trying to locate her grave or find out where her ashes were taken. I was told she was cremated."

"And her name was?" the man asked.

"Brenda Andrews," she said.

"Would you have a number?" he asked.

"No, sir, just that name," Ginger answered, wishing, not for the first time, she had more information.

"Let me go check our records." A thud signaled the phone being laid down.

It seemed to Ginger like it was an hour before he was back, but according to the clock beside her bed, it was only five minutes.

"I'm glad you called. We have those ashes stored here at our facility." He cleared his throat.

"How much do I send to have them shipped to me, and can I use a debit card?" she asked.

"Of course you can. It's a flat twenty-five-dollar fee, and I'll take your numbers right now if you'd like for me to send the ashes tomorrow. We have to send them by priority mail and mark them cremated remains, so look for a package like that," he said.

Ginger got her new debit card from her purse and gave him the numbers. She asked him to hold just a minute and she ran across the hall and knocked on Betsy's door.

"What is it?" Kate opened her bedroom door. "Is it the baby? Do we need to go to the hospital?"

"No. I need the address to the Banty House," Ginger said.

"It's 800 South Main, Rooster, Texas, 78862," Kate replied. "What do you need it for?"

Ginger rattled off the address into the phone and then said, "Is that all you need?"

"Yes, ma'am. They should arrive at your address in two days."

"Thank you so much. You wouldn't, by any chance, know how I could find my father's remains? His name was Larry Andrews," she said.

"I can check. We . . . Oh, yes, ma'am. He's here, too," the man said. "We often take care of people who aren't claimed in this area. Should we ship them to you, too? Same payment and address?"

"Yes, please," Ginger answered. "And thank you."

"I'll send you a receipt with the remains for your records. I can send you a copy of the death certificate for each for an additional ten dollars per person," he said.

"Please, I'd like that very much," she said.

"Anything else I can do for you?" he asked.

"That's all, and thank you again." She wasn't sure how she should feel, but it sure wasn't anything like what she was experiencing right then. Her chest had tightened, and tears rolled down her cheeks. She'd never known them, but between them, good or bad, they were her parents. Wherever she put their ashes would be the place where she settled down. No matter what their past was, she wanted her daughter to have ancestors that she could call her own.

She turned around to find all three sisters standing in their bedroom doors, staring at her.

"Are you okay, child?" Betsy asked. "You are pale as a ghost."

Chills ran down Ginger's back and she opened her mouth, but words wouldn't come out.

Betsy rushed to her side. "Is it the baby?"

Ginger shook her head. "I just found my parents. I'm having them shipped to me."

"Their bodies?" Connie frowned.

Ginger shook her head. This was all surreal. She would have death certificates and ashes. She might have been an orphan, but now she'd have parents, even if they had been dead for so long. "Their ashes," she whispered, breaking into sobs.

The other two sisters gathered around her like mother hens. Betsy was closest, so she wrapped her up in her arms, and Ginger didn't even care that she smelled like a van from the 1970s. Kate kissed her on the cheek, with a waft of blackberry moonshine. It didn't matter. Connie made it a four-way hug, and Sloan's words came back to Ginger about her being their sneaky child.

"I'm so sorry," she apologized. "I didn't even know my parents, but it's like they just died yesterday, and it hit me hard."

"Darlin', you can't mourn for something you never knew," Kate said. "You are grieving for what you wanted them to be, and that's all right. Just let it all out. When they get here, we'll bury them in the Cottonwood Cemetery and get a couple of memorial headstones so you can visit them from time to time."

"Can you bury ashes?" Ginger dried her eyes on the tail of her T-shirt.

"Of course you can," Connie reassured her.

"I just want my baby to know that she had grandparents." Ginger hiccuped.

"Honey, that sweet child will have three grannies who love her very much," Betsy said.

That brought on more sobs. "I can't ever repay y'all for giving me a home and . . ." Ginger laid her head on Betsy's shoulder, and the weeping began all over again. The sisters cried right along with her.

Chapter Seventeen

Rain poured out of dark clouds that hovered overhead when Sloan reached Randlett on Friday afternoon. His goal was to visit all his teammates' graves to put a measure of closure to the guilt he'd been carrying around with him for so long. So far he'd had fairly good experiences, but he wondered if the dark clouds were an omen.

He drove through the cemetery and located John Matthews's gravesite, but there was no way in the pouring-down rain that he could get out of the truck and lay a hand on it the way he'd done the others. Instead, he sat in his vehicle and thought about all the times John had told them he'd sell one of his kidneys for a good old Oklahoma rainstorm. Of all the things he'd missed when they were in Kuwait, he'd said that the smell of rain topped the list.

Sloan rolled down the window just enough to get a whiff and said, "I miss you, my friend. I hope, wherever you are, that you're enjoyin' this rainstorm. I'd like to say that I ordered it up special just for you, but I can't take the credit." The driving rain blew into the truck and got his shoulder wet, but he didn't care. Getting wet was well worth the price of saying a final goodbye to his old friend.

According to the map on his phone, it was only twenty-five miles to the hotel where he had reservations in Wichita Falls, Texas. That should have taken less than thirty minutes, but with the rain slowing the traffic down, it took him an hour to get to the hotel. Poor old Tinker whined the last ten minutes and squirmed over there in the passenger's seat. Sloan snapped the leash onto his collar and dreaded going out into the rain to the section marked for dogs, but Tinker took care of that problem in a hurry. He hiked his leg on the back tire of the truck, and Sloan could've sworn that the dog let out a long sigh when he finished his job.

He left Tinker in the truck and got checked in. Then he went back out to drive the truck around to the nearest entrance to his room. As luck would have it, there was no awning over that door, so he and the dog both got soaked again going from the vehicle into the hotel. Sloan was a little jealous of the dog when he shook from his head all the way to the tip of his tail in the hallway, slinging water everywhere. He had to wait until he was in the room to strip out of his own wet clothing.

As soon as he'd changed into dry pajama pants and a T-shirt, he sent a text to Ginger asking if she wanted to do some FaceTime with him. In seconds she called back, and he could see her bright smile right there on the screen.

"You're a sight for sore eyes," he said.

"I'm glad you think so. I see more life in your eyes than when you left," she told him.

"Oh, really? Want to tell me why you think that?" He knew that his heart had made peace with what happened, but what did that have to do with his eyes?

"When I first met you, there was a curtain over your eyes," she said. "You do know that the eyes are the windows to your soul, right?"

"Seems like I heard that somewhere." He grinned.

"So that meant you were holding sadness inside you that you didn't want anyone to see. Every so often a shimmer of light would come through, kind of like opening the curtains in a big auditorium just a crack. Then it would go away, but now it's like I can see the real Sloan Baker, and that's real nice," she told him.

"My granny used to talk about old souls," he said. "I think you must be one of those to be able to see and understand things the way you do."

"I read lots of self-help and psychology books when I was in high school. I so wanted to understand why my parents were the way they were and how it affected me," she said. "And speaking of parents . . ." She told him about the ashes that would be arriving in a couple of days.

"You do know that if you bury your folks in the Cottonwood Cemetery, it means you're probably going to be staying in Rooster." He got up and moved from the chair to the bed, where he could stretch out his legs.

"I've thought about that." Her expression changed from cheery to serious. "I love it here at the Banty House, and I love the ladies so much, but I think it would be best if I moved out when I can. Not moved on. I've figured out that someday I can take my daughter to visit the ocean and see other places, but she needs to have a permanent place to call home. And since my parents' ashes are coming here and the ladies have offered me space to put them in the Cottonwood Cemetery"—she paused—"I want to be near them even though I never knew them. I want my child to know that she had grandparents, no matter what kind of folks they were."

"Where would you move to if you did move out away from the Banty House?" he asked.

"Close by so all y'all can still be a part of my life," she answered. "I would love to work for the ladies forever if they want me to. I like it here." He could tell by her expression that she was struggling for words to explain the way she felt. "They want this baby to be their grandchild, and it would be ideal to be able to bring her to work with me every day."

"But they're overpowering sometimes, right?" he asked.

"I'd never talk about them behind their backs." She sighed. "I just want to be the mother the baby needs me to be. I'm fine with them seeing her all the time, and even spoiling her."

"I understand completely." Sloan nodded. "That's what my mama said when Granny kept me so much. Even when she was gone, she was the mother, and my granny pretty much abided by her rules."

"So it's not ugly of me to want to live somewhere other than the Banty House?" she asked.

"Not at all, and don't worry—the sisters will understand," he assured her.

"I don't want them to think that I don't want to raise my daughter here because it used to be a brothel. Or because"—she lowered her voice to a whisper—"because there's moonshine and pot in the place."

"Don't fret about it. It'll all work out, just like this trip has worked out for me," Sloan said. "We'll get through it together. I'm here for you."

"You can't know what that means to me," she told him.

"Right back at you. You've helped me through so much, too, you know."

"I'm here for you, too, Sloan." Hetty jumped up into her lap and laid a paw on the phone screen. "Looks like she wants to say hello."

"Where's Magic?"

"Right here beside me." She turned the phone so he could see the white cat curled up in a ball right next to her.

"Where's the ladies tonight?" he asked.

"They've already gone upstairs. I'm putting it off. It's gettin' harder and harder to lug this pregnant belly up the steps," she answered.

"I've got a spare bedroom," he said. "My house is small, but you could always move in with me."

"Don't tempt me," she laughed and then got serious. "Seriously, thank you for the offer. Someday I want a house like yours—a small, cozy place with pictures of family all around me."

"Even if it's right next door to a cemetery?" he asked.

"That makes it even better if I bury my folks there. Your grandparents and parents are right across the fence, too," she answered.

All the shackles around his soul fell away when she said that. The long, dark tunnel was behind him, and he stepped out into a light so bright that it was almost blinding. That cold rain was beating on the hotel window didn't matter one iota. Sloan Baker's heart and soul were basking in sunshine.

❖   ❖   ❖

Ginger awoke Saturday morning to the sound of Flora's and Betsy's voices down in the kitchen. She got out of bed as fast as she could, dressed in one of the three pairs of skinny jeans she owned—none of which would even come close to buttoning anymore but she'd fit back into them soon—and threw on a clean T-shirt. When she'd finished using the bathroom and brushing her teeth, she carefully took the steps one at a time and got a lecture ready to deliver to Betsy if she'd started breakfast without her. Betsy was alone now, but she was having a doughnut and a cup of coffee.

"Flora, God love her heart, brought us pastries for breakfast, and she even took them out of the bag and put them on a dish for me." Betsy pointed to the middle of the table. "We won't be cooking this morning, but you might get out the milk and juice and four glasses. Flora knows how much I love the fresh doughnuts from that little shop in Hondo, so she drove into town at six o'clock this morning to get them fresh. Ain't many friends would do something so sweet."

"You'd do that for her," Ginger said. "You keep potpies and cobblers in the freezer, ready to bake if someone is ailing or if there's a funeral. I bet you'd even send a pie to Edith if her son was to die."

"If I did, I'd add a tablespoon of rat poison to it." Betsy picked up a second glazed doughnut. "These may heal my wounds quicker than anything."

Ginger set a jug of milk and a pitcher of orange juice on the counter, poured herself a glass of milk and carried it to the table. She eased down into a chair and put a frosted doughnut with sprinkles on a napkin. "I used to splurge and get day-old doughnuts on the way home from work sometimes. Lucas said they weren't fit to eat, but I dunked them in my milk or coffee and they were fine."

"He wasn't a very nice person, was he?" Betsy asked.

"Not really, but I'd never had a boyfriend before, so I didn't have anything to compare him to." Ginger bit into the doughnut. "Mmmm." She made appreciative noises. "This is amazing."

"That little shop does a fine job, but I hardly ever get them this early. They're still good when we get into Hondo on Thursdays, but not like this." Betsy licked her fingers and then picked up her mug and took a sip of coffee.

"We'll never eat all of these," Ginger said.

"Speak for yourself." Connie entered the kitchen and went straight for the coffeepot. "I can put away four, and Kate . . ."

Kate butted in from right behind her. "Kate will eat until she's miserable." She filled a glass with juice and one with milk. "I'll have coffee afterwards. Did you drive to Hondo this morning, Ginger?"

"No, ma'am," Ginger answered. "Flora brought these to Betsy to help her get well."

"If I push her down the stairs and break her hip, do you reckon she'd bring more, like maybe twice a week?" Kate teased.

"No, but if I kick you down into the basement and you wind up with a busted hip or leg, she might bring them for you," Betsy shot back at her.

"Oh, stop your bitchin' and enjoy the bounty that is before us. Kate, you need to say grace even though Betsy has already stuffed her face," Connie said.

Ginger bowed her head and swallowed the bite that was in her mouth. Kate said a very short prayer, and as soon as she said, "Amen," Betsy reached for an apple fritter.

"Now that they're blessed, I get to start all over again." She grinned.

"Munchies, huh?" Connie asked.

"Well, I did share a joint with Flora. Poor darlin' needs a little something to help her get through the day with her mama's attitude, and the mellow is wearin' off, so yes, I'm just a little hungry," Betsy admitted. "And besides, it would be a sin to let these doughnuts get stale."

"Especially after Flora was good enough to go get them for us before daylight." Kate was already on her second one.

"Us, my butt," Betsy said. "She got them for me, and I'm being nice enough to share."

"And we thank you for that." Ginger reached for another one, then refilled her glass with milk. "Sloan called last night. He'll be home this evening. He said it's about a seven-hour drive from where he is and that he's kind of made peace with what happened to him over there in Kuwait."

"Can you tell us just exactly what *did* happen?" Kate asked.

Ginger nodded and started with when Sloan got the call from his granny telling him that his dog had died. When she ended, all the sisters were wiping tears on the cheap paper napkins that had come with the doughnuts. "And now he's found out that there was nothing—not one thing—he could've done to save his friends that awful day, so he's making peace with the past."

"You are a blessing to us," Kate said.

"Hey, I think you got that backwards," Ginger disagreed. "Y'all have given me more than I could ever give back to you."

"It's all in my stones," Connie said. "They've brought us spiritual guidance and emotional peace."

"Bullshit!" Kate said. "Them colored rocks didn't have jack squat to do with any of these past couple of weeks."

Connie shrugged and pulled a little bag from her pocket. "Don't swear at the stones."

Betsy's eyes grew wide, and her head bobbed up and down. "You better listen to her, Sister. I was tellin' her that those rocks ain't got power on Sunday afternoon about the time that Edith got here."

Kate picked up the bag and kissed it. "Forgive me, O mighty stones, and don't let me fall and break a leg or a hip. I don't want to have to slide down the steps to the basement on my butt."

Ginger couldn't imagine a life without these women in it—or without Sloan, either.

Chapter Eighteen

The sun was just past straight up in the sky when Sloan drove past the Banty House that afternoon. He wanted to stop right then, but he'd been driving for seven hours, stopping only once for poor old Tinker to water a bit of lawn at a rest stop. The dog wanted to be out in his own yard to chase a rabbit through the mesquite thickets from behind the house all the way to Hondo Creek.

Sloan turned him loose and then went into the house, started a load of laundry while he took a shower and shaved, and then dressed in a pair of faded jeans and a blue T-shirt. Tinker wasn't nearly ready to come inside, so Sloan filled his outdoor water bowl, got into his truck, and drove back up to the Banty House.

He parked at the curb and was halfway across the yard when the front door flew open and Ginger stepped out. "I was looking out the kitchen window, and you got here earlier than we expected."

He opened his arms and she walked right into them. "I'm so glad to be home," he whispered into her hair.

"I missed you." She hugged him as tightly as she could with a baby the size of a big fall pumpkin between them. "Come on inside. Betsy and I've made a chocolate cake, and we have ice cream to welcome you home."

"Just seeing you is enough of a welcome, but I wouldn't turn down cake and ice cream," he said.

"That's so sweet." She started to say something else, but the voices of the sisters arguing preceded them as they crowded into the foyer to greet him.

"Don't just stand there in the door," Betsy said. "Get on in here where I can hug you."

"Besides, you're letting the flies in," Connie scolded.

"I'm so glad you got here early," Kate yelled over from behind her two sisters. "Betsy wouldn't let us cut the chocolate cake at dinnertime. She said we had to wait until you got here."

"Oh, stop your bellyachin'," Betsy said. "You had half a dozen doughnuts for breakfast. That was enough sugar to last you until Sloan got here."

Both Sloan and Ginger stepped inside the house.

"Thank God that old truck made it." Connie shut the door behind them. "I worried about you the whole time. You should get a new one, maybe one of them with a back seat." She led the way into the dining room, where the table was already set with dessert plates and bowls.

"You drive a sixty-year-old car," Sloan reminded her.

"To Hondo and back, not halfway around the world." Connie continued to fuss.

"Besides, just how are you and Ginger going to take the baby for a snow cone when she's old enough to eat them? It's against all these new laws to have a kid in the front seat of a vehicle. Nowadays, you've got to put them in one of them newfangled car seats." Kate brought out a container of ice cream.

"Well, now, that puts a whole new light on the subject, doesn't it?" Sloan teased. "Do you think I should buy a pink one since the baby is a girl, and maybe put a gold crown hood ornament on it?"

Betsy shook her fist at him. "Don't you joke about this. It's serious stuff. We've got to think about the future. Did Ginger tell you that we're going to bury her folks' ashes in Cottonwood? We've decided to give her two of our plots. Grandpa bought too many for our family, so we're going to put her mama and daddy in with us."

"She told me." Sloan smiled. "That's pretty nice of y'all, and it'll put them pretty close to my family." Hopefully, that meant Ginger would stick around for a long time.

"Yep," Connie agreed. "The gravediggers will be there on Monday. That's the day you spend at the cemetery, so you can oversee it. They said they don't have to dig six feet for ashes, but you make sure it's deep enough. We want it done right."

"Eighteen inches is how deep it has to be." Sloan seated Ginger and turned to help Betsy, but she and Connie were already sitting. "I've been out there when they buried remains before. What kind of stone do you want?" he asked Ginger as he sat down.

"Just one of those little flat ones. Nothing big and fancy," she answered.

"We'll take care of that later," Kate said. "Right now, we want to hear all about your journey. Did Ginger tell you that when the baby is old enough to make a trip, we're all going to California to see the ocean? You'll have to come with us. Ginger can't take care of three old women and a baby all by herself."

"That sounds wonderful," Sloan agreed. "The trip was tiring, but I'm glad I went. I've got closure now, and I feel like I can move on. I need to do something meaningful with my life. My old commander talked about a job where I'd teach teamwork and about defusing bombs."

"That's amazing, but what will we do without you?" Betsy asked.

"Oh, darlin'," he said in his sexiest voice, "that job would have to be worked around the hours I work for you."

"Long as the general or commander or boss-lady understands that," Kate joked as she dipped ice cream for everyone.

Sloan looked around the table at the three senior citizens and the woman that wasn't even old enough to buy a drink in a Texas bar. The five of them were all misfits in their own way, but somehow they made a perfect family.

❖ ❖ ❖

Reality and fear hit Ginger smack between the eyes.

She was letting people take charge of her life again, just like Lucas had done. "Move into this apartment I found for us," he'd said. "It's not much, but I've got some deals going that'll put us in a nice home in six months. Trust me, darlin'."

She'd vowed that she'd never let that happen again, and here she was, living in the lap of luxury, letting people make choices for her. She loved all of them, especially Sloan, but if she didn't pack her parents' ashes into her ragged old suitcase and leave pretty soon, she'd be right there in Rooster forever. After all the sisters had done for her, she wouldn't be able to tell them no. The way she felt when Sloan got back to Rooster made her realize that she was falling in love with him. No absolutely wonderful man like Sloan would fall in love with a woman that was eight months pregnant, so she would just get her heart broken if she didn't cut the ties.

No. She fought with the voices in her head. *I am making my own choice right now. I'm choosing to stay with these wonderful people, and I'm choosing to see where this attraction between me and Sloan might go. These folks might want the same thing for me, but that doesn't mean they're wrong.*

Sloan nudged her. "You sure look serious. What's on your mind?"

"My parents' ashes." She admitted part of the internal fight she was having with herself. "Maybe I should just scatter them somewhere. It might have been easier to not know what happened to them. My father was dead before I was even born, and my mother died when I was in my first foster home, so it's kind of silly to . . . ," she stammered, ". . . have them close by, isn't it?"

"Nothing that brings you peace is ever silly," Sloan said. "I'm living proof of that right here tonight."

Kate stopped bickering with her sisters and asked, "Did I hear the word 'peace'?"

"Yep," Sloan answered. "I'm finally letting go of the guilt trip."

"I really hope that means you aren't thinkin' of reenlisting," Betsy told him. "We'd miss you so much."

"I would go back in if they'd let me, though as I understand it, they won't." Sloan held out his plate for a second slice of cake. "But this new idea of working for them in a civilian capacity is sure something to think about. Even if I took the job, I'd have to pass the psych evaluation."

Kate cut a wedge of cake and slid it over onto his plate. "Anyone else want more?"

Betsy shook her head. "The munchies are happy now."

Connie nodded. "Only half as much as you gave Sloan. I'll save the other half for dessert after supper. Are you going to have time to wash the car this afternoon, Sloan?"

"Yes, ma'am," he said. "Soon as we finish here, I'll get right on it. I can't be falling down on the job, or y'all might hire someone else."

Betsy snorted, and Kate giggled.

"Like that would ever happen," Connie said.

A wave of sorrow swept over Ginger. Leaving these sweet people would be worse than walking away from any foster home she'd ever been in.

So why are you going? the voice inside her head asked.

I just have to control my own life, she answered.

Sloan polished off his second piece of cake, took his plate to the kitchen, and was on his way out to the garage when a loud rap on the door made him stop. "Want me to get that?"

"I'm going that way." Ginger raised her voice. "I'll answer it." She opened the door, half expecting to see Flora, coming by with a couple dozen eggs to exchange for a jar of moonshine, but it was Gladys instead.

"Come right in." Ginger wasn't sure she'd done the right thing in inviting her in, especially after that incident with Edith.

The woman handed her a pan that was ice cold. "That's baked pasta, and it's frozen. Thaw it out, and then follow the directions on the top about how to heat it. I bet y'all are starving for good homemade food since Betsy has that busted arm. Poor dear, I came by to see how she's doin'."

"She's in the kitchen." Ginger led the way with the pan in her hand, reading the tape on the top as she went. "Preheat oven, then bake for thirty minutes." Maybe she should lace the casserole with some of Betsy's pot, then pass it off to Edith as a peace offering. She giggled at that idea. *Peace bitch,* she thought as she carried it into the kitchen.

Betsy was sitting at the table with a glass of sweet tea in front of her. "Hello, Gladys. Oh, my! Did you bring one of your baked spaghetti casseroles?"

"I sure did. I thought maybe y'all would like something homemade since we all know neither Kate nor Connie can boil water without settin' off the smoke alarm." Gladys laughed at her own joke.

"Well, that's right sweet of you," Betsy said in a sugary tone. "Won't you sit down and have a piece of cake and some tea?"

"I'd love to," Gladys said. "Who brought the cake?"

"Ginger made it." Betsy flashed a saccharine smile.

"With Betsy's recipe." Ginger cut a wedge of cake and filled a glass with ice and tea. "Ice cream?"

"Just cake." Gladys's tone was a bit flattened. "So you can cook?"

"More now than when I arrived." Ginger set the cake and tea on the table for Gladys, then handed her a folded linen napkin. "Betsy is a great teacher. I'm going to take Sloan a bottle of water. Holler right loud if you need me, Betsy. I can hear you through the door."

"I'll be fine. We don't have anything else to do until supper, and Gladys has brought us that. Connie has walked up to see Flora, and Kate is in the cellar, so you go on and take a little break," Betsy told her.

Ginger got a bottle of cold water from the refrigerator and left the two old gals to their gossip session. As she was leaving, she heard Gladys say that Flora had offered to bring the snacks for Sunday school the next day, and a bit of a chill chased down her back. Betsy was up to something, sure as shootin', and Ginger intended to find out what it was before she went to bed that night.

The garage door was up. A nice breeze kept the place from being too warm. Sloan had already filled a bucket with soapy water and was busy going over the top of the car.

"Why do you do that every week?" she asked.

"Because it's my job," he answered. "Before I took it over, they had an old guy from up the street taking care of it, but he died not long before I came home. Kate did it until they hired me. If they wanted me to wash it every day, I'd do it. They pay me well even though I don't need it—Granny left me well taken care of. But they knew I needed something to do with my days other than let guilt eat me up." He finished the top, rinsed it with a garden hose, and used a chamois cloth to dry it off. "Did you think about the baby's birth certificate?"

Ginger opened up a lawn chair and sat down. "I've got mixed feelings about staying here, Sloan."

He stopped what he was doing and pulled up an old straight-backed chair from the corner and sat down beside her. "I thought you had that part settled."

"So did I. But am I just letting someone else run my life like Lucas did? Am I taking the easy way out? This is a gravy job, and I love it here at the Banty House, but will I regret making such a quick decision? I know they mean well, but I promised myself I'd never let anyone"—she paused and searched for the right words—"make all my decisions for me again."

"Move in with me," Sloan said.

She wanted to pop herself on the ears to be sure she'd heard him right. Had the trip he had just made rendered him totally insane? Surely he hadn't just said that, had he? She stared at him for more than a minute, trying to figure out if aliens had abducted him and done something to his brain while he was gone. The last time a guy had said that to her, she'd wound up with more trouble than she could hardly handle.

"Think about it," he said. "If you decide not to stay in Texas, it would ease you out of their lives. It will break their hearts if you leave suddenly. Betsy has adopted you as her granddaughter. I haven't figured out why, but I think it has something to do with the past. This way, you can continue to work for them in the day and come home to my place at night."

She almost pinched herself to see if she was dreaming. "I'm eight months pregnant," she finally whispered.

"I can kind of see that." He grinned. "I'm not asking you to sleep with me. There's a spare bedroom in my house. It might not be as fancy as the one you're in now, but I reckon I can drag the old baby bed out of the barn out back, clean it up, and fit it in there. You don't have to make up your mind right now, but give it some thought. Not being here after you help get supper done would mean a little space between them and you. Then, when Betsy's well enough to take over the kitchen, you'd probably be done by midafternoon."

"Are you going to be mad at me if I say no and just leave on Monday?" she asked.

He covered her hand with his. "Ginger, I could never be mad at you. You're the angel who brought me up out of a deep depression. I owe you my happiness, my peace of mind—you're my saving-grace angel."

Twice now someone had called her an angel. *They must've gotten into Betsy's weed and Kate's shine to think that,* Ginger thought. She certainly didn't have a halo or wings either.

"So, will you think about it a day or two?" he asked.

"Yes, I will, and thank you for the offer, Sloan. You are a good man." She started to get up, but he was on his feet before she hardly moved. His big hand cupped her elbow and helped her to her feet. "You'd better get on back to washing the car, and I should go inside to see if Betsy needs anything. She's been taking a little hour-long nap in the afternoons, so she might want me to help her up the stairs."

Sloan chuckled. "Nap, my butt. She's probably having her midday smoke."

"Oh!" Ginger stopped after she'd taken a step. "That's it!"

"What's it?" Sloan asked.

"Remember when I told you about us making some wacky brownies, and then Flora bringing doughnuts real early this morning, and Dr. Emerson telling us about the restraining order Edith had drawn up?" Her mind was running in circles.

Sloan's expression was one of pure confusion. "You better back up and tie all that together for me."

"When I got a pan of lasagna out for dinner today, I noticed the brownies were gone," she said.

"Flora gets a pan full of them once in a while to help with her mother. The old gal won't take prescription medicine, says it's all poison, but she will nip a little moonshine or eat a funny brownie once in a while. She says that's all natural and won't destroy her insides," Sloan explained.

"But when I was leaving the kitchen to come out here just now, I overheard Gladys say that Flora was bringing the snacks for the Sunday-school class tomorrow," Ginger said. "When is Sunday school in y'all's church? Is it before or after the church services that we went to? I thought we were picking Flora up to go to church with us in Hondo, so would she be goin' to Sunday school in Rooster, and is Edith in that class? I'm confused."

"Sunday school is before church here in Rooster," Sloan explained. "Flora plans on going to that in our regular church, the one where you've gone with us. Soon as it's over, she'll hightail it down to the old post office and wait for us on the bench. We'll all be in our car and we'll pick her up to go with us to whatever church we decide on in Hondo." Sloan chuckled, then laughed, then guffawed. Ginger couldn't help but join him. They both had the hiccups when they finally got control. He pulled a handkerchief from his pocket, wiped his eyes, and handed it off to her.

"Our middle child is surely acting out, and there's not a damn thing we can do about it. You sure you want to move away and miss all this?" he asked.

"No, I'm not," she admitted. "I'd love to be a fly on the wall and see what happens in church tomorrow, but that restraining order is for everyone who lives in the Banty House."

"I don't live here," Sloan said. "I could go to church here in Rooster and report to you when we have dinner at the café there in Hondo. See what a nice guy I can be? I'd be the perfect roommate, and, honey, I do need help raising these old gals. What do you say?"

"I'll sleep on it," she promised. "But the sisters will be disappointed if you don't go with us. They've talked about what they're going to wear and how nice it'll be to have you walk in with us when we try out new churches. Besides, I'm sure Betsy and Flora have everything covered."

Sloan took a step forward, cupped her cheeks in his hands, and brought her lips to his in a long, lingering kiss that made her knees go weak. She leaned into him as far as her pregnant belly would let her when the kiss ended and splayed her hands out on his chest. She could feel his heart beating as wildly as hers and wished that he would kiss her again, but he just took a step back and said, "Think about that while you're sleeping on it."

"As if I could forget something that scorchin' hot," she said.

"So you felt it, too?" he said.

"Oh, yeah, I did," she told him. "And I liked it."

❖   ❖   ❖

Sloan whistled all evening as he brought his old baby bed from the barn and cleaned it up. He washed and rinsed each section, then propped them up against the house to dry. When he finished, he took all the pieces into the house, rubbed the oak wood down with lemon oil, and put them together. The assembled bed fit very well in Granny's old bedroom, over on the side with the window, so the newborn could get plenty of sunlight.

Babies change your life. Creed's voice was clear in his head.

"Maybe I need a big change," Sloan said.

Don't jump into the deep end if you can't swim, Bobby Joe said, joining Creed.

"Thanks for the advice, fellers, but I got this," he said.

The next morning he parked his truck outside the Banty House, and the garage door opened. Ginger and the ladies were already waiting in the car. "Y'all sure look pretty this mornin'," he said as he got in behind the wheel.

"Thank you," they all said at once.

"First time in our entire lives we've been to a different church," Connie said from the back seat. "We're a little bit nervous."

"I understand y'all are picking Flora up in front of the old post office, and I'm going to the church, right?" He started the engine and backed the vehicle out into the street. If Ginger was right and Flora really took funny brownies to Sunday school, then there might be some loud singing in the church services that morning.

"No. She changed her mind." Connie had entirely too much happiness in her tone. "I went to see her yesterday, because we were down to our last dozen eggs. I got the last that she had. She's sold her chickens and her cow. She said don't have time to work, take care of her mama, and run out to her place at the edge of town to milk a cow and take care of the livestock. She's going to our church in Rooster today, but she's going to meet us for lunch at Mama Rosa's Diner. She says they've got a chicken and dressin' special on Sundays, and she said you're supposed to drive us and go with us."

Rats! Sloan thought. *I was so looking forward to the circus.* But the way Ginger was grinning, he was kind of glad he'd get to sit beside her in services that morning. He gave Ginger a sly wink and smiled when she blushed. They were sharing thoughts, and to him, that meant they'd make fine roommates—at least for a while, but he was already making plans for the future.

Ginger chose the first church going into town, which turned out to be about twice the size of the one in Rooster but one of the smaller ones in Hondo. The congregation was already singing the first hymn when they walked into a packed house, so they had to go all the way to the front pew for a seat.

The ladies had decided to wear their pink Easter dresses from the year before, complete with hats and white gloves. It was truly by coincidence that Sloan had chosen a pink and green plaid shirt that morning and kind of matched them. The singing had been loud and lively when they first came in, but the noise dropped by 50 percent as the folks hushed and watched the newcomers take their seats. After the five of them had settled down on the pew right in front of the preacher, everyone began to pick up the volume again.

When the hymn was over, the preacher took his place behind the pulpit. "I'd like to welcome all our visitors this morning. We're glad for every single soul who comes to worship with us. Since these folks on the front row didn't get here in time to sing the first hymn with us, we'll sing another one this morning. So turn your hymn books to page one forty and let your voices ring all the way to heaven's gates."

"That's right sweet of him," Ginger whispered to Sloan.

Sloan leaned over and cupped his hand over her ear. "Maybe God whispered in his ear to do that so that you'll stay in this area and move in with me."

"I haven't made up my mind," she said.

"Mind about what?" Betsy asked from Sloan's other side.

"Shhh . . ." Kate poked Betsy in the ribs. "Mama taught us not to talk in church."

Sloan didn't even try to listen to the sermon. His mind went in circles, starting with what the commander had told him about a job and making its way around to how much he really did want Ginger to move in with him. That kiss the day before had told him that she was as attracted to him as he was to her. It was possible they could build a relationship out of the friendship they already had for sure.

Ginger must've gotten uncomfortable because she started to shift her weight from one hip to the other. He leaned over and said, "Are you okay?"

"Need to go to the bathroom, but I hate to walk past all these people," she told him.

"Tell Betsy we'll meet her in the car. I noticed the restrooms are right off the foyer. I'll go with you. I'm about to fall asleep." He laced his fingers in hers and pulled her up to a standing position.

Betsy gave him a sweet smile, and it almost seemed like lots of the people were enjoying having a little distraction from the pastor's dry sermon that morning. Sloan waited outside while she went into the ladies' room, and when she came out, he escorted her to the car.

"I didn't mean to squirm like a little kid, but sitting a whole hour is gettin' tougher and tougher. The baby tries to flatten my bladder sometimes. I'm sorry that you missed the last part of the sermon," she apologized.

"Honey, I wasn't listening to the sermon anyway," he admitted.

She removed her hat and laid it on the seat between them. "Me, either. Most of the time, the preachin' kind of bores me, and this morning I couldn't keep my mind off those brownies. One part of me hopes that they don't cause a problem. The bad part of my heart wants Edith to pay for insulting Belle. Did I tell you that I've picked out a name for my baby?" she asked, then fell silent.

"Nope, you did not." He started the car and turned up the AC to cool it down for the ladies. "Are you going to tell me what it is or make me wait until she's here?"

❖   ❖   ❖

"Martha Belle." It was the first time Ginger had said the name out loud, and it rolled off her tongue beautifully. She laid a hand on her stomach and said, "How do you like that name, little girl? Is it something you can love your whole life?"

"That was my grandmother's name." Sloan's voice went hoarse like he was talking around a lump in his throat. "You can't name the baby that and leave us, Ginger. We need you to be part of our lives."

Like every other child that was born into this world, she had needed care from the time she was born, but that was the first time anyone had ever said that they needed *her*. She wasn't sure what to do with the emotions inside her—did she run from them or to them?

"Are you sure about that? You'd forget me in a day or two, like the foster parents did when they said goodbye and I was taken away. It's the way of nature to forget those who are out of sight," she said.

"Honey, I'll never forget you, and neither will the sisters," he told her.

"Don't know about the rest of y'all, but I hope next week's church is better'n this one," Kate said as she got into the car. "That sermon was so dry it about put me to sleep."

"*About*, my ass." Betsy slid into the middle of the big bench seat. "I had to keep nudging you with my good arm to keep you awake."

"I heard her snore twice." Connie fastened her seat belt. "And there was dust on the arm of the pew. That's disgraceful. It's my turn next week, and I'm choosing that big, fancy church downtown."

"I'm going to ask Flora about all of them before I choose," Betsy said. "She's worked over here for more than forty years, so she'll know a little something about them—like how good the preacher is and how crowded they might be and such things."

They commented on every church they passed between the one they'd attended that morning and the café where they planned to have lunch. Flora had already arrived and gotten them a table, so they didn't have to stand around and wait like twenty other people.

"I slipped out fifteen minutes early," Flora said. "This place is pretty popular on Sundays."

Sloan patted her on the back. "Thank you. I didn't eat much breakfast, so I'm starving."

"Plus, it took everything in him to sit still during a boring sermon. How was church in Rooster?" Betsy asked.

Flora put her hand over her mouth and giggled like a schoolgirl. "Fantastic. Just flat-out wonderful."

Sloan squeezed Ginger's knee under the table. "Sermon was that good, huh?" Dammit! He knew there would be a fiasco, and he'd missed it.

"Don't have any idea what James talked about. Seems like he started off with something about loving thy neighbor, but then Edith"—Flora did a head wiggle—"who always has to sit on the front pew like the Queen of Sheba, just laid flat out on the pew and started snoring. I swear, I could almost see the roof risin' up and down every time she snorted."

"Oh, really?" Kate glared at Betsy. "What have you done?"

"I didn't do a damned thing," Betsy protested, holding both hands out. "You and Connie always blame me for everything."

"With good reason," Kate said. "If you didn't do anything, then what did you cause to get done?"

Ginger raised her hand. "I made the brownies. She's not lyin' about that. She didn't even touch the spoon I stirred them with or put in the wacky weed. I did it all by myself."

Flora's hand shot up. "And I'm the one who asked for them. I told her that my mama was feelin' poorly and a brownie might help her sleep. She's like Edith—she doesn't get funny or loud when she's high. She just goes to sleep."

Connie's hand was the third one to raise. "I'm the one who asked Flora to take the leftover brownies, which was all but one that her mama ate, to Sunday school, but Betsy told me to do it."

"Traitor." Betsy shot a mean look across the table. "I was almost home clear. Why'd you have to go and tattle on me?"

Ginger wanted independence, but she knew she could never leave this eccentric bunch of women. She leaned over and whispered into Sloan's ear, "Yes."

His eyes lit up like sparklers on the Fourth of July. "Do you mean it?" he asked.

"I do," she told him.

"What are you two whispering about?" Kate asked.

"Ginger is going to move in with me," Sloan said. "She'd love to continue to work for y'all, though."

"Praise the Lord!" Connie said. "Darlin', it's not that we don't love you."

"And we want to be grannies to the baby," Betsy said. "And I'd just lay down and die if you left us. But we're old and set in our ways. A baby would be more than we could handle, especially at night."

"We were thinkin' of building you a little house out back of ours," Kate said. "You need to raise your baby, and we're a controlling bunch of old gals. I'm afraid that we'd try to take over."

"We know our weaknesses. Look how we fight over the kittens." Betsy leaned forward. "Of course, they love me best, and the baby will, too."

"Why are you moving in with Sloan?" Flora asked.

"Because I asked her, and we're such good friends," Sloan said. "If that's all we ever are, then that's all right, but we've been a help to each other these past weeks, and I think we'll make good roommates."

"How's that going to work if you take that offer from the military?" Flora asked.

"We'll cross that bridge when we get to it." Sloan patted Ginger on the knee.

That had sure been easier than she'd thought it would be, but now she had to decide when to make the move. "I'll be there every morning to help you cook, Betsy. I promise."

Suddenly sadness filled her heart and soul. Sure, she was glad to be moving in with Sloan, but—why did there always have to be a *but?*—she'd miss the fun that she and the ladies had after supper each evening.

"You can't leave until Doc says I can use my arm," Betsy said. "Promise?"

"You've got my word." Ginger felt good about the decision and sent up a silent prayer that living in the house with Sloan, she would never feel the way she had felt in that apartment with Lucas.

"Oh, I forgot to tell you about Gladys," Flora laughed.

A waitress came to their table with a pad in her hand. "I'm so sorry y'all have had to wait. Can I start you off with something to drink or some appetizers? We've got fried green tomatoes, potato skins, fried okra, and mozzarella sticks."

"Sweet tea," Sloan said. "And please bring us an assortment of your appetizers."

The rest of the group all ordered either water or tea, and the waitress hurried off to wait on another table.

"Now, what's this about Gladys?" Sloan asked.

"Well, she got in on the brownies, too. Y'all ever heard that old song by Ray Stevens about the squirrel that got loose in the church down in Mississippi?"

Sloan chuckled. "Oh, yeah. When a bunch of soldiers from Oklahoma and Texas are stuck together over there in the sandbox, it don't take much to entertain them. That was one of our favorite songs."

"Well, honey, Gladys did not snore on the front pew. When James asked Mr. Raymond to deliver the benediction, she popped from her seat and declared in a loud voice that women could pray as good as a man, and she forevermore prayed. She asked God to forgive Edith for being a bitch, and then she lifted both her arms in the air and told God about all kinds of things. I half expected Ray Stevens to come in through the side door and start singing that song."

The waitress brought their drinks and appetizers and took their orders, and then Flora went on. "Mary Lou Bastrom started to cry and called nine-one-one on her cell phone because she thought Edith had died. And before Gladys could say, 'Amen,' the paramedics came in and loaded her up." She took a long drink of her tea. "James left the pulpit and went with them. The lights were flashing and the sirens were screaming and Gladys started praying again. Finally, her daughter and a friend got her by the arm, and they disappeared with her out a side door. Mary Lou's son put his arm around his mama and led her out the front door. Too bad those brownies don't affect my mama like that. It might be kind of amusing, but they just make her snore."

"Good Lord, when the folks at the hospital figure out that Edith was stoned, they'll come gunnin' for us." Kate dried her tears on a napkin. "I shouldn't be laughing, but she was hateful about my mama."

"I took what brownies weren't eaten back home with me, so the evidence is gone," Flora said. "But I don't have any doubt that Edith will trace it all back to Betsy, and she'll be furious."

"I hope she does," Betsy said. "She needs to know that she don't mess with the Banty House women. When we get mad, we get even."

"Are we going to grow up to be like them?" Ginger whispered to Sloan.

"I sure hope so. You reckon you can get Betsy to show you how to crossbreed weed? I'll see if Kate will teach me how to make good moonshine," Sloan answered.

"What are you two whispering about now?" Connie asked.

"We're wondering what your vice is," Sloan replied. "Kate's got her shine, and Betsy grows pot. What do you do?"

"Honey, I deal in stones for healing and candles for revenge." Connie tilted her chin up. "I light black candles if someone is mean to my sisters, and they never fail me. If you ever doubt that, just visualize Edith in her cute little suit, red lipstick runnin' into the lines around her prune mouth, all curled up on the front pew snoring like she was this morning."

The waitress brought out five plates of the Sunday special and set them around. Then she put a nice big basket of hot yeast rolls in the middle of the table. "Y'all enjoy, and when you're done, I'll bring out your blackberry cobbler. One check or separate ones?"

"Just one, and I'll take it," Sloan said.

"That's awful sweet. Thank you," Flora said. "Who's going to say grace over this food before we eat it?"

"It's my turn." Betsy bowed her head. "Thank you, Lord, for this food, and bless Sloan for paying for it. If you've a mind to keep Edith in the hospital a couple of days, then tell them to give her a colonoscopy. That way Doc can get that corncob out of her butt, so that she don't think she's so high-and-mighty. Amen." She raised her head and said, "Now let's eat before this good food gets cold."

"Holy crap!" Ginger muttered.

"At least she didn't say 'ass,'" Sloan said.

"Well, it is Sunday," Ginger said.

Chapter Nineteen

Ginger kept an eye out for the mail all day. Most of the time the postwoman was there by midmorning, but that day, noon rolled around and she still hadn't showed up. With Betsy's supervision, Ginger had made a hot chicken casserole for dinner, but she was too nervous to eat much of it.

"What's the matter with you, today?" Kate asked. "You've been like a worm in hot ashes all day, and now you're not eating."

"And last night you went up to bed early," Betsy said. "Did we hurt your feelings at dinner yesterday when we said we were glad you were moving out?"

Before Ginger could answer, Connie said, "Sometimes we have Banty House meetings, but they are only for the shareholders, which is the three of us now that Mama is gone. We discuss things that pertain to finances and the upkeep on this place. Our CPA, Suzanne, is invited to the meetings four times a year. That's when we have to pay our quarterly taxes."

"Stop beatin' around the bush, Connie. Next thing you know you'll tell her that you checked those rocks in your room before we had our meeting," Kate said.

"Well, for your information, I damn sure did," Connie snapped at her older sister. "On Saturday evening, after you went to your room, we met in Kate's room and decided that it would be better for you if we built a little guesthouse on the other side of the cornfield, so you could have some privacy. We all love you, but we want you to be the mother, and Betsy is controlling."

"So that's part of the reason why we were so excited to hear that you were moving in with Sloan," Connie said. "I've burned candles and even rubbed an amethyst on the chair where he sits to eat with us so he would have healing in his body, mind, and spirit. He needs someone in his life. Even if y'all are just friends forever, it'll be good for you to be with him."

"I'm not controlling." Betsy pouted. "It's just that, well, I went to Woodstock when I was twenty-eight, and . . ." She told Ginger the whole story of how much she'd wanted to be a mother and had lost her baby. "I'm convinced that God sent you to me in my old age so I could have the family I always wanted."

Tears ran down Ginger's cheeks and dripped onto her T-shirt. She'd never thought of losing her baby, not one time, but she could feel the pain that Betsy suffered even fifty years after the miscarriage.

"Mama used to say that once a mother always a mother, no matter how old the children are." Betsy hugged Ginger, mingling their tears together. "In my mind, a woman becomes a mother even before her child is born."

Ginger picked up a napkin and dried Betsy's cheeks first, then her own. "But you have had Sloan most of his life. He's like a grandson."

"Yes, he is and we love him." Kate sniffled. "But he had a grandmother. You don't. We just don't want you to think we don't want you in our lives because we were happy that you're moving in with Sloan."

No matter how many homes she'd lived in, or what had happened in them, she'd never known such unconditional love. "I've never done anything impulsive in my life," she said. "From the time I was a little girl, I learned not to get close to my foster parents or to the children in the homes where I lived. I knew I wouldn't be in one place long, so why make friends? The social workers tagged me as RAD—reactive attachment disorder. Most kids with that problem act out. I just withdrew into myself. When I was old enough, I got some books at the library so I could understand why I didn't want to be close to people. I made an effort to fit in more in my last foster home, and with Lucas. Neither worked out so well, but since I've come here, I've"—she paused and took a deep breath—"well, I've felt myself coming out of living inside myself, and I've learned to trust y'all and Sloan. I wasn't a bit offended when y'all said that yesterday. I was dreading telling you I was moving out, because for the first time in my life, it mattered to me what someone thought."

"Oh, honey." Betsy hugged her again. "We all love you so much, and you can always trust us, and you can always come to us with any problems, or just to talk."

"Words can't describe what's in my heart right now." Ginger saw a movement out the window in her peripheral vision and whipped around to see the mail lady bringing two boxes across the yard. "They're here."

"Well, darlin', let's go bring them inside." Kate pushed back her chair. "If you want to think about putting them in Cottonwood Cemetery, it's all right. You don't have to make the decision right now."

"I'd like to get them buried as soon as possible. They deserve to be either scattered or put into the ground, but I sure thank y'all for giving me plots." Ginger followed her to the door.

"Well, then, we'll do it at dusk tonight." Kate opened the door and took the boxes from the lady.

"I ain't never delivered anything with 'Cremated Remains' on the side," the lady said.

"It's my parents," Ginger told her.

"Well, it's my first." She laid a few pieces of mail on the top box. "I don't think we've met. I'm Laura Johnston. I saw you at church on Easter."

"Pleased to meet you," Ginger said.

"How's Edith this mornin'?" Connie asked. "I heard she had a spell at church yesterday mornin'."

"Aunt Edith is at home this morning. We aren't sure what happened, but when she woke up last evening, she was starving. Dr. Emerson said the only time he'd ever seen such a thing was when someone had gotten high on drugs, but we all know that Aunt Edith is a teetotaler. She won't even take a sip of champagne at a wedding. I'll tell her you asked about her. Sorry about the argument. I don't know what got into her." Laura turned around and hurried back to the mail truck.

"Good Lord, is everyone in town kin to each other?" Ginger asked.

"Just about." Kate set the two boxes on the credenza.

Ginger laid a hand on each box. "I expected them to be bigger."

"So did I," Kate said.

"Are you going to bury them in those boxes or take them out?" Betsy asked.

"I hadn't thought that far." Ginger tore the tape from one box and opened it to find a plastic bag full of gray ashes and an envelope with a death certificate inside. "This is my father. He died from a gunshot wound to the heart and was dead on arrival at the hospital. Should I put them in the ground inside the plastic bag or dump them out? What do y'all think?"

"I'd leave them in the bag," Betsy said. "I bet we can find something in the attic to use as urns or little coffins to put them in. That'd probably bring you more closure than just dropping a plastic bag in the ground."

"Can we go up there and look now?" Ginger asked.

"We sure can," Kate told her. "I'm remembering a metal box that Mama said Grandmother kept her egg money in. It even has a latch on it."

"I didn't get around to cleaning the attic last fall, so it's going to be dusty." Connie was apologetic.

"Don't know why you clean it anyway. No one ever goes up there but you," Kate fussed as she led the way up the stairs.

Ginger followed behind them. She'd expected an emotional roller coaster when she finally got the remains, maybe tears or anger or something. She'd cried over Betsy's story, so surely she should feel something looking at her parents' ashes, but she hadn't felt anything. Maybe when they buried them that evening, it would be different. As she climbed the second set of steps up into a pristinely organized attic, all she could think was that she was sure glad Sloan's house didn't have stairs.

The sun hung in the western sky like one of the big orange Nerf balls Sloan had played with as a kid when they gathered around the two shallow graves in the cemetery that evening. Ginger kneeled down and placed a cedar box in the first hole, then moved over to put a metal one in the second one.

Sloan extended both hands to help her up. She took them and stood to her feet, her belly throwing a wide shadow over both graves.

"My senior year in high school, we studied some poetry by Rod McKuen. A poem of his spoke to me so much. I can't quote it, but one of the lines in the poem about his father said that he envied the other children for their fathers because he never knew his. That has stuck in my head and made me wonder, if I'd known my parents, would I be a different person today, or was Fate or God or Destiny doing what was best for me even though the journey from birth to this moment hasn't been easy?"

Sloan swallowed twice to get rid of the lump in his throat. Ginger was definitely, beyond a doubt, an old soul, as his granny used to say of people who were wise beyond their years.

"I should feel pain today, but I don't. I feel happiness that I get to bury my parents and that I'll know where they are finally laid to rest. I feel good that my child will have at least this much of her grandparents close by, but what I feel most is relief. It's like, by doing this, I can finally put the past behind me and move on to the future. Thank all of you for being here with me today. Let me play a song on this new phone to finish off this service." She touched her phone and Sarah McLachlan's voice filled the cemetery with "Angel."

The words seemed so fitting to the situation that Sloan wondered if it had been written for a couple of folks just like Ginger's parents. A single tear traveled down Ginger's face when the lyrics said that in the arms of an angel maybe they would find some comfort. Sloan draped an arm around her and pulled her close.

"That was beautiful," he said.

"It was all I had, and the song seemed to be the right one." She sniffled. "I wish I would have known them, but if I had, I wouldn't be where I am today, and for the first time in my life, I really like my place in the universe," she said.

"Me too," Sloan said.

A soft breeze sent the scent of nearby honeysuckle floating across the whole cemetery. Sloan picked up the shovel that the gravediggers had left behind and filled in both graves. Then he stuck a marker that had the names and dates of birth and death in the place where the headstones would be set eventually.

Using the back of the shovel blade, Sloan patted the earth down as much as possible, then leaned the shovel against a big pecan tree that shaded all the graves in the plot. "I'll plant some grass seed on here later this week and keep it watered until it takes root."

"We should've brought flowers," Betsy moaned. "Mama's had pretty flowers on her grave ever since she passed away."

"We can do that when the headstones get here," Ginger said.

Kate went over to Belle's grave and laid a hand on the tombstone. "Sloan, the cemetery sure looks nice since you've taken it over."

"Are you ready to go home now?" Betsy asked.

"Y'all go on without me," Ginger told them. "I think I'll stay for a little while."

"I'll be glad to bring her home when she's ready," Sloan offered.

"All right, then," Kate said. "We'll leave the door unlocked in case you get home after we're already in bed."

"Thanks." Ginger waved as the three went to the car.

Sloan tucked her hand in his and together they walked across the cemetery, through the gate, crossed the yard to his house, and climbed the steps. "Want a glass of tea or a bottle of cold water?"

"Water would be good." She dropped his hand and sat down in one of the two old red rocking chairs on the porch. "I can see myself rocking the baby out here in the evenings."

"I hate to ask you to get up, but I've got something I want you show you," Sloan said. "We can come back out here after you see it."

He held out a hand. "Need some help?"

She tucked her hand into his, and he pulled her up. "I'll be glad when Dumbo gets here. It's gettin' harder and harder to get up and down."

"Hey, now, be careful." He smiled. "You might mark that sweet little girl by calling her that and she'll have big ears."

"I don't believe all that superstitious mumbo-jumbo," Ginger said.

Sloan led her through the small living room, down the hall, and into his granny's old bedroom. "I brought this out of the barn and cleaned it up. My grandfather slept in it when he was a baby and then my dad and me. I thought if we could put the new little girl in it, then . . ." He didn't get the rest of the sentence out before Ginger let go of his hand and grabbed him in a tight hug.

"Oh. My. Goodness." She pulled his face down to hers and kissed his cheeks, his eyelids, and his chin. Then she let go of him, went straight toward the bed, and put a hand on it. "It's beautiful, Sloan. I never dreamed that I'd have something like this for her."

"I'm glad you like it." He realized in that moment that he'd fallen in love with Ginger. Someday maybe she'd feel the same, but he was a patient man and willing to give her time to learn that she could love someone without fear of losing them.

"This is going to be my room? Do you think your granny would mind?" She went from the poster bed to the dresser to the rocking chair over by the window and back to the baby bed.

"Yes, this will be yours and Martha Belle's bedroom, and no, Granny won't mind at all. She'd be happy to have you here," he answered.

"I can feel her spirit in here." Ginger ran her hand over the wooden rail of the baby bed. "Everything is just perfect."

"Well, we do need a mattress for the bed, and I thought you didn't believe in mumbo-jumbo superstition," he teased.

"You don't mark a baby by calling her Dumbo, or eating strawberries, but it's okay to feel a sweet spirit in a room," she told him. "Martha Belle is going to love this room. See? She's tellin' us so." She picked up his hand and laid it on her belly. "Those kicks mean she wants to sleep in that bed the first night that she comes home from the hospital. She's trying to get right in it."

Sloan felt like he was the baby's biological father right at that moment—and it didn't scare him one little bit. Matter of fact, he felt ten feet tall and bulletproof, like the lyrics of the old country song.

Chapter Twenty

Ginger was so ready to move into Sloan's house by the end of the week that she could hardly wait, but she'd promised Betsy that she'd stay until the doctor said she could lift things again. Not that it would matter, since she'd be working there with the sisters every day anyway, but she'd keep her word. Still, every time she had to climb the stairs, she let out a little groan.

On Thursday morning, she checked to make sure she had everything she needed for the day and left her bedroom. She really hoped that the doctor would release Betsy that day. It didn't take a genius to tell that the woman was cranky from sitting around doing nothing for days on end.

"I want waffles for breakfast, and I can't even get the waffle iron out from under the cabinet. When I get well, I may walk right through that damn restraining order and tear Edith's arm off and whoop her with it," she fussed.

"I'll get things going," Ginger said. "Maybe today Doc Emerson will let you take the sling off."

"I've got two minds about that, too," Betsy continued to complain. "When he does, you'll move out, so it's going to be kind of bittersweet."

"But I'll be back every morning and stay until afternoon," she reminded Betsy. "Kate and I decided that I'd be here from eight until four. That way, I can have dinner with y'all and then Sloan and I can have supper together at his house."

"And you'll come for movie night some of the time, and maybe come play dominoes or cards with us once in a while?" Betsy asked.

"We'll be here so often that you'll want to kick us out." Ginger set up the waffle iron and got out a mixing bowl to stir up some batter. "What are we making to go with these?"

"Melted butter and syrup for me. Strawberries and whipped cream for Connie, and Kate likes peanut butter and honey on hers." Betsy removed her sling and threw it over in the corner. When the thing flew over Hetty and Magic, it startled them so badly that they jumped straight up in the air and then tackled the thing with more determination to kill it than they had her Easter hat.

"You think that's wise?" Ginger asked.

"Probably not." Kate had come into the kitchen just in time to see the sling go flying. She ignored the cats, her sister, and everything else, and headed straight for the coffee. "I love waffles. I'll get out the peanut butter and honey."

"You!" Betsy pointed at her. "Sit down with your coffee. I'll see Doc today because I promised I would, but I'm releasing me as of this very moment, and I'll get out the rest of the toppings for our waffles."

"You always were headstrong," Kate said.

"Well, you were always the bossy one," Betsy accused as she opened the refrigerator.

"I wish I had a sister." Ginger filled the waffle iron just right and closed the lid.

"You can have either one of mine," Connie told her, coming through the kitchen door. "They drive me so crazy that sometimes I have to sleep with at least a dozen stones under my pillow."

"That's why you need your hair done on Thursdays," Kate smarted off. "It gets all tangled up from them rocks under your head."

Ginger knew she would really miss all this, but she sure hoped that the cats killed the sling and that the doctor would agree with Betsy that morning. She was in what the baby books she'd read before she came to Rooster called the nesting mode. She wanted to get settled in her new room and get things gathered together for her daughter. Martha Belle needed more than that cute little bow for her hair.

❖   ❖   ❖

Lucy was glad to see them at the beauty shop that morning, and praised Betsy for having such thick hair that grew fast. "It's already covering where the stitches were," she said, "and in another month, it'll all be one length again."

"I'd still like to snatch Edith bald-headed," Betsy fumed. "I've decided that since I'm going to be a great-grandmother, I'll let it go gray. I'll bet you that Edith stops dyeing her hair if I do. How much you want to wager, Kate?"

"Not a cent." Kate picked up a magazine and began to leaf through it.

"You're not any fun at all anymore." Betsy pouted. "What about you, Ginger?"

"Oh, no." Ginger shook her head. "I'm saving all my money to buy things for the baby."

Kate held up her magazine showing a page of pictures of several different hairstyles. "What do you think about this one, Ginger?"

She had no idea what style would look good on Kate. "I like the way you wear your hair now."

"Not for me—for you. How long has it been since you had a cut and shampoo?" Kate asked.

"Since the last time I had dinner with the Queen of England," Ginger joked. "I do like that, but I want to be able to put my hair up in a ponytail, and that looks a little short for that, and I'm not spending money on a haircut when I can do it with manicure scissors."

"I can do that style a little longer," Lucy said. "And you do need to get those dead ends cut or they're going to split all the way to your scalp."

"Let's do it," Kate said, "and, Lucy, put Ginger on the books to get her hair done on Thursdays with the rest of us."

Ginger had no idea what that kind of thing cost, but she figured that amount of money would buy at least one little outfit for Martha Belle and maybe more if she shopped at a thrift store. She started to protest, but Betsy held up a hand.

"Consider it part of your benefit package."

"Y'all are spoiling me." Ginger smiled.

"Not as much as we're going to spoil the baby," Kate told her, then went back to flipping through the magazine.

Ginger almost went to sleep while Lucy was giving her a shampoo. When she had wrapped a warm towel around Ginger's head, she led her over to a chair, combed all the tangles out of her still damp hair, and then began to cut it.

"You've got really lovely hair," Lucy said. "I have a lot of customers who'd pay good money for this color. I can't even mix my own dyes to get this kind of true blonde. Now, let's blow-dry it and see what you think." When she finished, she turned the chair so Ginger could see herself in the mirror.

The girl's eyes widened and she threw her hand over her mouth. "It's so shiny and silky."

"Amazing what the right volumizing shampoo and a good cut will do, and you can still get it up in a ponytail," Lucy said. "Kate, you're next."

"Give us some of that shampoo you used on Ginger when we leave," Kate said as she took her place in the shampoo chair. "She's like most young girls this day and age. She washes her hair every night, so she'll need it."

Ginger found herself wishing she could sit in the chair and stare at her reflection all day. Even with her huge pregnant stomach pushing out the cape she still wore around her neck, she felt every bit as pretty as the girls who had gotten to go to prom when she was in high school.

❖   ❖   ❖

Ginger was afraid they'd be late to the doctor's appointment that day, but they arrived at the doctor's office right on time, and Linda, the nurse, ushered them right back to an exam room. She did all the preliminary vital signs and temperature checks, then said, "Doc wants to get away by noon so he can have lunch with his golfing buddies. Y'all are our last patients for today."

Doc Emerson came in and frowned when he saw that Betsy wasn't using her sling. "So you decided to be me and release yourself, did you?"

Betsy lifted her chin a notch and said, "Yes, I did, and I did fine all day. I even made a chocolate cream pie for you. It's out at the desk. The whisking went just fine."

"Well, then." He patted the table. "Let's look at your head and arm, and I'll see if I agree with you."

She eased onto the table. "My leg still looks like a three-hundred-pound football player tackled me, but it don't hurt no more."

He did a brief exam and said, "If you promise not to get into any more fights, I'll release you to do whatever you want."

"Can't make that promise, but I will tell you this." Betsy shook her finger at him. "If Edith wants another round, you'll be takin' care of her, not me."

Doc laughed and turned to Ginger. "Your turn."

Betsy left the table, and Ginger took her place.

Doc checked the baby's heartbeat, then measured her belly. "Girl, I hate to be the bearer of bad news, but there ain't no way around this."

Linda nodded. "I was thinking the same thing."

Betsy gasped.

Kate threw her hand over eyes.

Connie took Ginger's hand in hers. "Is there no heartbeat?"

"Oh, no," Doc said. "The baby is fine, but there's no way Ginger is going to deliver it naturally. It's just too big, so I'm going to have to order a cesarean section for this one."

All three sisters sighed.

Ginger felt like she might faint. "How am I ever going to pay for something like that?"

"I work for moonshine," Doc said. "And Kate always overpays me, so this one is on the house. We do this kind of delivery two weeks early, and I'm going out of town for a week on May tenth, so . . ." He looked at the calendar on the wall. "Linda, set this up for May sixth." He turned back to Ginger. "We'll check you into the hospital the night before, and keep you a couple of days afterwards. That way I'll be here until you go home."

"That's next week." Ginger suddenly felt light-headed, and woozy. She couldn't be ready for a baby in only a week. "I don't have things ready for her."

"Honey, it don't take much at the beginning," Linda reassured her.

All Ginger could think was that she had six days to get ready for a baby and that in between now and then, the ladies would be getting ready for the Rooster Romp. When the doctor helped her sit up, her thought pattern shifted to Sloan. He thought he had until the end of the month to get mentally prepared for a baby, and now it was coming in less than a week. What would he think of that?

❖　❖　❖

To Sloan, the week seemed to last forever. He could be patient, but only up to a point. Now that Ginger had agreed to move in with him, he was eager to get her settled into the house. The mattress for the baby bed had arrived on Tuesday, but they had no sheets for it. He and Ginger needed to visit about things, like whether she wanted a specific color or if pink was all right, and just how prissy Martha Belle's corner of the room should be.

He picked up the phone to call her at noon, but before he could hit the number for her, his phone rang. It startled him so badly that he fumbled the telephone and dropped it right on Tinker's head. The dog jumped up and growled at him. The phone scooted under the sofa, and Sloan had to get down on his hands and knees to even locate it. There it was all the way back against the wall. He had to lie on his belly and stretch his arm as far as it would go just to get a grip on the thing.

"Hello." He was breathless when he finally answered on the fifth ring.

"Well, at least you answered this time," Commander Watterson said. "Were you out doing PT? You sound out of breath."

"Dropped the phone," Sloan said.

"I was wondering if you'd thought about that idea of training guys for me and helping put teams together. I've been given the green light to pick a civilian assistant for that job. You'd have to pass the psych eval, and it's a seven-to-three job," the commander said.

"Where?" Sloan asked.

"San Antonio at the Bullis Army Base," he answered.

"Are you kiddin' me?" Sloan's heart kicked in an extra beat. "That's only half an hour from where I live."

"You'd start July the first. I've got a whole new bunch of recruits coming out of Lawton, Oklahoma, for training. That would give you plenty of time to come over here, get all the paperwork in order, and be ready if you want to give it a shot," Commander Watterson said. "Pay and benefits are pretty much the same as what they were when you were on active duty."

"Yes," Sloan said. "I would like that very much, and thank you, sir."

"Then I'll get the preliminary paperwork done and call you in a couple of weeks with the schedule for all your tests. Have you kept in shape, or am I going to see a beer belly?"

Sloan glanced down at his camouflage pants. "I'm still wearing the same clothes I came home with."

"Good," Commander Watterson said. "Then the only big hurdle will be that psych eval. Pass it and we're good to go. You told me once that your dream had been to make a career of the military. I can't get you back in with the discharge that you have, but I can give you a job within the ranks that will get you a twenty-year retirement."

"I can't tell you what this means to me, sir," Sloan said, "or thank you enough for the opportunity you're giving me. I'll be waiting for your call." He didn't even realize he was holding his breath until it all came out in a whoosh. Surely, he hoped to God, he would pass that evaluation exam.

"I'll send paperwork before I call," he said. "I've got your address right here in front of me. Talk to you soon."

Sloan had just ended the call when someone rapped on his door. He crossed the living room to open it and found Ginger on the other side. She looked like she was either scared out of her mind or about to explode in anger.

"I've got something to tell you," she said.

"I've got some news for you, too," he told her. "Do you want to sit on the porch or come inside?"

She brushed past him and went straight to what was to be her bedroom. "Oh, my! There's a mattress in the bed." Then she covered her face and broke into tears.

His first thought was that there was something wrong with the baby. She'd probably just come from the doctor's office. Cold chills chased down Sloan's back. What if it was going to be stillborn?

He took her by the hand and led her to the rocking chair. Then he sat down and pulled her onto on his lap. She buried her face in his shoulder and sobbed.

"Talk to me, Ginger. Tell me what's wrong," he said.

"The baby is coming in six days," she said between sobs. "And I don't have anything ready for her, and I don't even know what to buy or where to go to shop. I've never bought anything new in my life. I could get her things from a thrift shop, but I wanted her to have something new and pretty to come home from the hospital in, and . . ." She stopped to catch her breath.

He stood to his feet with her still in his arms, pushed up out of the chair, and took her into the living room. "If that's all it is, we can fix that problem. You scared the crap out of me. I thought you were going to tell me something was wrong with the baby." He set her down in a chair in front of his desk and opened his laptop.

She put her elbows on the desk and buried her head in her hands. "And now you've only got six days to get ready for this big change in your life, instead of three weeks. Are you sure you want me to move in here that quick?"

"Honey, we can go get your things this afternoon. You can sleep here tonight, and you'll have almost a week to get used to the place. Everything's goin' to be all right. And by the way, I like your new hairdo."

That made her cry even harder. "No one ever noticed me before. I don't deserve it."

He went to the kitchen, brought back a chair and pulled it up beside her as close as he could. "Now, dry up those tears." He reached to the back of the desk, jerked a tissue from a box, and wiped her face with it. "And let's get you some retail therapy."

"What's that?" she asked. "And yes, I would like to move in this afternoon. Those stairs at the Banty House are killing me."

"It's online shopping, and whatever we buy can be shipped here in two days. Let's start with sheets for the bed. Pink?" He hit a few keys and brought up a page with all kinds of baby things. "Let's start with basics and buy all the fancy swings and stuff like that as we figure out whether we need them or not. So sheets?"

"Pink." Ginger managed a smile. "I want her to be a princess."

"Oh, honey, there's no doubt that she's already that. I almost forgot to tell you my good news," he told her as they filled a virtual cart together.

"Sloan, that's wonderful." She wrapped her arms around his neck. "You'll be doing what you love, and it's not that far that you have to move. But if you just want a job, that big shot at the hospital offered you something there, and that's a lot closer."

"That's a job." He nodded. "But this is what I want to do. I loved the military, and working with them again would be like a dream come true. But I will have to change my car washing day to Saturday."

"Then that's exactly what you need to do, and, honey, I reckon the sisters won't mind you washing the car on Saturday." She smiled at him.

He could have easily drowned in her dark-brown eyes. Their gazes caught, and he tipped up her chin just slightly so he could kiss her. The first one was soft and sweet, but then they deepened until they were both panting for air. He held her close for another few seconds and felt like he could conquer anything—even a psych eval—if she was there every evening when he got home.

Chapter Twenty-One

*G*etting used to a different bedroom and a smaller house was more difficult than Ginger thought it would be. Although she was ready to get away from those killer stairs in the Banty House, she still didn't sleep well that first night. She dreamed all night that Lucas was back and he was furious with her for getting pregnant. He threw things and cussed so loudly that she thought for sure his voice would break the dirty windows in the apartment. He said that since it was too late to get rid of the thing, she'd have to give it away.

She told him to go to hell, stormed out into the night, and found a park bench, where she curled up and went to sleep. In the dream, Sloan drove up in his truck, and they were driving away when she awoke. When she finally opened her eyes and glanced around the room, she let out a long whoosh of air. The dream had been so real. She immediately curled up in a ball with her hand over her stomach to protect the baby. Then she heard Sloan whistling and pots and pans rattling together and caught the aromas of bacon and coffee. He had come to rescue her in the dream, but in real life, too.

She swung her feet out of the bed and padded across the hall to the bathroom in her bare feet. Her faded and worn nightshirt barely reached her knees and had stretched just about as far as it would go over her belly. Her reflection in the mirror showed dark circles under her eyes, but her hair still looked pretty dang good. She washed her hands and splashed cold water on her face, then went toward the kitchen.

"Good mornin'," Sloan said cheerfully. "Did you sleep well?" He filled a mug with coffee and handed it to her. "It's decaf. I stopped drinking caffeine when I came home. It seemed to add to my jitters."

"I've been using decaf when I can get it"—she blew on the top of the cup and took a sip—"and no, I didn't sleep too good, but then, I never do when I'm in a new place."

"Give it a day or two." Sloan took a pan of muffins from the oven and set it on the table beside a plateful of bacon.

"You don't have to wait on me," Ginger said. "We didn't talk about rent or bills last night. I should pay my half."

"The house and land were handed down to me by my granny, so there's no rent. The utilities are paid for through the company funds, so don't worry about all that," he said.

"What are you talking about?" she asked.

"It's complicated, but this place is actually Baker Oil Company. I don't have a formal office, but I do have a lawyer and a CPA who take care of things for me. I meet with them about once a month over in Hondo to sign papers," he explained as he buttered a muffin and put it on her plate.

"But . . . ," she started to argue.

He shrugged. "How about we make a deal? You get free room and board for making supper for us and helping with housework. I like a clean house, but I hate to dust. I could hire someone to clean for me, but I don't want people in my house that'll go out and tell what kind of toilet paper I use or whether I have steaks or chicken in my freezer. I figure those things are nobody's business but mine."

"I don't like to dust, either, but what you suggest is sure enough a fair deal." She took a bite of the muffin and a sip of her coffee. "What about breakfast and dinner? I'll be here until about eight o'clock, but

I'll be at the Banty House at noon, then back here at supper when I'm working for them."

"I like to make breakfast, so that's my job," he said. "Besides, when the baby gets here, there'll be times when you'll be up with night feedings, so I imagine it'll be nice for you to have it fixed for you. Anything else?"

"Yes." She reached for another muffin. "Can I have the recipe for these? I've got a collection of Betsy's, and I'd like to add this to my book."

Sloan pushed back his chair and went to the utility room. She expected him to return with a recipe card or maybe a cookbook, but he set a box on the table in front of her. "Use this. The recipe is on the back. It says to add an egg and some milk. Stir and bake at three hundred fifty degrees for twenty minutes. There's a whole selection of things like this in the pantry if you ever want to whip some up for yourself."

"I reckon that recipe is simple enough that I can master it." She finally smiled.

"If I can follow it, I know you can," he said.

"And if I have trouble, I'll just yell at you." She ate a fourth piece of bacon and finished off her coffee. She stole glances over at him. A tiny dot of toilet paper was stuck to his chin where he'd cut himself when he shaved that morning. His dark hair was combed straight back, and his shoulders were squared off, even when he sat at the table. Military was written all over him. She was glad that he had the chance of a job doing what he loved, but suddenly a jolt of pure fear went through her. She had thought she would faint when he had defused that bomb in the hospital, and he would be doing that all day every day if he went to work for the military.

"Hey, what's the matter? Are you okay? Is it the baby?" He reached across the table and laid a hand on hers.

"I'm not askin' for anything, honest," she whispered, "but what happens to me and Martha Belle if . . ." The words wouldn't come out of her mouth.

"If what?" Sloan asked.

"You'll be working with bombs all day"—she gulped a few times before she could go on—"and what if one of them blows up?"

"Honey, I won't be working with live bombs. I'll be training guys on how to identify different explosive devices and how to disarm them, but I shouldn't be in any danger," he told her. "And if you'll put my name on the birth certificate, then everything I have will go to the baby if I did die."

"Do you even know what you're saying? That's crazy talk," she said.

"Why is it? You're naming the baby after Granny, and I have no children, so the company will have to go to someone. I can't think of anyone better than someone who's named after my granny." He shrugged. "Besides, it's just money. That ain't nothing but dirty paper with dead presidents on it."

"You've known me less than a month, and this baby isn't biologically yours," she said.

"Want to know a great big secret? One that no one in the whole world—not even the sisters in the Banty House—knows."

"I don't know," she answered.

"My daddy couldn't have children. Granny told me that he had a high fever as a child. Doc Emerson said that it could have made him sterile, and so they did some tests when he was in high school. Sure enough, Doc Emerson was right. My dad fell in love with my mama when they were still in school, and she knew about the problem. They married young and thought about adopting, but Daddy wanted his baby to have my mama's DNA. So they went through a fertility clinic, and here I am. If they ever did a DNA test on me, they'd find that my father was number seven-two-eight-six. Blood don't always mean family."

Ginger was stunned speechless for several minutes. She'd thought that he looked just like the picture of his father that was hanging on the living room wall. When she could speak, she asked, "How did you find out about that?"

"Granny told me on her deathbed, because with all this new DNA testing going on, she was afraid I'd find out on my own. She didn't want me to think my mama had been unfaithful to my daddy. She said I was the product of my father's undying love for my mama and that there had never been a child who'd been more wanted than I was."

After the dream she'd had just before she awoke that morning, she could hardly wrap her mind around that much love. "Do you ever wonder about your father?"

"Nope." He shook his head. "My daddy was my granny's son for all I care."

"Do you want children of your own?" she asked.

"Martha Belle could be mine if you will let her be. Maybe someday she'll have a sibling or two. Who knows what the future might hold?" he said. "But I do know what the present holds. We've got about thirty minutes to get ready and go to work. You don't want to be late on your first day, and I don't want to have to rush with washing the car."

Ginger got up, carried her dirty dishes to the dishwasher, and then went to her room to get ready for work. She stopped and placed her hands on the rail of the baby bed. "Your biological father is dead, and I don't even know if he'd want a child if he was alive, and a man I met only a few weeks ago is asking me to name him as your father. It would be a lie, but it would secure your future forever. What do I do?"

❖　❖　❖

"Hey, hey." Betsy gave Ginger a hug when she arrived that at the Banty House. "We missed you at breakfast this morning. How'd you do on your first night at Sloan's?"

"Not so good." Ginger tied an apron around her body above the baby. "What are we doing today?"

"Making dozens and dozens of cookies for the Romp tomorrow," Betsy said. "We'll spend the day on the porch and serve cookies and lemonade to anyone who wants to sit a spell and visit with us. Last year, we went through twenty dozen cookies and so many gallons of lemonade that I lost count. The folks appreciate free refreshments." She talked as she stirred up a batch of peanut butter cookies. "And, honey, there's some folks who can't afford to buy off them high-dollar vendors. Now tell me why you didn't sleep good."

"I had a bad dream and Sloan is asking me to do something I'm not sure about," she said.

Betsy whipped around with narrowed eyes, pursed lips, brows drawn down so hard that the wrinkles in her forehead deepened. "What's he done?"

"It's complicated, but you got to understand the nightmare first." Ginger told her about the dream and then what Sloan had said.

Betsy pulled out a kitchen chair and sat down somewhere in the middle of the story. Ginger told her everything except the part about the fertility clinic. "So what do you think? Give me some advice."

"Oh, Ginger, that's the sweetest thing I've ever heard." Betsy wiped tears from her cheeks with the tail of her apron. "That's such a sweet thing for him to do. You've got to think about it . . ."

"Think about what?" Kate came in from the living room. "I've got the chairs and the card table all set up for the Romp. I thought you might have some cookies already out of the oven. I was going to steal one."

"You got to tell her and Connie," Betsy said.

"Tell me what?" Connie walked into the kitchen and set a can of dust spray on the table. "When's the cookies going to start coming out of the oven?"

Ginger told the story again. "What do I do? I never set out to take advantage of anyone, and if I do what he's asking, I feel like I am. I'd love for Martha Belle to have a father listed on her birth certificate, but it doesn't seem right to lie."

"Martha Belle?" Betsy whispered.

"You're naming the baby for our mama?" Kate asked.

"I picked out Belle first, and then I saw the name Martha on Sloan's granny's tombstone and they kind of went together. I plan to call her Belle," she answered.

"Mama would be so proud, and so would Martha. Since you're doin' that, I think you should do what Sloan asked," Connie said. "His granny would be so proud to know that she had a granddaughter named for her."

"I'd like our baby to be called by both names. There ain't nothing sounds more Texan or Southern than a double name," Kate said, "and when she gets old enough, I'm going to teach her to make shine just like my mama taught me. I went to the basement with her the first time when I was twelve. By the time I was fifteen, I could make a run all by myself."

"Martha Belle." Connie smiled. "It rolls off the tongue so well. I can see Mama smiling up there in heaven right now."

"But she's not blood kin to either his granny or your mama," Ginger argued.

"Honey, do you think that makes a bit of difference to either of them? No, ma'am, it don't. You think on it for a while and make up your own mind." Betsy stood up and set about getting a pan of cookies ready to go in the oven. "And while you're thinkin', we'll get cookies made."

"I got one more thing to say," Kate said. "You ain't blood kin to us, either, but we couldn't be happier that you're in our lives or prouder to have you for our adopted granddaughter if you was our very own. Blood don't always make families. Hearts do."

The only thing that came to Ginger's mind was "Amen!"

Chapter Twenty-Two

*G*inger didn't have to worry about what she'd wear to the Rooster Romp. Betsy had remodeled a dress for her—one of the remaining white cotton dresses that the last round of working girls had left at the Banty House. It had been decided that she would sit on the porch with the ladies in the afternoon, but until noon, she could go with Sloan down to Main Street. Betsy said that she needed to see all the vendors and maybe get some cotton candy at the carnival, but she warned her about riding the Ferris wheel.

"What if something crazy happened and you couldn't get down off that thing?" Betsy asked. "It happened to me one year, and I was stuck up there for a whole hour. Connie got really bitchy by the time that stupid thing started to move again."

Ginger hadn't ever been to a carnival, so she made no promises. She'd imagined the whole thing would be much bigger than it was, but it was actually quite small. Everything was set up right on Main Street and covered only two blocks, with the Ferris wheel sitting in front of the old post office.

"Let's do that," she said.

"Oh, no, ma'am," Sloan said emphatically. "Betsy gave me my orders. You can ride a horse on the merry-go-round, but you're not to get on that thing. She'll take a switch to me if I don't take care of you."

Ginger wasn't sure if it was the result of pregnancy brain, or if she'd had enough of men telling her what she could or could not do. She handed Sloan what was left of her cotton candy and marched right over to the Ferris wheel. She handed the man enough money to purchase a ticket and sat down in the seat he held for her.

Sloan dropped the paper cone of pink candy and raced over to the teenage kid who was operating the Ferris wheel. "She can't ride this. She's going to have that baby in four days. So make her get off."

"Sorry, sir, but my manager says anyone can ride this, including pregnant women, and I'd get in trouble if I made her get off. She could sue the carnival, and I'd lose my job," the kid said as he pushed the button to bring the next seat into play. "Next?"

A couple of lovestruck teenagers got into the seat and huddled up next to each other. Ginger heard the ticket taker tell Sloan that he'd have to wait until the next ride, and then the wheel began to turn. She didn't realize that she was afraid of heights until the swinging seat reached the top of the wheel. She looked out over the town of Rooster, and her stomach started to clinch up into a knot. The nausea hit on the second round, and even though she closed her eyes at the top, the swaying motion reminded her of just how high she was. By the fifth round, she absolutely hated the thing and its lively music. If she could have reached the kid who had insisted that it was all right that she rode the thing, she would have slapped him for selling her a ticket. She prayed to God that she hadn't caused her baby any harm and vowed to never ride anything at a carnival again if she could just put her feet on solid ground.

When it finally stopped, Sloan was there for her, and she was glad to have him to hang on to because her knees were weak and she was sweating bullets. "Just take me to the Banty House," she whispered. "I feel sick, and I need to lie down."

"Do you need to go to the emergency room?" Sloan asked.

"No. I've just never been that high up off the ground, and I found out the hard way that I don't like heights," she admitted honestly. "If I can just lie down for a little while, I'll be fine."

"Just lean on me, and we'll get you out of this crowd," he said.

She'd never appreciated anyone as much as she did Sloan right then. He never said that he told her so, not even once. He kept his arm tightly around her until he could flag down a golf cart and help her into the back seat. Five minutes later he was leading her up the porch steps to the Banty House.

"Good God!" Betsy jumped up from her rocking chair. "Is she in labor? Doc said she can't deliver the baby naturally, that he'll have to take it."

Kate was on her feet next. "Take her into the parlor and put her on the sofa. I'll call Doc. He's at the Romp, so he can come on down here and check her." She hurried into the house and headed for the kitchen telephone.

"Why haven't you already called him on your fancy phone?" Connie fussed at Sloan as she followed everyone into the house.

"Didn't even think of it," Sloan said.

"I did it to myself," Ginger whispered. "I've never been that high and the bucket thing was rocking back and forth and"—she grabbed her stomach—"I think I just had a contraction."

"We're going straight to the hospital," Kate yelled into the phone and hung it up. "Get her out to the car, Sloan. I'll lock the doors, and we'll be there by the time you get the engine started."

"I'm fine," Ginger protested just as her stomach knotted up again.

❖   ❖   ❖

Sloan picked her up like she was nothing more than a baby and carried her through the kitchen and out the garage door. He set her down in the passenger seat and hurried around to get behind the wheel, making plans about how to get out of town the whole time. Main Street was blocked, so he'd have to make a right turn before the old post office and circle around until he could get onto the road up to the highway.

The sisters crawled into the back seat, and Kate said, "Just get us to the hospital. Don't pay a bit of attention to the speed limit signs."

He had to go slowly in town, so as not to hit anyone, but when he got the big car out on the highway, he floored it. The five-minute trip to the hospital took less than three, and Doc Emerson even beat them there. He met them in the emergency-room lobby and started asking questions while the nurse put Ginger into a wheelchair and rolled her through a set of double doors and back to a cubicle.

"Okay, ladies and Sloan, get out of here and go to the waiting room. I'm going to see what's going on. I'll be out to tell you in a few minutes," Doc Emerson said.

Sloan led the ladies out to the empty waiting area. They all three sat down in chairs next to each other and clutched their oversize handbags to their chests.

"I told you not to let her—" Betsy started.

"You know how stubborn she is," Kate butted in.

Connie pointed right at Kate. "She gets that from you."

"It's my fault. I should've argued with her more," Sloan lamented. "I told her not to get on the Ferris wheel, but she marched right over there and bought a ticket, and the guy rolled her up and let the last ones on, and it was too late for me to even get on it." He plopped down in a chair with a thud and put his head in his hands. "The kid said it was safe for pregnant women."

"You are not to blame yourself," Kate said. "She's a grown woman, not a child."

"But I talked down to her like she was a kid," Sloan said. "She was bullied by the baby's father, and I'm sure she's made up her mind not to let anyone do that to her again. I shouldn't have pushed her like that."

The double doors opened and Sloan jumped up, but it was only a nurse. She went over to another family and said a few words to them. One of the guys in that group broke down and then the rest of the group was suddenly trying to comfort each other. Sloan was familiar with the heavy cloak of guilt landing on his shoulders, and he accepted it. No matter what the ladies said to encourage him, he knew that he could have kept Ginger from getting on that ride if he'd gone about it differently. He could have told her that he hated rides, that they made him sick, and asked her to please do something with him instead of going on the Ferris wheel. But oh, no! He had to demand that she not go, and she had to prove to him that she could do whatever she wanted and take care of herself.

He got up and started to pace back and forth, from the doorway to the other side of the room and back again. On one of his trips, he heard the other group of people talking about how lucky they'd been. On another, he got a second tidbit. Evidently, a two-year-old had swallowed something poisonous, but the doctors were able to save the child's life. Their tears had been ones of joy, not sorrow.

If Ginger lost this baby because of him, she'd never forgive him, but worse yet, he'd never forgive himself. This time, visiting a grave like he'd done with his old teammates wouldn't work—the guilt would stay with him forever.

He was just past the doors going back into the emergency room when they swung open and Dr. Emerson came into the waiting room. The sisters, still wearing their long white dresses, had rushed to his side by the time Sloan could get whipped around and take a few steps back to him.

"Is she all right?" Betsy and Connie asked at the same time.

"Is the baby all right?" Kate laid a hand on Doc's arm.

Sloan just stood there, speechless, and waited for the bomb to explode.

"Her blood pressure is way too high and the baby is in a little bit of distress, so it's best that we go ahead with the cesarean today. We're taking her to surgery now. She's asked to see Sloan. I've told her five minutes, and she informed me that if she didn't see him, she was going home. Sassy little piece of baggage," he chuckled. "Reminds me so much of Betsy when she was young."

Betsy slumped into a nearby chair. "We're gettin' a baby today. Doc, please tell me that Ginger will be all right."

Kate and Connie sat on either side of her and looked up at the doctor with wide eyes.

"She'll be just fine. This would probably have happened no matter where she was or what she was doing. I'll either come out as soon as I can to give you the news or else I'll send a nurse, and y'all can move down to the surgery waiting room. Now, come on with me, Sloan. He'll be back with you in a few minutes."

Sloan followed the doctor, but he was now convinced that there was definitely something wrong. Ginger would have asked to speak to Betsy and comfort her so she wouldn't worry before she would have asked for Sloan if everything was really all right. He was sure that he was about to be told some bad news and then be asked to break it to the sisters.

Doc pulled back a curtain and motioned Sloan forward. "Five minutes, and then you'll have to suit up if you agree with her," he said, then disappeared. "The nurse will be here to tell you what to do. I'm going to scrub up."

Sloan took a step into the tiny curtained area. Ginger had an IV in one arm, and a blood pressure cuff was fastened around the other. "I'm so sorry," he whispered, taking her hand in his.

"What for?" Ginger asked. "I did this—you didn't, and it's going to be all right, but I'm scared. Doc says that if you put on a gown and mask, you can go into the delivery room with me. Please, Sloan. I'm terrified. If you're there, I'll be fine." Her grip on his hand tightened.

"Yes, I'd love to go with you," Sloan said without hesitating for a second.

"Okay, it's time to gown up or get out." An older nurse pushed the curtain all the way back.

"I'm going with her." Sloan took Ginger's hand in his.

"Then follow me." The nurse started pushing the bed out of that area and down a hallway. "I'll talk while we walk. You will get into a surgical gown, cap, and mask, and you will stand behind a screen. The surgical area is sterile, so you can't be in that part. You won't see us take the baby out, and you won't be able to cut the cord. Once we do the necessary things, like weighing, measuring, and cleaning her up a bit, one of you will have a two-hour bonding time with the baby, skin to skin. If the mother is awake and able, that's her job, but if she gets tired, then you will take over. When that time is over, we'll get her dressed and ready for other folks to hold her. Do y'all understand all that?"

"Yes, ma'am," Sloan said.

"What is skin to skin?" Ginger asked.

"It's a naked mama's or daddy's chest with the naked baby laid against it. We've found that it helps the baby bond and makes babies that are calmer than if we just take them away to the nursery," she explained as she pushed Ginger into the surgery room and pointed to a small closet with an open door. "I'm going to get her prepped for this. You'll find everything you need waiting in that room with the instructions about how to put it all on. Someone will come get you when it's time."

Sloan let go of Ginger's hand and leaned over the bed to give her a kiss. "I'm still scared. What if she don't bond with me? What if I fall asleep and drop her? Doc said I'll be awake but kind of drowsy."

"I'll be right here with you until we take her home, I promise. If you get drowsy, I'll take off my shirt and put her next to my skin," he promised.

"If the offer still stands, I think that your name should be on the birth certificate," she said.

"Okay, one more kiss and I'm turning her over to the surgical team," the nurse said to Sloan.

Ginger cupped Sloan's face with both her hands, brought it to hers, and said, "Don't take too long. I feel better when you're holding my hand."

"I'll be there as soon as they let me through the doors," he promised.

He rushed into the small room, scanned the directions on the wall, and shook a paper gown out of a wrapper. He had no trouble with the hat since it worked like a shower cap, but how did he tie the gown when the strings were behind him?

"I've dismantled bombs," he muttered. "I can figure this out."

Finally, he tied all four of the ties but the one near his neck and then slipped the thing over his head like a shirt. That done, he managed to tie the last one without too much trouble. He was pulling booties over his shoes when a nurse arrived.

"Need me to . . . ?" She stopped and stared at the gown. "I see you've already got it done. We're ready for you to join us. She's been given an epidural, and it'll only be a few minutes before we begin. By the way, how did you get that thing tied?"

"Tied it first and then put it on," he answered as he followed her out of the room.

"You must work well under pressure," she said. "Most fathers are so nervous they can't even figure out the part about it tying in the back."

"My heart is racing, and my stomach is tied in knots," he said.

"Well, you'd never know it. You stay behind this screen. Your job is to hold your wife's hand and keep her calm," she said.

"I'll do the first and give the second my best shot." He bent to kiss Ginger on the forehead and took her hand in his. Holding her hand wouldn't be a tough job. He was already doing that. But keeping her calm might be harder, especially when he was more nervous than he'd ever been in his life—even when he dismantled bombs.

The nurse disappeared, and Ginger giggled. "Love your new hat. It's a little lighter shade, but it matches your eyes. I think I fell in love with your eyes even before I fell in love with you. I never believed in all that hogwash about love at first sight until . . ." She frowned. "I can't feel my legs."

"Is that normal?" Sloan asked the nurse closest to him.

Dr. Emerson chuckled. "That's exactly what we want. Ginger, you will feel a little pressure."

Her eyes popped wide open and locked with Sloan's. "I'm glad you're here."

Should he believe what she had said about falling in love with him? Or was it nothing more than the ramblings of a person under the influence of drugs and stress? Hopefully, she had meant what she told him and would put his name on the birth certificate.

"I told you it was a big one." Doc's voice came through the screen. A baby's healthy screams followed right after his statement.

Ginger's big brown eyes opened again and tears flowed down her cheeks. "Sloan, do something. They're hurting our baby. Give her to me."

"Eight pounds, four ounces," the nurse said. "Twenty inches long. Look at all this black hair."

"I guess she got something from me." Sloan smiled down at Ginger.

"Of course she did." Ginger yawned. "You're her father. Just look at the birth certificate. When can I see her?"

"We'll get her cleaned up and lay her on your chest in a few minutes," Doc answered.

"We did it, Sloan," Ginger said. "Even though I did a stupid thing, we got through it together."

"We sure did," he said. "And, darlin', we'll get through whatever the universe throws at us in the future. As long as we've got each other, we'll jump every single hurdle. I promise not to try to boss you anymore."

"I will try to not be so bullheaded," she told him.

"Sounds like a plan to me," Doc said from the other side of the curtain. "Now, go on out to the waiting room and tell the Banty House girls the news. They'll be nervous as old mama hens in a room full of coyotes. We'll have Ginger settled into a recovery room in a few minutes. There's only supposed to be two at a time until she's in a room in the maternity wing, but I'm going to bend the rules."

A nurse came from around the screen with the new baby in her arms. "Time for skin to skin. You ready to hold your daughter, Ginger?"

"Oh, Sloan, look at all her dark hair. She looks like you," she said as she opened her arms.

In that moment, he wanted to be the father, not just on paper but for real.

The nurse unsnapped one side of Ginger's hospital gown and laid the baby next to the new mother's bare skin. Then she covered them both with a soft, warm blanket. "I'll stay with her until we get her into a room," the nurse told him, "and then you can be there in case she gets tired."

"Thank you." Sloan touched the baby's face and fell in love with her that very instant. "God almighty! She's beautiful, Ginger."

"Tell them everything went perfectly. A nurse will come get you soon."

Sloan bent to kiss Ginger on the cheek. "I'll only be away from you a few minutes."

"Thank you," she whispered, "for everything."

"Rightbackatcha." He felt like he was walking on air as he headed for the waiting room. The three sisters were the only ones there, and they all met him halfway across the room.

"Sweet Jesus! We've been in here for hours," Betsy said.

"It's only been thirty minutes," Kate argued.

"Well, it seemed like an eternity. Is she all right? Is the baby here? Is anything wrong? Please tell us that it all went well." Connie finally stopped for a breath.

"Ginger is holding the baby right now. Doc was right about it being a big baby. She weighed over eight pounds and is twenty inches long, and she's got a lot of black hair." He removed the cap from his head and ran his fingers through his own dark hair.

Betsy sank into a chair and let out a whoosh of air. "Are you sure Ginger is going to be all right?"

"Doc Emerson says it went well." Sloan sat down beside Betsy and draped his arm around her shoulder. "I promise I won't leave her side until Doc says she's able to do whatever she wants."

Betsy patted his hand. "I'm holdin' you to that. If you have to go anywhere, you call us and one or all of us will come and stay with her."

"When can we see her?" Kate asked.

"As soon as they get her into a recovery room," Sloan answered.

"I call dibs on going in first," Connie said.

"Doc says he'll bend the rules so we can all go in, and then, when she's in the maternity wing, we can all stay as long as we want. But I'll be staying in the room with her until I take her home," Sloan answered.

"You are a good man, Sloan," Kate said.

❖ ❖ ❖

Ginger peeled back the blanket and counted Martha Belle's toes and fingers. Then she covered her back up and said, "I wonder if my mother had a bonding time with me like this."

The nurse turned from checking her vital signs and said, "Were you talking to me?"

"No, ma'am," Ginger said.

"Do you feel like you're drifting off to sleep?" the nurse asked.

Ginger shook her head. "I want to stay awake forever. I don't want to miss a single thing that happens in her life."

The nurse giggled. "Girl, I've got four kids, and believe me, you will want to sleep. Matter of fact, you may decide you love to sleep more than you love chocolate."

But I won't love it more than I love Sloan, she thought, and then sucked in a lungful of air. Had she really told him that during the birth? She drew her eyes down until her brows were a solid line. *Maybe I was just thinking it. Everything is a little bit of a blur.*

The door opened and Sloan ushered the ladies into the small room. They tiptoed close to the bed in their white dresses, and all three of them had big smiles on their faces. Betsy was the first to reach the bed, and tears welled up in her eyes as she looked down at the baby. "She looks like Kate's baby pictures."

"How can you say that?" Connie asked. "We all looked just alike at birth. If Mama hadn't put names on the back of the pictures, we wouldn't know which of us was which."

"I think she looks exactly like Martha Belle Baker," Sloan said.

Kate smiled and nodded. "That's a good solid name. I'm going to teach her to make moonshine when she's old enough."

"And you're not going to teach her to grow pot." Connie shook a finger at Betsy.

"Okay, ladies, time to go." Doc Emerson broke up the impending argument when he came into the room. "We should have her in a room within the hour. Why don't y'all go on home or get something to eat?"

"I *would* like to get out of this dress, but how can we leave this baby?" Betsy asked.

"She's not going anywhere," Ginger said. "Would you bring me some of those cookies we made when you come back? I'm starving."

"Not yet," Doc said. "First you'll get some liquids—broth, juice, and Jell-O—then at supper you can have some light food. Tomorrow you can get back on a regular diet. You just had surgery, young lady. You need to take it slow." He motioned for the ladies to leave the room.

"Thank God I'm living in your house," she said when she and Sloan were alone. "I love them all, but they would smother me."

"Honey," he chuckled. "It don't matter where we live; it's going to happen."

"My arms are so tired," she said. "I hate to ask, but just for five minutes . . ."

Sloan ripped the robe he was still wearing right down the front, unbuttoned his shirt, and took the baby into his arms. When he laid Martha Belle against his chest, she looked up at him with soul-searching eyes, as if she were studying his face.

"Hello, punkin," Sloan said. "Welcome to the Baker family."

"We may be a *strange* family, but we are one, aren't we?" Ginger said.

"Yes, darlin', we are." Sloan nodded.

Chapter Twenty-Three

Ginger dressed Martha Belle in a frilly little pink dress for church that morning and put the band with the bow that Sloan had bought around her head. She had just finished putting a pair of booties on her when Sloan came into the bedroom.

"Happy Mother's Day," he said. "I forgot to tell you that this morning at breakfast."

"Thank you. It is my first Mother's Day, isn't it?" She kissed the baby on the cheek. "And you are the reason I get to celebrate this day, you sweet little doll." She turned her attention back to Sloan. "Are the presents and the diaper bag ready to go? I'm so eager to get out of the house for a few hours. It's only been eight days, and I know that we've had company every day, but I'm ready to get out, get a ride somewhere in the new vehicle."

"The gifts are in the back of the SUV, all ready to deliver to the Banty House ladies after we have dinner, and the diaper bag is right behind the passenger seat. Honey, we can go anywhere you want," he said.

"I still can't believe that you went out and bought an SUV," she said.

"If the ladies hadn't let us borrow their car, we'd have had to hire a taxi to get us home. Besides, you'll need it when you go back to work.

I can take the truck to San Antonio, and you and Miz Punkin can use the SUV." He picked the baby up and settled her into her car seat. "I'm not sure the world is ready for all your beauty this mornin'," he told her as he gripped the handle with one hand and crooked his other arm for Ginger.

She looped her arm into his, and they went out into the bright sunshiny morning. "I'm glad Edith dropped that restraining order so we can go to our own church."

"Flora said that James told her to drop it or else he'd have to leave town and find a church that he could afford to preach at," Ginger said.

"I bet the ladies got a kick out of that." Sloan took care of getting Martha Belle's car seat clicked into the base, and then he opened the door for Ginger.

"Kate said that she laughed so hard that she got the hiccups and that Betsy said she'd go back if Edith apologized to her in public at church in front of the whole congregation. Connie wanted her to stand on the altar and ask God Himself to forgive her for judging their mother. Flora convinced them all that it would do more good for them to be ladies than to demand stuff like that," Ginger explained.

Sloan laughed at the visions in his head of the old gals making Edith do all that, but he was most interested in Ginger that morning. "You sure look cute this morning in that dress."

"Thank you. I'm glad you like it. I did some online retail therapy for it, like you taught me. It just came in yesterday. I wanted me and Martha Belle to wear the same color on Mother's Day. It may turn out to be a tradition, like Easter at the Banty House."

Sloan made his way around the SUV and got behind the wheel. "Then I'll be sure to take a picture of the two of you before the day is over. You can put it in the book that you're making for her. Maybe we can talk Kate into taking one of the three of us."

"I'd like that." Ginger had to say what was in her heart or else she was going to flat-out explode. "I love you, Sloan. I think I fell in love with you that first day when you came to the Banty House to work for the sisters. I don't want you to think I'm saying this because of a new car or what all you've done for me this past week since the baby was born. I couldn't ask for a better friend, but I want you to know that I love you"—she stopped and took a long breath, then blurted out—"for more than just a friend."

The way he whipped around and looked at her made her wonder if he'd even heard her. Finally, just when she'd begun to think that he was trying to figure out how to let her down gently, he said, "Are you sure about that?"

"We can stay just friends. I guess everything depends on what you want. I have no right to ask for more. I was eight months pregnant when we met, and all we've shared is a few kisses," she answered.

"Well, honey, those few kisses about knocked my socks off, and I've dreamed about you every night." He started the engine of the new SUV.

Her heart fluttered like it might jump right out of her chest. She laid a hand on his shoulder. "Me too. What are we going to do about us?"

"Well, I could make a suggestion, but you might think it's too soon. After all we've both been through, I don't believe in wasting time. We're living together, and we're getting along really, really good." He drove from the house to the church and found a parking spot not far from the door. "Except when you get all stubborn with me about Ferris wheels and how much work you can do after surgery."

"You can't expect to live with someone twenty-four hours a day and not have a few arguments," she told him. "I bet you and your granny even had words at times."

"Oh, yeah." He smiled, turned off the engine, and faced her. He took both her hands in his and gazed into her eyes. "This isn't a very romantic time or place, and church starts in ten minutes so we're a little rushed for time. But here goes: Ginger Andrews, I love you. I don't know what the future holds, and I'm willing to wait until you are ready, but will you marry me?"

"Yes!" She unfastened her seat belt and leaned over the console to seal her answer with a long, passionate kiss that left them both breathless.

Epilogue

Twenty years later

*G*inger dressed in a cute little pink sundress and matching sandals. She'd just finished running a brush through her shoulder-length blonde hair when Sloan came into their bedroom and slipped his arms around her waist from behind.

"Happy early anniversary," he said.

"Thank you, darlin'." She wrapped her arms around his neck. "It hasn't been a good twenty years. It's been a wonderful twenty years. Did you calm our oldest daughter down?"

"I tried, but she's pretty nervous. It's a dream come true for her and Kate both. I swear she was marked from birth. I wanted her to go to college, but oh, no, she and her Nanny Kate had different plans." He kissed Ginger on the forehead. "We'd better round up the crew and start moving in that direction."

"I just have to get my purse," Ginger said. "You get the SUV started, and I'll yell at the girls. You know, we could try one more time for a boy. I'm not quite forty yet, and more and more women older than I am are having babies."

"No, thank you," Sloan chuckled. "I'm happy with our three girls. In a few years, they'll probably all be living at the Banty House and we'll finally have time just for each other. When we get Lizzy and Annie raised, I'm going to retire, and we're going to do some traveling."

"That sounds exciting, but, Sloan, I don't want them to be old maids like the nannies were. I want them to have what we've had all these years," she said.

"Don't worry, honey." He brought her hand to his lips and kissed the knuckles. "They'll find their way, just like we did. If we don't leave pretty soon, I'm going to lock the door and crumple up that pretty dress you're wearing."

She shoved him out the door with a giggle, picked up her purse, and yelled down the hallway of the new addition they'd built onto the house when the twins were born.

"All right, girls. The wagon train leaves in two minutes."

Martha Belle came out of her bedroom with a worried look on her face. At almost twenty, she looked more like Sloan than she did her mother. Even though he wasn't her biological father, her blue eyes were almost the same color as his. She was six inches taller than Ginger and built with curves in all the right places.

"Mama, you'll be where I can see you when they interview us, won't you? I'm so nervous that my hands will be shaking." Martha Belle slung her arm around Ginger's shoulders.

"I promise that your daddy and I'll be standing right behind the cameras so you can see us both," Ginger told her. "You've got this. You're as strong as all three of your nannies put together."

"I'm so glad that Nanny Kate and Nanny Betsy are here to see this day." Martha Belle sighed. "But I miss Nanny Connie so much."

"Don't you dare start crying," Ginger scolded. "You know I can't let anyone cry alone, and tears will ruin our makeup."

"Who's cryin'?" Lizzie asked, coming out of her bedroom. Even with three-inch wedge heels, the seventeen-year-old wasn't as tall as her older sister. Her blonde hair was pinned up in a messy twist, and she wore a bright-yellow dress that skimmed her knees. "Don't any of y'all dare start that crap in front of Nanny Kate. She shouldn't cry on her birthday. And if she cries, so will Nanny Betsy."

"Or on the day that our sister launches her first legal batch of moonshine." Annie joined them. If it hadn't been for the fact that she and Lizzy had such different fashion styles, few people could have told them apart. Ginger smiled at Annie, who reminded her of all three of the sisters that day. Her daughter had chosen a long white dress for the party like the one Connie had worn on the festival days. The hot-pink cowboy boots that peeked out from under the lace at the hem definitely had come from Kate. And Ginger would bet that her daughter's hot-pink fingernail polish was the same color as Betsy's.

"That's right," Ginger said. "Now go get in the vehicle. We're all going together."

"Ahhh, Mama." Lizzie pouted. "I wanted to take my own car."

"Not today," Ginger said. "Today we're going as a family."

❖ ❖ ❖

Change was a good thing.

Kate remembered thinking that was a bullshit statement twenty years ago, when she and her sisters drove down to Hondo to their new hairdresser's place.

"I was wrong to argue with those words," Kate told herself as she got dressed that morning in a pink pantsuit that Martha Belle had picked out for her. According to her granddaughter, they needed to wear the same color for the television crew. Today, she and Martha Belle were cutting the ribbon on the brand-new building back behind the cornfield that was their artisanal moonshine business. It was a dream come true for both of them, and Kate was glad she'd lived long enough to see the time come. Martha Belle was being hailed as the youngest entrepreneur ever to start such a business. Of course on paper it belonged to Kate, but as soon as Martha Belle turned twenty-one, it would all shift over to her.

While she waited for Ginger and the whole family to arrive, she picked up the picture book that her mama had started a hundred years ago and flipped through it. She and Betsy had lost Connie ten years ago to a heart attack. Kate was thankful that it had been quick and that Connie had died with a dustrag in her hand.

"Poor little Martha Belle, Lizzy, and Annie," she whispered. "They took it so hard. Betsy and I couldn't have gotten over it if it hadn't been for those girls being here with us so much."

She touched the next picture and smiled at the expression on Connie's face. "The house ain't as clean as when you took care of it, sister, but you trained Lizzy and Annie well. They've each bought a car with the money they saved from helping me and Betsy out in this old house. You'd be proud of them. I'm glad you went fast and doin' what you loved to do. I hope I have a heart attack just like you did when it's my time to go. Or that I drown in a vat of moonshine," she giggled.

"Nanny Kate! Nanny Betsy! Are y'all ready?" Martha Belle yelled as she entered the house through the kitchen. "I saw the television van drive past just when Daddy parked out front. Get your cane, and let's go tell them all about our new moonshine business."

"I was reminiscing about Connie." Kate picked up her cane and followed Martha Belle outside.

"I was doing the same thing." Betsy came from the living room with a cane in her hand. "I hope she's lookin' down from heaven and smiling today."

"I miss her so much," Martha Belle said.

"I tell you one thing," Betsy said as she headed outside. "Heaven ain't never been cleaner. I bet she's got some kind of fancy stuff that even shines the angel's wings. When I get there, I just hope they let me grow weed."

"They ain't goin' to give you no lip about it if you do." Martha Belle helped Kate into the SUV.

"Why's that?" Kate asked.

"Because," Annie said from the back seat, "Nanny Connie already got them under her thumb with the cleanin' business, so if her sister wants to grow weed, ain't nobody goin' to say a word."

Kate laid a veined hand on Martha Belle's arm as she got into the back seat of the SUV. "I love all of you, and I'm so glad that your mama came into our lives when she did."

"Hey," Ginger said from the front seat, "that goes double for me. The Banty House was my salvation."

Sloan looked over at her and smiled. "And it's where I met the love of my life."

Acknowledgments

Dear Readers,

Kate, Betsy, Connie, Ginger, and Sloan, all characters in the Banty House, have stopped talking to me now that the book is finished. I have to admit that we became pretty good friends during the writing process, and I really do miss them. More than once one of the older women would wake me up in the middle of the night to fuss at me because I didn't get her part of the story told just right.

I'm grateful for the voices in my head and for the ideas that come from everywhere and anywhere. I often tell folks that my love for storytelling comes from my Grandmother Gray, who could mesmerize me with her stories. As I was writing, I could imagine her as mother to Kate, Connie, and Betsy, and that's why this book is dedicated to her.

Speaking of being thankful, sometimes it's difficult to express just how much I appreciate my readers who listen to or read my stories. I want to thank you all for buying my books, reading them, talking about them, sharing them, writing reviews, and sending notes to me. Please know that each and every one of you holds a special place in my heart.

I'm a very fortunate author to have such an amazing team at Montlake. They take my ideas and help me turn them into a finished product for my readers. From edits to covers to publicity, they are all amazing, and I appreciate them more than words could ever express.

Special thanks to my editor, Anh Schluep, who continues to believe in my stories; to my developmental editor, Krista Stroever, who always manages to help bring out every emotion and detail in my books; to my awesome agent, Erin Niumata, and to Folio Literary Management; and once again, my undying love to my husband, Mr. B, who is and always has been my number-one supporter.

Until next time,

Carolyn Brown

About the Author

Photo © 2015 Charles Brown

Carolyn Brown is a *New York Times*, *USA Today*, *Publishers Weekly*, and *Wall Street Journal* bestselling author and a RITA finalist with more than one hundred published books and more than five million sold. Her novels include romantic women's fiction, historical, contemporary, and cowboys and country music mass-market paperbacks. She and her husband live in the small town of Davis, Oklahoma, where everyone knows everyone else and knows what they are doing and when—and they read the local newspaper on Wednesday to see who got caught. They have three grown children and enough grandchildren and great-grandchildren to keep them young. Visit Carolyn at www.carolynbrownbooks.com.